LOVE ME

A SHE'S MINE NOVEL

Jennifer Ryan

Cover design by Angela Haddon – www.angelahaddon.com

Edited by Susan Barnes – www.susanbarnesediting.com

Copyeditor – Melissa Frain – www.melissafrain.com

For all of you holding out for the happy ever after everyone deserves.

This book contains stalking, violence, rape (off the page),

a baby's death, murder, suicide, trauma,

sex, true love, and a happy ending.

Chapter One

T he silence might kill her.

Where was the wail of her baby crying?

When would she feel something other than the smothering of her grief?

Heartbreak. That's just how it started.

Agony was where she was stuck between the physical and emotional pain writhing inside her.

She could hear the scream lodged in her throat. Feel the emptiness in her belly like a living thing clawing at her.

She couldn't escape the loss she felt of someone there, then gone, but never here.

The agony crashed over her, then receded into a throbbing ache before it built again as she considered what was gone. What would never be. Hopes and dreams and a life barely lived.

The spark ignited by love and passion snuffed out by twisted desire turned to rage.

He killed my baby!

The words were a scream in her mind. An echo that sounded over and over again with each tear that fell.

She's gone, and I am empty.

The deep, dark pit of despair held her locked tight against its silent, heartless soul, aching to be free of the pain and resigned to feeling it forever.

Chapter Two

Adam winced at the bright light in his eyes and the pain in his wrists. He tried to lift his arm to see why it hurt and discovered the padded band around his forearm was actually strapped to the bedrail.

What the fuck!

He was restrained to the bed by both arms and ankles. He struggled against his bonds. A sense of déjà vu came over him.

Someone trying to get away from *him*.

Oh shit!

It all came back in a flash of nightmare images. Brooke! His beautiful Brooke.

His heart thrashed in his chest, pounding so hard he could barely catch his breath.

He'd almost had her. She was right there. His for the taking.

I was so close.

She wanted it.

He knew she did.

She'd been waiting for him.

But no. She fought him.

Fury seared through his veins. The cunt! She'd given herself to someone else. He tugged at the restraints again, wanting to flee this place and find her, hunt her down and get his hands on her.

More images flooded his mind. She fought him, trying to push him away. Holding her hands up to ward him off. But he kept attacking.

Blood. Dripping down her arms. Soaking her clothes. His vision a red haze of rage.

Oh God, no. More blood. Pumping out of her round belly.

Her agonizing screams echoed in his ears.

He hurt her.

He never wanted to hurt *her*.

"What have I done?" Shame. Guilt. Utter sorrow washed through him.

He'd killed a baby.

Her baby.

Tears leaked from his eyes, down his cheeks, and drenched the hospital gown he wore.

He didn't deserve to live. Not now. Not after what he'd done to her.

Trapped, he flailed in the bed, desperately trying to get free so he could end it. He didn't deserve to live. Not after what he'd done to the woman he loved.

Brooke. His beautiful Brooke.

He spotted the bandages over his wrists, sat up, and tried to lean forward enough to bite them off.

Monitors shrieked.

The door flew open.

His father stood there, his mother behind and to the side of him.

She looked shocked and anguished. Sad. Lines wrinkling her forehead and around her tight lips.

His father looked pissed and horrified.

Can't have this, can you, asshole?

What will people think?

How many votes will this cost you?

"Adam. Stop struggling," his father commanded. Like his order, his rule, was law.

"Fuck you! Untie me and get out." Adam pinned his mother in his gaze. "Why the fuck did you save me?"

"We love you," his mother wailed, tears raining down her face.

"Bullshit. I'm nothing more than a prop." Adrenaline cleared even more of the fog from his mind. "Where is she? Is she here? Is she alive? I need to see her. I need to tell her I'm sorry. I NEED TO SEE HER!"

A nurse burst in holding a syringe.

He leaned forward, his arms drawn tight by the restraints. "Don't even fucking think of coming near me with that," he snapped at the nurse, staring down his father. "You can make this happen. I need to see her."

"Calm down." His father eyed the nurse. Then Adam again. The silent message: *Not in front of witnesses.* He cocked his head at the nurse. "Please excuse us. We'd like to be alone with our son."

The nurse hesitated but ultimately followed his order and scurried out.

Adam wondered what fucked-up tale he'd told everyone about what happened tonight. "Is she alive?" She had to be alive. *Please.*

"Yes," his father bit out. "Though I guarantee she doesn't want to see *you*." His father stepped into the room, his mother following, then leaned against the door, barring anyone from coming in. Voice low, his eyes narrowed, he gave Adam the cold, hard truth. "You fucked me."

"Of course you think this is all about *you*." Adam fell back in the bed, exhaustion clawing at him. Probably from the blood loss after he tried to end it all.

I couldn't even get that right.

"Why didn't you just let me go? It would have been so much easier for you to use your fake heartbreak over your loss to gain voter sympathy. And don't think I don't know you've already ordered your lapdogs to tell the press how distraught you are over your son's mental health and how hard it's been on *you*. You'll be able to milk this for weeks. Because I know you'd never let it get out that I was the one who went after those stupid girls and nearly killed Brooke."

"Why?" His mother's anguished voice broke him out of his sorrowful fury.

"Because I love her. I wanted her. She saw me for who I really am." He glared at his father. "Not your fucking son. Not some actor in your fucking political play. She liked *me*."

"So why go after those other women?" his mother asked, seeing that she got him talking when all he wanted to do was rail at his father.

Not that he liked her much better. She played her part and it usually meant her making him go along with everything his father wanted. She was his fucking puppet.

"I wanted to be my best for her." He settled back into the pillow, unclenching his fists to relieve the pain in his wrists. "I need to see her."

His father left the door and came to his bedside. "You will never see her again." *Because you can't be linked to her*, his eyes said.

He held his father's hard gaze. "I *need* to see her."

"You will keep your mouth shut about what you did. You will tell the doctors, anyone who asks, that you tried to take your own life tonight because you've been over- whelmed by school and struggling with depression that you never disclosed because you feared what people would say."

He glared his father down. "I could give a fuck what you or anyone else thinks. I. Need. To. See. Her!"

"If you don't follow this order, there will be nothing I can do. You'll either play along and stay in this very *nice*, very *expensive private* hospital for the rest of your life, or you'll go to prison, where God knows what you'll suffer."

"I. Need. To. See. Her."

His father stared him down, thinking of all the possi- bilities and ways this could play out. He liked control. He needed it. And he forced others to his will with a smile, a handshake, and a few direct words that left others clamor- ing to do his bidding.

"She's asked to see me."

Adam gasped. "When? I want to go with you."

He shook his head. "I'll go alone. If she decides to go public, I won't be able to help you."

"No, you'll do and say whatever you have to do to dis- tance yourself from me. Your son. Because we both know all you care about is your fucking career and getting more power."

His father grabbed the guardrails on the bed, his knuck- les going white as his eyes narrowed. "Believe it or not,

Adam, I love you. Maybe I didn't always understand you, or give you what you needed, but I did the best I could." He rubbed his hand over the back of his neck, tension around his tired eyes and body. "I know, I should have made more time for you. But I can't change that now. All I can do is help you." He dropped his hand and pinned Adam in his gaze. "But that doesn't mean I'm going down with you. So you'll have to do what you've always done and get on board with the plan before your fate is out of my hands. Please." For a brief second, Adam saw the fear and concern in his father's eyes before he locked it down and turned for the door.

"Take me with you. I need to see her," he begged, tears welling in his eyes.

His father walked back to him. "Get this straight. You are never getting out of here. You are never going to see her again. After what you did, she's never going to want to see you again. *You* did that. Now accept it and play your part before you end up locked in a cage the rest of your life."

I'm already in one.

But I will get out.

I will see her again.

Chapter Three

I t was late. The hospital quiet.

Mindy Sue slept in the chair beside Brooke. She looked so peaceful.

She hadn't lost her whole world tonight.

But maybe she'd lost her best friend. Because Brooke didn't think any part of who she was had survived Adam's wrath.

He tried to kill me.

Why?

What did I ever do to him?

Brooke shifted her gaze to the other side of her bed. Mr. Wagner sat in a chair in the dark, the light from his phone screen lighting up his face. He'd come through for her tonight. He'd ensured her wishes were carried out by the hospital staff.

He'd held Mindy Sue as she cried for Brooke and her baby.

Such a good father. A good friend to Brooke, too.

He looked like he was answering emails or something on his phone when it vibrated with an incoming call or text. His head snapped up and his gaze met Brooke's. "He's here. He wants to see you." Mr. Wagner had done it.

The governor had arrived.

She turned her head away, a new wave of tears threatening, but she just didn't have the strength to weep anymore.

Mr. Wagner touched Mindy Sue's shoulder, waking her gently. "Come with me, sweetheart. You can't be here for this. I don't want you involved."

"But I want to stay with Brooke. She shouldn't be alone." Mindy Sue squeezed Brooke's fingers, avoiding the bandages covering the many lacerations on her palm and arm.

Brooke saw the worry in Mr. Wagner's eyes. "Go," she choked out, not wanting to involve her best friend in this very dangerous situation.

Brooke was the only one who could identify her attacker.

Mr. Wagner looked at her one last time. "Are you sure you want to do this?"

Brooke nodded. It had to be done. Adam had to be stopped.

Minutes after they left, the governor walked in and stood at the end of her bed, his shoulders slumped, dress shirt collar unbuttoned, tieless, and his hands deep in his slack's pockets. Pale, weary, his face deeply lined with a haggard expression. With bloodshot eyes, he let his gaze roam over her battered body, wincing at the bandages covering her arms and the brace on her broken wrist and ankle, never really looking her in the eyes.

Silence stretched as he seemed to shrink in on himself.

Then he pulled himself up to his full height with an inhaled breath and his rough voice rasped out. "He left a very disturbing and anguished message for his mother." Governor Harris rubbed his hand over the back of his neck. "We rushed to his apartment." Whatever he was remembering shone as pure torment in his eyes. "He...he slit his wrists." His gaze landed on her abdomen and stayed there, though he couldn't see the damage his son had done to her. To her baby. The fact that he couldn't only served to prove the devastating loss she'd suffered at his son's hands. "We barely got there in time."

No one got to me in time to save me—her—from him!

"He's been taken to a secure, private mental health facility."

Not jail.

"Doctors there will treat him for his wounds and the obvious psychological breakdown he's suffered." The governor put both hands on the bed's frame and hung his head, his knuckles white from holding on so tightly. His gaze came up filled with remorse and a plea. "I beg you. Please. Allow us to get Adam the help he needs. Prison will only leave him broken. Please. I'm begging. Don't point the finger at him."

The cover-up had already begun the second the governor admitted Adam to the private hospital, and unless Brooke blew the story wide open, Adam Harris's suicide attempt would be recorded as a tragic symptom of mental illness and nothing more.

She stared right through him. She didn't care about his pain, what he wanted, or what happened next.

Adam was locked up.

But not where he belonged.

Even in her devastated state, she knew she'd never get justice. Nothing would ever be enough to compensate for the loss of her daughter.

"Do you see me?"

The governor swallowed so hard she heard the click of his throat and stared down at her. "Yes, Brooke. I see you. I know exactly what he did."

"I am not the only one."

He flinched a second before resolve hardened his eyes. "You will be the last. He will never get out. I promise you that."

"That better be the one promise you keep for the rest of your life."

Air whooshed out of his lungs in a deep sigh. He ground the heels of his hands into his damp eyes, then raked his fingers through his close-cut, silver-threaded brown hair. He gave her one last once-over, straightened his shoulders and spine, then walked out of her room completely poised and in control once more.

She seethed and grieved and hated with her broken heart as her never-ending tears fell and she tried to believe in the promise he'd made even as he carried out his self-serving agenda.

If he didn't keep his promise, she wouldn't keep her mouth shut.

And that made her a serious threat and him a very dangerous enemy.

Chapter Four

Brooke hadn't been left alone since she'd been admitted. She knew what everyone was worried about. It worried her, too, that she so easily thought about ending it. What did she have to live for now?

In the back of her mind, a whisper said, *A lot.*

At the moment, it was hard to conjure something, anything that made her feel even a glimmer of hope that she wouldn't feel this grief and loss and rage for the rest of her life.

They told her she was well enough to go home today.

Home.

The dorm? The ranch? Not with Cody and Kristi there. Where exactly was home?

She'd planned to make a home with her daughter in the apartment she was having set up for them. Now, she could care less about her plans for the future. What did they matter when her daughter was gone, the dreams and plans she'd made nothing but fantasy, washed away by absence and aching sadness.

A knock sounded on the door.

The nurse who helped her shower, redress her wounds, and dress herself had left a few moments ago. The nurses usually gave a cursory knock before stepping in, but whoever was on the other side of the door waited for permission.

"Come in." Was that her raspy voice? She remembered screaming and wailing when she found out her baby died. Until now, she hadn't realized how much her throat ached.

Mindy Sue walked in with her father.

"You look better." Mindy Sue tried to smile, but it didn't reach her eyes.

"No, I don't."

Mindy Sue held something clasped in her hands. A round silver box. It could be mistaken for a trinket or music box. But no. It held something more precious to Brooke than anything else in this world.

She held out her trembling hands.

Mindy Sue stepped forward to place the vessel in her hands and covered Brooke's with hers. "I'm so sorry."

Brooke clutched her daughter to her chest and broke down in wracking sobs.

Mindy Sue wrapped her in a tight hug.

Doug stepped forward and brushed his hand down her hair.

Brooke flinched from the contact, but he didn't say anything and only brushed his hand over her head again, offering her comfort as the tears fell like rain.

She held the vessel to her chest, sniffled back her remaining tears, and stared up at him. "Please. I need to get out of here."

Doug's eyes filled with understanding. "The car is downstairs at a side entrance just in case there are any media out front. The nurse will be here with a wheelchair any moment."

Brooke wasn't concerned about the media. Yes, they knew someone had been attacked on campus again, but they didn't have her name. She could be anyone leaving the hospital, but Doug was being cautious and she appreciated it.

She didn't have the strength or brain power to deal with anything more than getting from the hospital to her dorm room, where she could crawl into her bed and try not to think about anything anymore.

Mindy Sue stuffed the paper bag of meds and clean bandages the nurse had left for Brooke into the duffel Mindy Sue had packed and brought from their dorm room this morning. Her clothes had been cut off her body in the emergency room the night of the attack, so Mindy Sue had brought her some spare clothes and toiletries.

"Thank you for bringing my clothes and stuff."

"Of course." Mindy Sue hooked the bag strap over her shoulder and grabbed the bag of personal effects the emergency room staff had taken off Brooke the night she arrived here.

How long had she been here?

She wasn't quite sure. The last couple days bled into each other.

The heavy-duty pain meds didn't help her keep things straight either.

The nurse backed into the room with the wheelchair.

Mindy Sue steadied Brooke as she moved to the wheelchair on rubbery legs. The brace on her sprained ankle kept her off-balance. She settled in the seat and held up her feet as the nurse adjusted the footrests.

Doug and Mindy Sue stepped out of the room ahead of her. The nurse pushed her toward the elevator, where Doug punched the button.

She had a sinking feeling that it didn't matter if she left this place where her trauma and injuries and loss had been tended and mended in some ways that she'd never escape. The cuts would scar. Her heart would forever be missing a broken piece. Her mind would never forget Adam, the attack, the death of more than her sweet little girl, but the loss of a life never lived and memories never made.

Would she spend forever wondering what might have been, daydreaming about what could have been?

What was better? These moments of sad realities or the fog that encased her in shell where she thought about and felt nothing?

Somehow, she found herself in the sunlight, blinding her. She winced and shied away from the brightness and heat that reminded her how cold she felt inside and out.

She didn't remember the elevator ride or getting into Doug's car as they pulled up in front of the dorms. She barely registered walking into her dorm room and lying on her bed, Doug and Mindy Sue whispering.

But she welcomed the shadows when Mindy Sue closed the blinds, the brush of her lips on Brooke's forehead before she went to her own bed and lay down. And then she let the fatigue take her down deep, where nothing mattered except the feel of the silver box resting on her chest over her aching heart. Maybe in her dreams she'd see her baby girl and tell her she loved her and missed her and was so sorry she hadn't been strong enough, fast enough, to save her.

Maybe then she wouldn't blame herself for letting a monster so close he could take the one thing she loved above everything else.

I'm sorry.

And how was she supposed to tell Cody he'd lost another child? Not because nature had deemed it unviable but because of the violence unleashed by a man's obsession.

Cody would hate her for not telling him, for not allowing him to be a part of the pregnancy and sharing their little girl with him.

He'd hate Brooke for not protecting her.

She truly had lost everything.

Chapter Five

"*Thank you for joining KNTB News. Tonight's top story...*"

A picture of the UT San Antonio school logo popped up on the screen next to the news anchor's face.

"*As we've been reporting, the University of Texas at San Antonio campus attacker assaulted another woman. His fifth victim was found near the campus library and taken to the hospital with life-threatening injuries five days ago. We are happy to report that after two surgeries, the victim was released this afternoon from the hospital. The woman's name and details about her condition have not been released to the public. Police still do not know the identity of her attacker, who fled the scene prior to police arriving to help the victim, though they have released some details. He is believed to be approximately five-foot-nine, with a slim build, wearing all black, including the ski mask he wears to conceal his identity. Campus police and San Antonio PD are asking all female students on campus to remain vigilant and stay in groups.*"

The camera panned over to the female news anchor.

"*We also have an update on Governor Harris's son, Adam, who was found in his apartment several nights ago after he tried to take his own life. He remains at a private hospital receiving treatment for his injuries and mental health. Today, Governor Harris spoke to reporters outside his office."*

Cody leaned forward on the couch as the TV screen switched to video of Governor Harris's comments. *"My son, like so many other Texans, is suffering from depression. He's struggled with his mental health for a long time. We are so grateful to the doctors and nurses taking such good care of him right now. He's receiving the best treatment available, something not everyone has access to but deserves, just like my son. That's why I'm working with our public health department to come up with funding and a new initiative to help those in need. I hope to have something in place very soon because people struggling with mental health issues need help now. Thank you."*

Cody's heart went out to the governor and his family. It hadn't been that long since the governor, his wife, and Adam were all here celebrating Christmas with them.

The governor stepped back from the reporters, who shouted out questions. The governor held up his hands. *"Please, I ask that you give me, my wife, and Adam our privacy at this time so that we can focus on Adam's needs and helping him heal."*

Cody hoped the governor made mental health a priority and he wasn't just paying lip service to something that was desperately needed for underserved communities, where folks couldn't afford therapy that was often not covered by insurance.

Kristi glanced over at him. "I still can't believe the governor's son attempted suicide. It's so sad. It's all anyone is talking about. On one show yesterday, they had people from his classes talking about him. Everyone said he was quiet and had few friends."

Cody wondered if that was true. "I think Brooke was friends with him. I saw them talking at the Fourth of July picnic and at Christmas when he was here."

Susanne came up behind them. "Dinner is served."

Cody turned off the TV, stood, and held his hand out to Kristi to help her up. The last few days had proven to be a reversal of their schedules, where Kristi had been working nonstop and helping her mother on some charitable project. They'd barely spoken on the phone, let alone texted. If he didn't know any better, he'd think she was purposely avoiding him.

The thought that maybe she knew he wanted to end things and was stalling crossed his mind more than once. Not that he'd given her any indication of that since he'd made up his mind just days ago. Still, it seemed odd. And the longer she made him wait to see her, the closer they got to the wedding date.

But tonight was the night. He'd invited her over, hoping to talk and end things amicably. But Susanne opened the door to Kristi when she arrived and invited her to stay for dinner before Cody could say anything. So he was stuck waiting until after their meal to have the private talk. It needed to be done today. He didn't want to wait any longer. Kristi deserved to know he'd changed his mind, so she could break it to her family and they could cancel all the wedding plans. And he desperately wanted to see Brooke and tell her he loved her and wanted to be with her.

Kristi took her seat and looked across at Susanne. "You heard about the governor's son, right?"

Susanne never said anything to him about how she felt about Kristi being at the table when Brooke hadn't been home in months. It had to wear on her. She had to be upset with him for the way things had changed.

He sensed she didn't say anything because she knew he didn't like Brooke's absence any more than she did. But he hoped to change that very soon.

Tonight would be the first step in getting Brooke back.

Susanne nodded. "That poor boy. I thought about calling his mother, but decided to give them some time before I reached out."

Kristi loaded a slab of lasagna onto her plate. "They've got their hands full right now, that's for sure."

Cody handed the salad bowl to Susanne. "Everything seemed fine at the Christmas party. But I guess you never really know what someone is going through on the inside when everything on the outside seems fine."

Thinking about the Christmas party made him think of Brooke. Memories of her lingered in his mind and popped up all the time.

Was she upset about what happened to Adam?

Were they close enough that she'd know if something was wrong?

Was she sad for her friend right now?

He didn't want to think about her being upset. He wanted her to be happy. Always.

She hadn't come home for her twenty-first birthday. He'd always thought they'd share that special day together. He'd get her drunk. Keep her safe. Show her a good time.

Right. The last time he shared a drink with her, they'd had a good time that ended in disaster.

The last time he spoke to her was on her birthday. He'd wanted to reach out so many times, to let her know he'd changed his mind about marrying Kristi. He wanted to tell her how much he loved her. But he needed to end things with Kristi first.

It felt deceitful to sit next to Kristi now, when she was oblivious to what was going to happen after dinner. His appetite shriveled up. He didn't want to hurt her. He was doing this so he didn't hurt her more in the long run by lying about his feelings.

Kristi added lasagna to his plate, but spoke to Susanne. "How was your day?"

"I went by Brooke's building to check on the progress of the renovation. She's going to love all the changes. I sent her some pictures of the café space. Then I did some shopping. I thought I'd send Brooke a little something to cheer her up."

What? Why? "Is something wrong with Brooke?" Cody tried to sound casual and not as desperate as he was for any information about her.

"I've gotten the feeling she's not been herself lately. I think she might be homesick and stressed about finals over the next few days."

The upcoming wedding probably weighed heavily on her. Cody wished he wasn't the cause of her upset. He'd make it up to her. Soon. He couldn't wait to see her. He couldn't wait until she was home. With him. Finally.

Their housekeeper, Janie, walked in from the kitchen with a stack of mail. She clutched several envelopes to her chest, her eyes filled with dread and worry.

"What's the matter, Janie?" Susanne asked, her voice urgent.

"I'd forgotten to get the mail earlier and went out to retrieve it now. There's something odd. Is Brooke sick?"

Susanne set her fork down with a clatter on her plate. "No. I don't think so. Why?"

"There're several statements from the insurance company and a hospital addressed to her. And this." She held up the cream-colored envelope. "A card from a funeral home."

"What?" Susanne snatched the mail from Janie. "Thank you."

Janie walked away, leaving the family to deal with their own business.

Cody's stomach went tight as Susanne opened the first envelope, scanned the statement, pushed her plate away, and tore open another envelope. Then another. And another. And another, until they were all spread out before her on the table.

She opened the card and tears fell from her eyes as she covered her gaping mouth with her fingertips, making Cody's heart race.

"Susanne, what is it?"

She held out her hand, waving her fingers in a gimme motion, her gaze filled with a panic that set off all kinds of alarms inside him. "Your phone. I left mine upstairs. Give it to me."

Cody handed it over into Susanne's shaking hands. She tapped at the phone, fumbled the number, and had to try again. She held the phone in a death grip as she listened. "Voicemail. Voicemail. Damnit, Brooke, answer the phone. Answer the phone."

She dialed again and listened, then slammed the phone on the table.

He snatched back his phone. "Susanne." Even his sharp tone didn't get her attention as he tried to see what the statements said without pulling them out from under Susanne's hands.

Openly crying now, Susanne shook her head from side to side.

Kristi's gaze bounced from him, to her, then back again.

Cody's gut twisted, his chest so tight he could barely take in a breath. He desperately needed Susanne to tell him what happened. "What's wrong with Brooke?" His mind spun tales of what might have happened to her. Everything his mind conjured scared him half to death.

"This can't be true." She slammed her hands down on the papers. "This can't be true!" She picked up the papers. "Blood work. A gestational diabetes test."

He didn't know what that was.

"Obstetrician visits."

Oh God. Cody's mind reeled as his stomach knotted.

"This is why she hasn't come home for months. Not for a weekend, or her birthday. This is why she planned to stay with Mindy Sue for a few weeks before coming home after she graduates. All this time...she was pregnant."

With my baby. It has to be mine.

Wait. *Was pregnant.*

Cody went stone still.

Tears streamed down Susanne's face. She held up the card. "Condolences on the loss of her child." Misery filled her every word. "This can't be true."

Cody felt the cold reality of it sink into his bones, like claws biting into him.

"No!" he wailed and swept his arm across the table, sending his plate, wineglass, and silverware flying across the room and shattering on the floor.

Kristi flinched and stared at him, eyes wide with shock.

He grabbed the papers and tried to concentrate and sort out what he read in black-and-white, but couldn't seem to take in as real.

This can't be happening. Not again.

Why didn't she tell me?

Maybe it wasn't his.

No. It had to be his.

And I wasn't there when she needed me.

He jumped up from his seat and ran to his office. He pulled out the folder he kept in his desk with all the information for Brooke's school in case of emergency. He called the dorm advisor first, since Brooke wasn't answering her phone and going through Mindy Sue probably wouldn't get him anywhere.

"Hello."

"Andrew. This is Cody Jansen. I'm trying to reach my sister, Brooke Banks, but I can't seem to get ahold of her. Is she in the dorm right now?"

"Uh..." The pause lasted so long, Cody thought maybe the connection had cut out.

"Andrew? Are you still there?"

"Sorry. I've been instructed by campus security not to give out any information on Brooke's whereabouts."

That set off all kinds of red flags. "Why?"

"I'm sorry, I can't say. You'll need to call the dean for more information."

Cody hung up, found the dean's number, and dialed.

"Hello."

"This is Cody Jansen. I'm calling about my sister, Brooke Banks." He never called Brooke his sister, but he'd use the family connection and whatever means necessary to get answers.

"Mr. Jansen, I'm so sorry. It's terrible what happened. I assure you, we are doing everything possible to keep her safe and find the perpetrator."

Confirmation that something terrible had happened to Brooke sent a shockwave of dread through his system. He pressed his palm to his desk to steady himself. "Is she all right? Why weren't we notified that something happened?"

"She gave strict instructions when they admitted her to the hospital that no one was to call her family. I'm sorry. She's an adult. My hands were tied."

"What can you tell me about her condition? About the baby?"

"Well...I need to be sure you're really who you say you are. We've had a lot of calls from reporters."

"I know the baby didn't make it." He hoped that assured the dean that Cody was really who he said he was.

"They've kept that information in the strictest confidence. I've not seen Brooke, but have been told her injuries are quite extensive. Worse than any of the other victims. She fought for her life and that of her baby, but the man had a knife. I don't know the exact details of her injuries because of the privacy laws. You'll have to speak to her. She returned to campus just a few hours ago with her roommate. We have security outside her building. I'm sorry, but that's all I know."

"I'm on my way." Cody hung up, pulled his keys from his pocket, and started for the door, passing Susanne and

Kristi on his way. "Keep trying to call her. Tell her I'm on my way." He thought about that, and then changed his mind. "On second thought, don't tell her I'm coming. She might not like it. Call me as soon as you reach her. I need to know that you talked to her. I need to know that she's okay."

Susanne caught up to him, grabbed his shoulder, and pulled him around. "I'm coming with you."

"No." He couldn't think past getting to Brooke. Right now. Ten minutes ago. Three days ago. Six months ago. He met Susanne's gaze. "*I* need to do this. Please," he begged, hoping if he got to Brooke first, he'd have a chance to salvage something, anything of their relationship.

If Susanne came along, Brooke would lean on her and probably shut Cody out. He wanted to be there for her, to share the pain of losing *their* child. To help her in any way he could and pull her back to him and the love they shared. He wanted to prove to her that she hadn't lost him or that love.

She needed him. He needed her more than ever.

"She's *my* daughter." Tears gently rolled down her cheeks.

He put his hand to her arm and squeezed. "I know."

"Her baby died!" Susanne wailed and the tears came in a torrent. She cried so hard, she started to hyperventilate.

Cody took her by the shoulders and practically held her up. "Susanne, take a slow breath. You're going to—"

Her eyes rolled back and she passed out. It was all he could do to wrap one arm around her and ease her to the floor without her bumping her head.

"Oh my God." Kristi rushed forward and dropped to her knees beside him.

Susanne was already waking up and mumbling, "What happened?"

"You fainted."

She tried to get up.

Cody gently helped her sit and kept his hand at her back to ensure she didn't pass out again and crack her head on the marble floor. "Give yourself a minute."

The tears had slowed but not stopped. "I need to see her."

"You're in no shape to go anywhere right now. And what if she's already on the way home and we miss her?" The dean said she was in her dorm with security outside, but Brooke could decide to leave campus and come home to her mother. He doubted it, but it was a possibility.

Susanne pressed her hand to her forehead. "I need to be there for her." Her voice came out soft and made her sound lost.

"I need you to let me do this. You understand, right?" He didn't have time to go into what happened between him and Brooke at Christmas. At this point, Susanne had to know the baby was his.

He didn't even look at Kristi. That was a conversation for another day, to go along with the end of them.

"I just..." She looked at him with teary eyes filled with worry. "I feel sick about all of this."

He got that when she fainted on him. He'd never seen her do that, but she'd never been rocked by such terrible news like she was today.

"You need to rest." He hugged Susanne, hoping to reassure her. "Wait here in case she comes home. Please."

Susanne begrudgingly nodded as he let her go. "Bring her home."

He gave Susanne a quick kiss on the cheek, so grateful she'd let him go to Brooke alone. "I'll call you as soon as I see her." He helped her up and didn't let go until he was sure she was steady.

"I'm fine. Go. Hurry."

He took two steps toward the door before Kristi stepped into his line of sight and said under her breath, "Let Susanne go and take care of Brooke."

He met her angry gaze. "I can't. Not now. Please take care of Susanne. Brooke needs me." He slammed the door behind him and ran to his car. The long drive would test his patience. Strained and anxious, he drove, fast and nearly reckless, his focus on getting to Brooke and discovering exactly what happened to her and his baby.

Chapter Six

The normally two-hour drive took him one and a half. By the time he reached campus, he knew several things. The hospital refused to give him any information. They wouldn't even confirm Brooke had been admitted. He'd called the local police and campus security. Even though he was a lawyer and Brooke's stepbrother—technically—he couldn't get any information. Everywhere he turned, he met a brick wall.

No wonder the reporters didn't have Brooke's name as the latest victim. The police, the school, the hospital, all of them protected her identity. Cody could only think of one reason they'd do that. Brooke could identify the campus stalker. Also apparently, someone had shut everyone up. That meant money. That meant power. Whoever was behind this had both and was using them to keep everyone quiet. Including Brooke.

Two security guards met him outside the dorm entrance.

"I'm sorry, sir. Only students who live here and have ID are allowed in the building."

"My name is Cody Jansen. I'm here to see Brooke Banks."

The two guards exchanged a telling look and turned back to him.

"Are you with the press?" one of them asked.

"No. I'm her stepbrother." He hated using that to get to her.

"We can't let you in without her authorization."

"Go in and get her. Tell her I'm here. She'll want to see me." He hoped that didn't turn out to be a lie.

"She's not to be disturbed tonight."

The hospital had released her earlier today. The dean had given up that much, but Cody knew nothing of her condition or the severity of her injuries. Or what her injuries were to begin with. She'd presumably given birth prematurely, and the baby hadn't made it.

He imagined that alone was horrific enough for her to deal with on her own.

That she'd been attacked by the campus stalker with a knife made matters worse.

Had he raped her like he had the last student?

The rage that had been smoldering inside him since he found out what happened flared to life yet again, but he held it together so the security guards didn't send him away for good.

Cody had no idea what to expect when he saw her, but he couldn't let his mind go down that road or he'd do something rash and upset her more. She needed him calm. She needed him to take care of her.

He kept his cool. Barely. "Brooke is family. She needs me." *And I need her.* "So, please, let me in."

"Listen, Mr. Jansen, we have strict orders from campus security and her lawyer that no one gets in to see her. Why don't you talk to her lawyer and have him put you on the list of people allowed in? They'll give you a visitor's pass."

He held up a hand. "Wait a second. She has a lawyer." That shocked him.

Who the hell did she hire? And why?

The guard nodded, then looked past him toward the parking lot. "Yes. You just missed him."

"Who is he?"

"Mr. Doug Wagner. He just left with his daughter. She'll be back shortly."

Doug Wagner, the top defense attorney in San Antonio and Mindy Sue's father. No wonder everyone had sealed their lips. No one would go against Wagner. If he wanted the case handled discreetly, he'd get his way. Even the police chief was afraid of being sued by Wagner. Cody wanted to know just what the hell had happened to get him to shut everyone up.

Cody took out his cell phone and called the dean. "Dean Fitzpatrick. This is Cody Jansen again. I can't get into Brooke's dorm because two guards are stopping me. Take care of it." Cody hung up and paced in front of the two security guards while he waited. It didn't take long for one of their radios to beep. The security office had called to allow him entrance to the building. The guard verified Cody's ID, then swiped his card down the lock. Cody ran in and rushed up the three flights of stairs to Brooke's floor.

He walked the long hall. Unusually quiet. No one on this floor played their music too loud or ran up and down the halls between friends' rooms. A few students eyed him suspiciously as he passed open doors. He stood outside Brooke's door at the end of the hall and stared at the many get-well messages on her white board. Below it, several photos of Brooke, Mindy Sue, and lots of other girls covered a bulletin board. Brooke had a lot of friends.

He raised his hand to knock, but stopped at the last second when someone pounded up the stairs and yelled, "Stop." He turned and found Mindy Sue jogging toward him with Brooke's messenger bag over her shoulder, hair disheveled. Blue smudges darkened the underside of her eyes, and even the weary way she moved told him how bad things had been over the last few days.

"Don't knock. You'll wake her up. It took me forty-five minutes and a sedative to get her to go to sleep."

Cody put his palm to the door with his fingers splayed. He leaned forward and rested his head on the back of his hand.

She was right behind this door. It had been months since he'd seen her. He didn't want to wait a second longer.

Mindy Sue's hand pressed on his shoulder. "Let her sleep. I'll let you in to see her after we talk. Okay?"

What choice did he have? Two brand-new deadbolts on the door were a cold, grim reminder of the reason he was here. He wasn't getting in unless he woke up Brooke, or Mindy Sue opened the door.

He stuffed his hands in his pockets and followed Mindy Sue down the hallway. She took him to a small room that served as a kitchenette with cupboards, microwaves, and two refrigerators that all the students shared. They both took a seat at the small, round table by the only window. Mindy Sue set the bag on the table between them, running her hands over the material. He'd given the bag to Brooke right before she'd left home for her freshman year.

"She has a term paper due in one of her classes, but the police had her bag. My father got it back along with her laptop."

He looked up at her then. He didn't really care about the bag. "Start with when she came back from Christmas break and work your way up to what happened five days ago, and why no one called her mother, or me." Controlled rage laced his voice, but it didn't deter Mindy Sue's cold stare.

"I understand that kind of fury. I've felt it for the last five days. The last six months that asshole stalked and terrorized her."

Those words fell on Cody like a ton of bricks. "Are you serious?"

"Yes."

"Why didn't she tell me? Her mom? The police?"

"You know why she didn't want either of you to know. She reported it to both campus security and local law enforcement. They've been investigating. A fat lot of good that did. They couldn't trace the gifts he sent because he paid with cash or gift cards for everything. The pictures...well, any number of people could have taken them on campus, in town, anywhere and everywhere she went. He never relented. It never stopped. He just let her know he was out there, watching her, knowing her every move. And then he nearly killed her."

"Start at the beginning," Cody demanded, trying to understand how this happened.

Mindy Sue glared harder.

He fisted his hands on the table, feeling helpless. "Please."

"Brooke came back to school early. You know that. She was upset you'd decided to marry Kristi."

"Kristi was pregnant," he defended himself. But there was no defense for the way he'd treated Brooke, his best friend. She'd left home, pregnant with his baby, without saying a word. For months. Did he have a right to be angry? Yes. No. How was she supposed to tell him after he chose another woman? Not once. But twice.

Fuck!

"I'm sorry for your loss." She was the first to say that to him since Susanne held him after he confessed the loss to her. He and Kristi had kept the pregnancy mostly a secret. No one outside of Brooke and Susanne knew about it and the miscarriage.

Well, and Mindy Sue. Because Brooke told her best friend everything.

Which meant Mindy Sue knew what happened between him and Brooke and how Brooke had been feeling about everything these last many months.

It hit him all of a sudden that Kristi had simply moved on like the miscarriage never happened. He supposed it could have been because it was so early in the pregnancy, she never actually felt like it was real. The end of the pregnancy happened because nature took its course.

He still felt the weight of the loss.

Kristi never wanted to talk about it. For him, it faded into the background, then popped into his mind at odd moments. Once, he'd told Kristi that and asked if it was the same for her. She said no. It just wasn't meant to be. She looked forward to the wedding and their life together. He supposed that was one way to cope. He wallowed in the what ifs and what could have been if only their child were here.

How did Brooke feel?

The miscarriage hurt but it was nothing compared to seeing that condolence card and knowing that his baby, six months along in Brooke's belly, died without ever taking a breath.

Mindy Sue brought him back to the present. "Brooke listened to your message...I don't know how many times. It killed her to know that after Kristi lost the baby, you still chose her."

"Kristi and I... It doesn't matter now." The reality was, he'd feared that Brooke wouldn't take him back after what happened.

That was just an excuse for not trying and risking the rejection and possibly making things worse between him and Brooke.

He'd thought things couldn't get any worse than them not speaking anymore.

He'd been wrong.

This was so much worse.

Now that he'd decided to end things with Kristi, did this change whether or not Brooke would take him back?

No. He wouldn't let anything stand in his way.

She loved him. He knew she did. All he had to do was convince her that he loved her and no one else.

Mindy Sue sat back in her chair and took a deep breath. "She had no reason to believe you wanted her after..."

"I asked Kristi to marry me." He'd given up Brooke, and true love and happiness, to give his child a whole family.

"The way Brooke explained it, you didn't ask so much as tell Kristi that's what would happen."

"I thought it was the right thing to do."

"We'll agree to disagree on that," she snapped. "Anyway, Brooke understood you wanted to do the right thing by Kristi and the baby. It hurt. But those were the circumstances, and Brooke made it easy for you by stepping out of the picture."

"When did she find out she was pregnant?"

"I imagine she figured it out when she started throwing up, then feeling fine, then feeling sick again. But she realized she didn't just have a bug one afternoon when we went out with Julie for lunch." Mindy Sue turned thoughtful for a moment. "Adam, Jeremiah, and Simon showed up and joined us. She ordered the fried chicken salad. Her favorite. But when the waitress set it in front of her...the smell made her sick. She ran to the bathroom. I followed her to make sure she was okay. We both suspected she was pregnant. We left the restaurant, hit the drugstore, went back to the dorms, she peed on the stick, we celebrated."

He would have loved to be there for that.

Mindy Sue smiled softly over the memory. "Beyond excited, she didn't care about feeling sick or tired all the time. Even in her sadness over you, she was happy about the baby." Mindy Sue met his gaze. "Really, really happy, Cody."

His heart ached with that news. "Why didn't she tell me?"

"She expected you to get married within a few weeks of her discovering she was carrying your child. She didn't want to ruin your wedding to Kristi, so she planned to tell you when you returned from your honeymoon."

"She had to know I'd have changed my plans and been there for her and the baby."

"She didn't know that. She thought you loved Kristi more because you chose her," Mindy Sue shot back, staring him down. "You and Brooke had an amazing night. You knew she was in love with you, but you never said anything about how you really felt about her. Kristi turns up the next morning pregnant, you bought her a ring, told her parents, and started planning your wedding within hours. You told Brooke that's the way it had to be and sent her back to school."

"I didn't want to. I wanted her." *I still want her.* He fisted his hands again, feeling like he should have done something. He would have if he'd known any of this.

"She woke up to you telling her you'd figure everything out, so you could be together, and then you put a ring on Kristi's finger. But for you, Brooke held off telling you about the baby, so that *you* didn't feel like you had to choose between her and Kristi. She didn't want to put you through that, and she didn't want to put herself through hearing you choose Kristi. *Again.*" Mindy Sue smacked her hand on the table. "You can't blame her for trying to salvage a little of her pride."

No. He couldn't. He didn't know what he'd have done in her place. "I hoped we could work things out. That's why I texted her after Kristi lost the baby, asking if we could talk. But she said she was already having enough trouble with her boyfriend and didn't want any more Kristi drama."

Mindy Sue's eyes went wide. "She told you she had a boyfriend? That can't be right."

"She said something about having trouble with some-one else. I just assumed that's what she meant."

Mindy Sue shook her head. "I'm guessing she said someone else instead of stalker to tell you something was going on without lying to you outright. She hasn't been seeing anyone. Not while pregnant with your baby."

"Well, I didn't fucking know that because she wouldn't talk to me," he snapped and ran his fingers roughly through his hair. "Fuck. If she hadn't said that, I wouldn't have stayed with Kristi. I wanted to ask if she still loved me. If she wanted us to try again."

Tears welled in Mindy Sue's eyes. "Text messages are not how you ask that."

"She wouldn't answer my calls."

Mindy Sue stared up at the ceiling for a moment and let out a heavy sigh. "All this over a miscommunication." Mindy Sue shook her head. "You two could have been together all this time. She would have opened up to you about what was happening."

Cody scrubbed his hands over his face. "All I had to go on was what she said in those messages."

"Yeah, well, you were very clear when you said you were still marrying Kristi. Brooke didn't fit in your world. Right?" She rolled her eyes.

Cody had to admit, it sounded rather lame. Another excuse.

But he'd stopped making those five days ago when he had that bad dream and decided to end things with Kristi.

Wait.

Five days ago.

The night Brooke was attacked.

Fuck.

That was some kind of kismet or cosmic nudge.

He felt more connected to Brooke than ever.

He hated that she thought he loved Kristi more than he loved her. And why wouldn't she? He'd made it seem that way by continuing his relationship with Kristi for all the wrong reasons when deep down he wanted to be with Brooke.

Mindy Sue sighed, fatigue sinking her shoulders. "I told her to call you. She refused. She didn't want to use the baby and make you think you had some obligation to her."

"She and my child are not an obligation. They're...everything."

"Then maybe you should have taken a breath after Kristi told you her news, given yourself a day or two to think about all your options, and told Brooke what that night meant to you and that things had changed about how you felt about her, even if you felt like you couldn't be with her."

Cody wanted to slam his head into a wall. So many small mistakes added up to one huge one with Brooke. He could have been with her all these months. He could have helped her through the pregnancy. He would have married her. Because he loved her. Not because of the baby. Months of scattered thoughts and emotions crystallized into true reality.

"I should have just told her about Kristi losing the baby and asked her to call me. She would have, and we'd have talked, and there's no way I wouldn't have begged her to come home."

"Shoulda, coulda, woulda." Mindy Sue shrugged. "It's too late for all that. You two weren't talking. You stayed with Kristi and set a new wedding date, so Brooke planned to tell you right after your honeymoon, so you two could figure out how you'd share custody of her."

"Her?" Cody asked, the single word clogging his throat.

Mindy Sue smiled sadly. "Yes. Her. A girl. We went to the ultrasound a few weeks ago and the doctor was able to see the sex. Brooke was over the moon in love with that baby. While the doctor did the ultrasound, Brooke sat talking to the baby. She would move around, and we watched her. It was the most amazing thing I've ever seen. Brooke has the pictures and a short video. They're all that's left of her. And her ashes."

"Brooke had her cremated?"

Mindy Sue nodded. "We'll get to that."

"Why didn't Brooke tell her mom about the baby? She must have wanted to share that with Susanne and get her mom's advice." The wedge between Brooke and Susanne was his fault.

"She didn't want to put her mom in that position. And...she wanted to tell you first."

Susanne probably wouldn't have kept the secret from him and would have demanded that he do right by her daughter.

"We celebrated her birthday with a few friends at an ice cream parlor. She's had the biggest craving you've ever seen for ice cream almost the entire pregnancy." Mindy Sue pulled out her cell phone and showed him the picture of Brooke at her birthday party.

She stood sideways, showing off her baby bump, with a hot fudge sundae in her hand. She held the spoon with a big bite about to go into her mouth. She smiled brightly, her whole face aglow.

He took the phone and stared at Brooke, so carefree and happy. Nothing else had really changed in her appearance, except for her rounded belly.

She looked lovely pregnant.

And now, she wasn't, and their baby was dead.

He put his head on his arms on the table and just took it all in. Tears came to his eyes, but he wasn't able to shed a single one. He looked up at Mindy Sue, now crying herself. She took the phone from him and glanced at the picture again before tucking it away.

He waited, but Mindy Sue sat silently looking out the window. "She didn't like going out anymore, but that night, she put you and her stalker out of her mind for just a little while. She didn't look over her shoulder every five seconds or let her anxiety drive her back to our room where she locked herself away all the time." Mindy Sue finally looked at him again. "You made her night when you called. She loved the gift you sent. She's still wearing your earrings."

His chest went tight, knowing that he'd brightened her birthday and that she'd been happy to hear from him.

Mindy Sue's gaze darkened with rage again. "Then we came back here, found yet another present *he* left for her, and the next morning she found out he'd raped someone at the same time we were out celebrating her birthday."

Whoever was doing this was sick in the head.

"Had this stalker tried to hurt her before? Did he threaten her?"

Mindy Sue frowned. "No. That's why campus security and the local police couldn't really do anything. But it freaked her out to know someone was out there, watching her all the time. The gifts he sent, they were things she'd see in a store but didn't buy herself. A scarf. A pair of earrings. A bracelet. He'd leave her favorite donuts at our door. He'd have her favorite pizza delivered for her lunch while she sat in the quad working on a paper. Things that on the surface seem nice, but when done without you knowing who is doing it, why, and what they want from you..."

"It's creepy. I'd have been just as concerned as her. I'd have probably made her come home." He'd have protected her.

"She wanted to go home, but she knew she couldn't hide. What good would that do? He hadn't done anything really threatening, except follow her around."

Cody thought about it. "But she knew, like you and I know, he'd eventually approach her. And she didn't want me to find out about the baby."

Brooke had handled all of this on her own. He should have been there for her. He shouldn't have allowed this many months to go by without checking in with her in person and seeing for himself that everything was okay.

"After the first three campus stalker attacks, the police told Brooke they suspected her stalker was the guy attacking those women."

That spiked his attention. "Why did they think that?"

"Because all the girls looked like Brooke."

Fuck. That hit him hard. While the news had reported the attacks, none of the victims were shown on TV, only the description of the stalker. "She knew they all looked like her but still didn't come home. She didn't call to tell us she was in danger."

Mindy Sue didn't respond.

How could she? He'd done this to Brooke and himself. He'd left her no way to come home or talk to him.

"He wore a mask, so none of his victims could ID him. He picked easy targets. All the girls were drunk and walking alone. So Brooke never went anywhere alone anymore." Mindy Sue's gaze drifted back out the window and her eyes filled with tears.

"If Brooke never went anywhere alone, how did he get his hands on her? What happened, Mindy Sue? What happened to Brooke and my baby?"

She finally turned back to look at him. The tremendous guilt in her eyes unsettled him. "It's my fault. I was late. I had a movie date with Tony. We were on our way to pick up Brooke at the library. Brooke was there working on her term paper and studying for a final exam. It's tomorrow," she said absently.

"Everyone on campus was warned not to walk alone at night. That's when all the attacks happened. She waited inside the library as long as she could, but they closed. I spoke to her on the phone. I was only minutes away. To save time, she said she'd walk to the parking lot behind the library, and we'd meet there. She followed a few other students out." Mindy Sue's voice drifted off, then came back on a whisper. "We should have gotten there just a minute or two after her. We hit every red light on the way, delaying us even more." Her watery gaze met his again. "That's all it took. Just her falling behind those other students, and he grabbed her and dragged her into the bushes and trees."

Cody scooted his chair around the table, close to Mindy Sue's, and took her hands. They were as cold as his whole being felt from the inside out. "Go on. What happened next?"

The tears swimming in her eyes fell one after the next. "He grabbed her as she came around the side of the building. He said he had a surprise for her, or something. She tried to play along. It seemed like he thought she knew who he was, but he was behind her so she couldn't see him. But she thought she recognized his voice."

Cody waited. Whatever was coming was difficult for Mindy Sue to say, and it was going to be even harder to hear.

"My father thinks she was his ultimate goal. The other girls were just...practice. He wanted her, had fixated on her. He dragged her farther away from the library. He told her he had a car. But then..."

"What?"

"She begged him not to hurt her or the baby, and he snapped. He didn't know she was pregnant. She hadn't gained a lot of weight, and all of it was in her boobs and belly. We joked that being pregnant would be the only time we'd ever have a really great rack."

Cody almost found a smile. Brooke had a good sense of humor. It sounded like she was happy with the pregnancy and looking forward to the baby coming, even though she didn't have his support. She had her friends. She had Mindy Sue.

"She only really popped in the last few weeks. Besides that, to be more comfortable, she mostly wore loose dresses and a cardigan. I think you gave it to her for Christmas and her mom sent it because she'd left all her gifts at the ranch. Anyway...the clothes made it hard to tell if she was pregnant, which is what the police advised her to do."

Cody got the gist of that statement. The police thought the stalker would take exception to Brooke being pregnant with someone else's baby.

Mindy Sue carried on with the disturbing story. "That night, she was wearing leggings and a tunic that showed everything off. My father thinks until that moment and because he grabbed her from behind, he didn't get a good look at her until he turned her around." She stopped and wiped away tears. "He went nuts and said she'd betrayed him. He stabbed her twice in the shoulder."

Cody gasped and rocked back into the seat.

Mindy Sue went silent.

"Go on. I need to know everything." So he could help Brooke get through this.

Mindy Sue sucked in a breath. "The stabbings didn't stop her. She fought hard to save herself and the baby. At one point, she ripped off the ski mask. She knew him. She said something to him, I'm not sure what, and it sent him into a rage again. He still had the knife and sliced up her hands and arms as she tried to fend him off. She never gave up. Not even when...he stabbed her in the stomach."

Cody's heart slammed against his chest in deep aching beats. He couldn't breathe. He couldn't think past the grotesque images assailing his mind.

Mindy Sue's voice droned on and echoed through his mind. "The knife came out of his grip, so he grabbed her arm and threw her to the ground. He broke her wrist. She tried to get away even then. He held on to her foot and twisted it pretty good. It's in a brace now. When he got her back under him, he looked down at her and realized what he'd done. She said he looked horrified. He ran. She heard the sirens and the police calling for her. She called out to them but there was nothing they could do to save *her*."

Her. His daughter.

Tears fell down Cody's face. His heart barely beat. He couldn't get a breath. "He stabbed the baby?" Cody asked, not really believing that's what happened.

"I'm so sorry. The umbilical cord had been severed. Brooke's heart was literally pumping the blood right out of her."

Cody shook with the revelation of how close he'd come to losing Brooke, too.

"They delivered the baby by C-section. It's left a large scar. All her other wounds weren't life threatening. Her shoulder required some surgical repair to the muscle and tissue and another bad bleed. Her broken wrist will be in a brace for several weeks. They stitched the worst of the cuts on her hands and arms. The others were minor and will heal on their own. And none of those things is as bad as looking into her empty eyes."

Mindy Sue raked her fingers through her already disheveled hair. "In the hospital...even now...I feel so inadequate to take care of her. Nothing I say or do will make Brooke feel better. She hasn't slept much. She's in a lot of pain, but even that doesn't compare to how much she misses the baby. They wouldn't let Brooke hold her, or see her. They said it was for the best. My father and I set up the cremation at her request. He got the funeral home to do it immediately, so she could have her baby back. My father and I picked up the ashes today and delivered them to Brooke before she left the hospital. I think it broke her, holding her baby for the first time, only she was in a silver vessel and not a pink blanket."

Cody wiped away more tears. "Who did this to her? Who killed our baby?"

"She made me promise not to call you or her mom before they loaded her into the ambulance. I wasn't sure she was going to make it. Not with that much blood loss. As soon as I got to the hospital, I called my dad. He arrived immediately and shut everyone up. Her name was kept quiet. He made sure she got everything medically necessary. The police weren't able to see her that first night. In the morning, they tried to talk to her, but her baby was gone, and she only stared into space. She wouldn't speak. They asked me to go in, and my father thought it was a good idea if I tried to find out what happened, and who attacked her.

"When I went into the room, she had her eyes closed and tears ran down her face and into her hair like a river. She told me her baby was gone and I held her."

Tears continued to run down her face and she could barely speak anymore. She swiped at them, but more came.

Cody wiped his own face, crying with her. All of this pain because a madman wanted to possess someone.

"She asked my father if he'd help her. He agreed and no one has been allowed to speak to her again. No one, except one man. He came to see her that night, although my father made sure no one saw him come or go."

"Who came to see her?"

She met his gaze. "The governor."

It took Cody only a second to realize the implications of that visit. Rage exploded through him in an eruption of fury and heat. That fucking little punk hurt Brooke and killed his baby. "Adam."

Mindy Sue nodded that she'd come to the same conclusion. "I'll remind you that Adam was at the Fourth of July picnic and the Christmas party. Right before the fireworks went off at the picnic, Brooke thought she saw someone upstairs in her bedroom window. At the Christmas party, the person she believed was just a follower on her social media left a message about how good she looked in her dress."

"He was already stalking her."

"She thinks it started at the picnic. We knew it was someone there, but there were so many people, several of them friends of ours. We knew it could be one of them, but they never gave us any kind of strange vibes."

"You said Adam showed up that day you went out to eat and she got sick, then took the pregnancy test."

"Yes. We'd met up with him a few times. But he was always with Jeremiah and Simon. They were all so nice. Shy. Well, not Jeremiah, but Adam and Simon. She was never alone with him. She never got a weird vibe from him. He was so careful. I mean, you could tell he liked her, but he never flirted or anything. He never asked her out." Mindy Sue tilted her head. "Why didn't he just ask her out?"

Cody didn't get it either. "I don't know."

Brooke was kind. She'd have tried to spare his feelings and let him down easy. She'd have still been his friend.

Fuck!

All this time, Adam had been close to her. Right in front of her.

Cody wanted to hit something. Preferably the asshole responsible for tormenting Brooke.

But he was out of reach, wasn't he? The governor had already taken care of that. And he had the audacity to sneak into Brooke's room in the dead of night to...what? What could he possibly say to her after she lost her child?

Had he threatened her? If he had, Cody would put him in the ground.

The governor and his people were working with the police and the hospital to cover up the real story of what happened that night. A man had gotten away with murder and attacking five women all because his father was the governor of the state.

Mindy Sue's furious voice broke the silence. "No one will ever know the governor's son attempted suicide because he couldn't live with what he'd done to Brooke."

Cody couldn't believe this was truly happening. No wonder no one was talking. It was a cover-up of monumental proportions. The governor lied and hid his son in a private hospital.

Cody wanted to get his hands on the son of a bitch, so he could kill him. Slowly. Painfully.

If Adam went to trial and got the death penalty, would his own father pardon him?

Unreasonable and selfish things ran through Cody's mind about what he'd like to happen to the governor's son. He indulged in them for a moment before realizing there was nothing he could do while Adam was locked away in a mental ward. No one, not even Cody, would ever get to him.

It was futile to try to go after Adam now. But somehow, some way, very soon, he'd get justice for Brooke and his daughter.

Right now Cody needed to protect and take care of Brooke. She needed him.

They'd lost their daughter.

He had to see her.

"Is that everything?"

Mindy Sue swept her blonde hair back over her shoulder. "That's all I know. She's determined to turn in her term paper and take her exam tomorrow, though I don't know how she'll do it. She's a basket case. She can't hold a thought for more than a moment. She sits for long periods just staring into nothing and cries for hours. The doctors say she needs time to process everything that's happened and to grieve for her daughter. I've spent the last few days with her, and I can tell you, she's only gotten worse."

"I'll take her back to the ranch. I'll get her whatever help she needs. I'll take care of her."

"I don't think taking her back to the ranch is a good idea. Not with Kristi there and the wedding in a couple weeks."

He didn't want to think about anything but Brooke. The wedding, everything, everyone could go to hell. He'd lost a daughter, and all he wanted to do was take care of his baby girl's mother.

Chapter Seven

Cody slid off the stool. "I need to see her now."

Tired beyond words, Mindy Sue's fatigue mirrored his own. The last several days had taken a toll on her. The last few hours had worn him down, even more than the last six months without Brooke had.

"I don't think it's a good idea to wake her. Her meds finally kicked in, and she was sleeping well when I left. I wasn't planning on leaving her alone this long, but I didn't want to tell you what happened where she could overhear us if she woke up."

"I just need to see her, so I'll know that she's really okay."

"I don't think seeing her will ease your mind." Mindy Sue stood and started back down the hall.

He followed. "I know she's injured."

"There's just no way to prepare yourself to see her. Believe me. Before I walked into her hospital room, the doctor tried to warn me. You just can't believe it until you see it."

Cody walked beside Mindy Sue to their room. She unlocked the door as quietly as she could. The deadbolts clicked and slid out of place. Opening the door slowly, she peeked in to see if Brooke was awake. Mindy Sue sighed with relief.

Cody looked past her and got his first look at Brooke. He moved farther into the small room. A lamp shone on the desk. A scarf over it cast a blue glow, soft, but enough light that he could see her. Her chest rose and fell as she breathed, disrupted by soft hiccups from crying herself to sleep. Wadded-up tissues lay beside her on the bed. Mindy Sue gathered them up and tossed them into a wastebasket under the desk that separated her bed from Brooke's.

He took a moment to catalogue Brooke's injuries. Her face was pale as death with dark circles under her eyes. A long, stitched cut on her cheek. She wore a tank top, allowing him to see a large bandage on her shoulder. Her left arm was bandaged. He couldn't see the cuts, but the fact that it was bandaged from her elbow down to her hand told him they were serious. Her hand rested over a silver-covered oval dish.

"Is that my daughter?" Cody whispered.

Mindy Sue touched her fingertips to Brooke's hand over the too-small vessel that held a tiny life that had never gotten a chance to really live. "Yes. She won't let go of her."

Cody wanted to pick her up and hold her. This was as close to his daughter as he would ever get. He knew that would wake Brooke, so he stuffed his hands in his pockets and continued to stare down at her.

Her right arm was bandaged much in the same way as her left, but it was in a strapped brace that served as a cast. He guessed despite her broken wrist, she still needed to be able to clean and re-bandage the stitched cuts. The tank top covered the bandages around her midsection. The outline of them showed through the material. Her leg, encased in a heavy black brace, lay outside the blankets that slightly covered her to the waist. She couldn't be comfortable, though pillows kept her propped up. Her right arm rested on a pillow by her side. He bet any time she moved her arm, it sent pain through her shoulder.

He had no idea how to get her back to the ranch without subjecting her to more agonizing pain.

The thought of hurting her made him ill.

"Why did they let her out of the hospital so soon? Shouldn't they have waited a few more days at least? Kept an eye on her injuries?"

Mindy Sue gathered some clothes from her closet and whispered over her shoulder. "She didn't need to be there anymore. The surgery went well. They patched her up and put her back together. She can walk and get around on her own. It's not easy, and it's painful. She can't use her hands and arms very well, but she'll manage with help."

"But the C-section," he protested.

"Most women who have one spend only three days in the hospital; she was there nearly five. She's okay, Cody. Physically, she's healing well."

Mindy Sue came over and stood beside him. They whispered, but even that small sound made Brooke squirm and mumble in her sleep. Her shirt turned wet over her left breast. He gave Mindy Sue a questioning look.

"Her milk came in. That's why her breasts are so big. Can you imagine your own body rebelling against you? You know there's no baby in your head, but your body insists there is. The doctor said her milk will dry up in a few more days."

Mindy Sue took a washcloth from a drawer and folded it in half. She gently raised Brooke's tank top enough to put it over her breasts. He guessed it was the best she could do without waking Brooke completely.

"Her pills are on the desk. She can't have anything else until two in the morning. If she wakes up, help her the best you can. I'll be downstairs on the second floor in room twelve. That's Julie's room. You remember her from summer last year. We all hung out at the ranch for a week."

Cody remembered the petite blonde with the giggling personality. She was a sweet kid. *Kid*, he thought. She was only a year younger than Brooke. Brooke seemed to age before his eyes. He saw her now for the woman she was: a badass mother, who fought for her life and that of her child. He was sorry it had taken him this long to see how tough, resilient, and strong she'd become.

"I don't know how she's going to react to seeing you."

"It'll be fine. I love her. I'll give her whatever she needs. But I'm not leaving her side for anything. Not now. Never again."

Mindy Sue stared at Brooke, then him again. "Okay. You can have my bed for the night. If you need me, come down and get me. We'll figure out what comes next in the morning." She bit her bottom lip, obviously reluctant to leave.

"I'll be gentle with her. You can trust me. She does." He hoped that was still true. If not, he'd spend the rest of his life proving it to her.

Mindy Sue came to Cody and gave him a hug, holding him tight for a moment. He needed it. He gave her a squeeze. "Thank you for taking care of her, for being the friend she needed, for watching out for her, for...everything." It should have been him with her, but he was glad Brooke had Mindy Sue.

She hugged him harder. "Make her happy again."

He held her at arm's length. "I won't stop trying until I do."

She nodded with a look in her eye that said she'd hold him to that. "I'll see you in the morning." Mindy Sue moved toward the door.

He waited for her to leave. The locks clicked into place with her key. He wondered if Brooke needed that sense of security even now, after Adam had been locked up.

Toeing off his shoes, he sat heavily on Mindy Sue's bed. Pulling his cell phone out of his pocket, he dialed Susanne. Well after ten, but he knew she wouldn't care about the time, and only needed to hear from him about her daughter.

He didn't want to wake Brooke and walked to the door, undid the locks, then stepped out.

Susanne answered on the first ring, and he said the only thing that mattered. "She's going to be okay. I swear it." He would do anything to help Brooke heal. "I have to whisper. She's asleep." He didn't want his voice to carry through the door or to others on the floor.

"What happened?

"She was attacked by the campus stalker." He let that sink in for a moment. "But it's a lot more complicated than just that."

"Did they catch him? Who was it?"

"You can't tell anyone for a lot of reasons."

"I won't. Just tell me."

"Governor Harris's son, Adam." He paused and looked through the crack in the door at Brooke, twitching in her sleep. He wanted to go back in and softly touch her shoulder to try to soothe her but knew nothing he did would help her. "I'll explain when I have more time."

"And your baby?"

Your baby.

"Our little girl was killed during the attack," he said, choked up, and let the tears fall.

Susanne's tears and grief drifted through the phone. "No, Cody. No," she sobbed. "I didn't want it to be true."

"It is." He needed to face reality and be strong for Brooke. She needed him to hold it together so she could fall apart and he'd be there to pick up the pieces. "I spoke with Mindy Sue. She told me everything. I'll fill you in on the details when I can. I want to bring her home tomorrow, but I'm not sure I can because of her injuries. They're bad. The drive will be hard on her. She might fight me about coming home to the ranch after...everything that's happened."

"If she can't come here, I'll go there. We can stay in a hotel until she can travel. In the meantime, take care of my girl, Cody. Tell her I love her. Tell her I want her home. Tell her nothing else matters. We'll take care of her."

Nothing else matters, as in it didn't matter that she hadn't told them about the baby. No one would be upset with her over it.

Cody had to agree. He'd made it impossible for Brooke to come to him.

Shaking off his misery, he remembered the most important thing was getting her well.

"I'll call you in the morning. Mindy Sue said Brooke needs to turn in a term paper and take her last final exam. I'll see if she's up to it. No matter what, I'm staying until I can bring her home."

Susanne knew him well enough to know he wouldn't leave Brooke alone anytime soon.

"I wish I was there, but I don't think I'd have been able to keep myself together. She needs us to be strong for her. I can't imagine her grief. The thought of losing her...I can't go there. She's my heart, Cody. And so are you. I hurt for the both of you."

Cody could barely get his next words past the lump in his throat. "You need to prepare yourself to see her. She's hurt badly. It's going to take her weeks to heal." He took a minute to calm himself before he went on. "Susanne, I'm sorry. This is my fault. If I'd talked to her after we... If I didn't let this thing with Kristi roll on, even when I knew..."

"You shouldn't have crossed the line if you only intended to hurt her," she snapped.

"I didn't want to hurt her. Kristi was pregnant. What else could I do, but be there for her and the baby?"

Susanne cried harder. "I'm s-sorry. I know y-you'd n-never hurt her intentionally. I'm just so an-angry about her st-staying away, and not confiding in me. I feel so helpless to h-help her now."

"It's going to be okay. This is my fault and I'll fix it."

Susanne let out a heavy sigh. "Cody, don't do that to yourself. Blaming yourself won't help her. Even if Brooke had told you about the baby, she probably still would have returned to school to finish her semester. The person stalking her would have found her here, there, wherever she went. It isn't your fault."

He appreciated that she said that, even if he didn't believe it.

"Sometimes, terrible things happen. We can only do our best for her now. She needs us, our love and support."

"I know. And I promise I will give her all of that and more."

"I know you will. Call me in the morning. Kiss her goodnight for me."

"I will." He ended the call, walked back into the room, locked the door again, crossed to her bed, and leaned over Brooke, kissing her softly on the forehead. "Your mom told me to tell you she loves you, sweetheart." Because she was asleep, he added, "I love you, too," and pressed his lips to her forehead, hoping that when she woke up, she'd be happy to see him.

Stretched out on Mindy Sue's bed, he lay on his side, just looking at her sleep beside him. In the more than ten years he'd known her, he'd never told her he loved her even in a non-romantic way. She'd told him all the time how she felt. She made a point of showing him how much she cared. Maybe not always in the best way—she could be a little forward at times—but she'd been young and determined.

He had to admit, even when her antics to win him were comical, he was flattered.

It hit him hard that he'd almost lost her, and he'd never told her how he felt about her. Maybe he hadn't known how deep his feelings ran. Maybe he'd denied them for so long, he couldn't see them for what they were.

Everything had come clear that night they shared together, five days ago, and now. He didn't want to waste another day of his life without her. He needed to be loved by her. He wanted to spend every day, every hour, every second loving her. Because he did. Deeply. Wholeheartedly. And he was ready to make sure she knew and felt it every day for the rest of their lives.

If she'd let him.

Chapter Eight

B eyond tired. Everything hurt. Every big and little cut and bruise and broken bone. Her muscles still ached from the fight. Nothing felt normal. Brooke wanted to wake up from this nightmare. But she was already awake and still drowning in misery and heartache.

She opened her eyes and stared across at Cody, lying on his back on Mindy Sue's bed, his forearm over his eyes, the other arm draped across his flat belly.

Sometime in the middle of the night, she'd woken to the pain radiating through her whole body. His deep, gentle voice whispered in her ear that she was safe. She'd be okay. Then he gave her the blessed pills that sent her back into oblivion.

She remembered feeling his lips pressed to her forehead and how it paused everything else and gave her a moment of joy before it crashed into pain once again.

He didn't belong to her.

He'd leave and go back to Kristi and his life with *her*.

She had nothing left of her old life. Not even her baby.

And if Cody was here, that meant he knew what had happened. What she'd failed to do. She didn't have to tell him.

All she had to do was face the kindness he'd show her, because he was a good guy. She didn't deserve his kindness. She'd failed. And they'd lost the precious soul she didn't protect.

She clenched her hand over the tiny vessel that held her daughter's ashes and turned away from Cody. It hurt to look at him, to know that the piece of him he'd given her was gone.

Moving set off a quake of pain that sent one aftershock after another of spasms and agony through her system. She tried to settle into a position that didn't press on any injury, but with so many, that was hard to do.

The tears came again in a wave of sadness that washed over her. She tried to be quiet and not wake Cody. She didn't need or want his sympathy. Even worse, his pity.

She just wanted to be left alone to grieve and disappear into nothing so she didn't feel anything anymore.

A hand settled on her shoulder. She nearly jumped out of her skin and sucked in a gasp, ready to scream as a shockwave of pain radiated through her whole body. "Hey, sweetheart."

She flinched at the sound of his voice and his light touch.

Adam had done this to her. He'd taken her sense of security. For months now, she'd lived in a constant state of fear.

"It's okay, sweetheart." Cody brushed his fingers through her tangled hair. "It's just me. It's Cody. Remember? I came last night."

Her tears subsided and she tensed even more under his soft touch.

He didn't mean it.

She met his blue gaze. "Let's get this over with, so we can both end this."

Cody's brows shot up. "What are you talking about?"

"Do whatever you need to do. Yell. Rage. Tell me how you think I'm a terrible friend for keeping her from you. Tell me it's my fault she's g-gone. I didn't p-protect h-h-er. I...I d-didn't s-save h-her." She choked out one sobbing cry after the next. "Go ahead! Say it! I deserve it. I can take it."

Cody shook his head. "You couldn't take a gentle breeze right now, sweetheart."

"How can you call me that?"

"Because none of this is your fault. It's mine. But I'm going to fix it. I promise."

"You can't fix this." Tears welled in her eyes. "She's gone! And it's not your fault." Her words showed her rising agitation.

Cody hung his head. "Maybe you're right. It's *his*. But the divide between you and me...that's *my* fault."

Brooke turned away from him. "It doesn't matter now."

"Yes, it fucking does." He leaned over the bed so he could see her face. "It matters more than anything. And I'm going to prove it to you."

The tears wouldn't stop. It was too late. There'd been too much damage, too much loss to go back. "I just want to be left alone."

He shook his head. "No, you don't."

She tried to roll away from him and ended up hurting herself. She groaned in agony as another wave of tears hit.

Cody softly brushed his fingertips over her hair. "Hey, baby, come on now. Be still. Take a breath. Just one. Nice and slow."

She tried as she shifted over to her back again and settled into the pillows surrounding her.

"That's it. There now. One more." His fingers sifting through her hair settled her even more. "That's better. Relax. It's just after six. You can have another round of meds." Cody uncapped bottles and shook out pills next to her. The mini fridge under the desk opened and closed. "I'm going to slip my arm under your shoulders and lift you up a bit so you can take these."

He moved her slow and easy, lifting her head, handing her the pills, then the bottle of water.

She downed all three, then settled back on the bed and laid her hand over their daughter on her belly. She needed to keep her close to help ease the overwhelming sense of loss.

"Those should kick in soon. You'll feel better."

"Not likely." *Not ever.*

Cody's gaze swept over her, landing on all the injuries and evidence of the brutal attack she'd survived only to wish she were dead.

"Go away." She wanted to be left alone. That's how she felt. So alone. So empty.

Cody hung his head again, then met her sullen gaze. "I'm not going anywhere." He dug his fingers into his bloodshot eyes and rubbed. "So stop telling me to go." It sounded like she'd hurt his feelings.

She really couldn't deal with the loss of her child and her broken friendship with Cody right now. "There's a donut shop half a block away. Go. Get some coffee. Leave me alone." She tried to roll over, but pain shot through her abdomen and her shoulder. She moaned and moved back, closed her eyes, and focused on trying to relax through the pain.

Cody brushed his hand over her head again. "Be still, sweetheart. Let me help you. Do you want to get up?"

She needed to pee, but she didn't want his help. She didn't want him to see just how bad she felt. The last thing she wanted or needed was his pity.

"I can do it."

"Honey, you couldn't swat a fly in the shape you're in."

"Fine. You want to play Prince Charming with a stick up his ass, let's do that." It hurt to have him so close and not have their daughter here. She'd waited too long, wasted too much time, and she'd denied him any chance of being a part of the pregnancy. He'd have no memory of her kicking against Brooke's belly, or seeing her bump grow each month. They'd never talked about names. Brooke had a few in mind but had wanted to wait until after she told Cody. Now it was too late.

She wished she could just curl up in his arms and cry and let him take some of the pain she was feeling away. She wanted to tell him so many things, and all of them were stuck in her throat and muddled in her mind. The only clear thing she could remember at the moment was he was going to marry Kristi in two weeks.

He'd chosen her.

And with the loss of their baby, Brooke had no place in Cody's future.

He was only here out of obligation.

"Just go, Cody. Go get some coffee. Get something to eat. Let me get up and figure out how I'm going to get through this day."

"We can't keep doing this, Brooke, acting like we're okay without the other person in our life. I'm sorry for the way things went over Christmas. I'm sorry that you thought you couldn't tell me you were pregnant. I know why you did it, but you still should have told me." The choked-up words made her already broken heart ache even more. "I'm even sorrier you spent the last few days in the hospital grieving for our girl all alone. I should have been there. I should have been with you." He leaned down and pressed his head to hers and whispered, "All this time, I should have been with you. I'm so sorry."

She didn't know what to do with those heartfelt words. Or the tears that dripped from his cheek onto her skin. She wanted to believe he meant it, that he wanted to be with her, but that was just his grief and emotions getting away from him.

Right?

She turned and found tears sliding down his cheeks, her sorrow reflected back to her from his watery eyes.

"I'm sorry," he said again, then leaned over and kissed the back of her hand where she held their daughter against her belly. Then he whispered to her. "I wish you were still here."

Brooke lost it and broke down again.

Cody softly kissed her tear-drenched lips. "I'm sorry she's gone, sweetheart. I'm sorry more than you know. I didn't know she was on the way, but I miss her so much already."

He hadn't moved more than a few inches from her face. Just enough for her to see he truly meant what he said. "We have a lot to talk about. One of those things is Kristi and the wedding. Right now, though, I just want to take care of you. Please. Let me do that."

Overwhelmed, she simply couldn't think and process what he was trying to tell her. This was his guilt and grief and pain making him talk and act like this.

Mindy Sue walked in, giving her a reprieve from having to confront her past with Cody again. "Hey, sweetie, you're up. How are you this morning?" Mindy Sue stood behind Cody, staring down at her.

"You called him," she accused.

"No. He just showed up."

Cody sighed and planted his hands on his hips. "We received a bunch of insurance statements for Brooke's prenatal care and a condolence card from the funeral home."

Guilt swamped Brooke.

"Oh God, Cody. I'm sorry that's how you found out." Mindy Sue said exactly what Brooke wanted to say.

She never meant for him or her mom to hear what happened from anyone but her. She simply didn't have the strength or emotional capacity to call them yet.

Cody continued to stare at her. "If not for the mail, that card, I might not have found out about any of this for days. I would have…"

"Married Kristi and been on your honeymoon," Mindy Sue finished for him. "Yeah. Great. Good for you," she said sarcastically. "Come on, Brooke. I'll help you change the bandages and get dressed. Do you want to wash your hair today?"

"I want to cut it off and hang myself with it."

Cody and Mindy Sue understood she wasn't entirely joking and exchanged concerned looks.

She leaned up on her elbow and tried to lever herself up without hurting anything. No such luck. Everything hurt first thing in the morning. By the afternoon, she'd be better. Once her body started moving, it seemed to do better to just keep moving. Too bad it was only a milder pain than overwhelming like now.

She struggled, and Cody gently put his hands at the back of her shoulders and pushed her up until she was sitting. She sucked in a breath and pressed a hand to her abdomen.

"Okay?" he asked, concerned.

"No. I am not okay. They practically cut me in half." Okay, that was a little dramatic and an exaggeration, but that's how it felt, like she'd been gutted. "Just move back and let me get up."

Cody did what she asked, but with little room to maneuver, he remained close. She stood and swayed and almost fell down. Cody's strong but gentle hands gripped her hips to steady her. "Easy, sweetheart."

Brooke put a hand to her head and waited for the room to stop spinning.

"You need to eat, Brooke. You barely touched anything yesterday. I'll go out and get us something. You shouldn't take those meds without food anyway."

"I'm not hungry," she said automatically.

"I'll get your favorite. Bacon, egg, and cheese biscuits. You can even have coffee again."

She'd given up caffeine when she'd found out she was pregnant. She hadn't had a cup in months, or a soda for that matter. She'd tried to eat as healthy as possible. Ice cream had been the one craving for sugary treats she'd allowed herself, telling herself that at least it had protein and calcium in it.

Mindy Sue put her hand on Brooke's shoulder. "Sweet-ie, please don't start crying again. I just put on my makeup, and I'd like it to last at least an hour before we start again. Deal?"

Brooke took a deep breath and swallowed the lump in her throat. "Deal."

She felt it then. Her breasts tingled and the warm, wet milk soaked through the cloth Mindy Sue must have put over her during the night. Her breasts were so full they actually hurt to the touch.

Tears welled in her eyes. She couldn't speak. She stum-bled her way to her dresser and found a new shirt, a bra, and the pads Mindy Sue had gotten at the drugstore to absorb the leaking milk. Without a word, she hobbled to the door and walked out, leaving Cody behind.

Mindy Sue followed. "You know you can't change on your own."

She stopped in the hallway and hung her head, her ankle aching, arms throbbing and stinging. "I can't believe he came."

"Of course he came. He loves you, Brooke. I saw it writ-ten all over his face last night. He was scared and desperate to see you. He knew he almost lost you forever and it devastated him."

They'd been friends forever. Of course he cared. That hadn't ended when he proposed to Kristi. Brooke had just gotten too caught up in thinking it had turned into some-thing more, and when she didn't get what she wanted, she couldn't accept anything less.

"I needed some space."

"Right now, you need him and your mom. You need to go home and give yourself the time and space you need to heal. You can't do that here, where it all happened."

"I'm not sure I can do it there either with him and Kristi in my face." The ranch wasn't home anymore. Not with them living there together. And even if she stayed at the new apartment, Cody would still be checking in. She recognized that from the way he was acting now. That would only make Kristi angry and stir up even more animosity and trouble between all of them.

"I wouldn't be too sure about that. Cody said some things last night, things you need to hear from him."

"About Kristi?"

"And about how he really feels about you."

Brooke couldn't even process that piece of information. "What do you mean?"

"It's for him to say. And I'm sure he will, once you're home. Plus, you'll be with your mom."

Brooke desperately wanted to see her.

The rest, she'd have to figure out later, when she had a clearer head and heart.

Mindy Sue helped her to the bathroom. Brooke had the use of her left hand, though her fingers were cut and swollen. It hurt to move her arm and pull on the stitches, but it was better than nothing.

She used the restroom, then Mindy Sue helped wipe her body down with a washcloth, wash her face, brush her teeth, tie her hair in a ponytail, and change her clothes.

It sucked that she couldn't manage on her own, but Mindy Sue was quick and efficient and Brooke felt a hell of a lot better.

And exhausted, though she'd barely done anything.

Slow going with the brace on her leg, but she managed to get back to their room while Mindy Sue ran out to get food.

Brooke opened the door and found Cody still there waiting for her.

"You look better. I called your mom and gave her an update. She can't wait to see you. Do you want me to call her back so you can speak to her?"

"No. I...I just can't yet."

Cody stuffed his hands in his pockets. "Okay."

"That's it?"

"I'm letting you lead here, Brooke. Whatever you need, I'll make sure you get it."

She needed help with the bandages. It was nearly time to turn in her term paper; maybe she'd ask Mindy Sue to do it after she returned with breakfast. The dean had notified all her professors she might not be up to attending the last few remaining classes. She wanted to take her final and just leave.

She'd miss graduation.

She tried to tell herself it didn't matter. But she couldn't go through with it because everyone would know she'd been attacked by the campus stalker.

One more thing Adam had taken from her.

Cody obviously wanted to take her back to the ranch. She wanted to see her mom, but...yeah, not a good idea. Too many memories. Too much quiet to think.

And the upcoming wedding on the ranch. All those people coming to wish the happy couple a happy life. All of it made her want to scream.

Cody sat on her bed, looking through her notebook. "You had everything planned. A budget for daycare, diapers, formula. Everything to raise our daughter on your own." He held up some printouts. "Cars for sale. Local mechanics to check them out before you bought one. A shopping list. A car seat, crib, dresser, changing table, a baby bathtub."

He shook his head. "When Kristi told me she was pregnant, she started planning a wedding. We didn't have a single conversation about buying a car seat for the baby, or getting a bathtub especially for them."

Brooke didn't know what to say. She didn't care what he and Kristi talked about, or didn't.

"You found out you were pregnant and started planning how you'd finish school, provide for and care for our baby, and focused on being a mom."

She still didn't say anything, because her throat closed and tears threatened. Yes, she had plans, but she didn't need any of them anymore because she wasn't going to be a mother.

But Brooke could do one thing for Cody. She opened the desk drawer and pulled out the framed photos of their baby's ultrasound.

She handed one to him.

He touched his fingers to the black and white image. "Look at her." He traced his fingers over her little face in the one image, and her little feet pressed to Brooke's abdomen in another. She loved that picture. Cody seemed to count out her little toes.

"It took Kristi weeks to tell me she'd lost the baby. You were going to wait nearly seven months to tell me I was going to be a father." He looked up at her. "Am I really that hard to talk to, Brooke? Do I make it impossible for the people closest to me to tell me things they think I don't want to hear?"

"I've never had trouble telling you what I think, even if you are stubborn and don't listen sometimes."

He met her gaze, the anger she'd been waiting for front and center in his eyes. "But you couldn't tell me you were pregnant."

"Circumstances, Cody. There were reasons, and you know them all. I was going to tell you in July," she said, choked up. "I hoped you'd be there for the delivery. I thought we could pick out her name. I was going to help you put together a room at the ranch for her when she stayed with you and Kristi. I made plans for you and me to be her parents *together*, even if we lived apart."

Brooke couldn't stand to see the pain in his eyes. She turned to her dresser to put away her things and tossed her dirty tank top and washcloth in the laundry basket.

"You were waiting for the wedding to be over and for Kristi and me to come back from our honeymoon. Mindy Sue told me last night. She also told me you almost called to tell me you were pregnant after I left you that damn message telling you Kristi lost the baby. But you didn't. You love me that much, you'd let me marry another woman, even though you were pregnant with my baby."

"I wish I had called." Immediately, she wanted to take that back. She couldn't let him think that anything would have been different. She turned and faced him, even though she couldn't look at him. "It wouldn't have changed what happened." She sighed and spilled the truth. "Adam Harris and I met at the Fourth of July picnic at the ranch. He'd been there several times before, I just never really talked to him until then. We talked about school and how he lived in his father's shadow, always falling short of his family's expectations. I don't think anyone really listened to him or cared about how he felt. I did. It was that simple, and he warped it into something that wasn't real."

"Mindy Sue told me he's been stalking you this whole time. Terrorizing you. Still, you didn't call me. You never said anything to your mom."

"What was the point of making you and Mom worry about something that seemed creepy, yes, but also innocuous? He sent me flowers to the house after the Christmas party, remember?"

Cody's eyes went wide. "The roses you thought I sent you?"

"The note said, 'You made last night remarkable.'"

His mouth fell open. "Of course you thought they were from me."

She nodded. "Then it was gifts and nice notes when I returned to campus. He did seem like a secret admirer with an undertone of something scary because of the way he followed me around without my knowing. It unnerved me. It made me paranoid. I suffered overwhelming anxiety. After a couple weeks without the person coming forward to ask me out, it went from odd to a warning of something ominous."

She sat slowly and carefully in the chair at the desk. "The detective who came to see me in the hospital said even if he hadn't attacked me that night and got me to wherever he planned to take me, that he probably would have killed me eventually." She shook off the chill that ran down her spine and invaded all her bones. "Adam imagined us in love, that I was his perfect woman. The second I didn't live up to the fantasy, he attacked me. He said I was supposed to be his. He stared at my baby bump and couldn't believe I'd let another man touch me."

"Not just another man, sweetheart. Me. I got you pregnant. She was *our* baby. We'll get through this together."

She ignored the last part, too aware that there was nothing left between them, not when the Brooke he'd known had died along with their daughter. She felt like an empty shell. Or rather, one filled with nothing but heartache and pain.

It hurt to breathe.

She didn't want to be here.

But she trudged on anyway and cocked her chin toward the closet. "Could you get that bag for me?" Too tired to get up, she waited for him to retrieve it for her. It took too much effort to simply exist through the emotional and physical pain.

A fine sheen of sweat covered her skin. Getting herself cleaned up and talking about what happened had sapped every ounce of energy she'd stored up after her fitful night of sleep. She needed to take a nap, and she'd only been up for an hour.

He grabbed the paper bag from the closet and dumped the contents on her bed, then rubbed his hand over the back of his neck, hesitation in his eyes. "I'm afraid to see what's under all those bandages."

"It's not pretty." She tried to use her right hand to unwind the bandages on her left arm, the one less injured, but it hurt to move her swollen fingers and hold her arm up at all.

Cody lightly touched her hand to still it. "Let me help you, honey. Just sit and rest. I'll do it."

He took the strand of bandage in one hand, her wrist in the other, and continued what she'd started. As he went, he removed the gauze pads covering long and short gashes that had been stitched closed. The sight of them made Cody's eyes cloud with concern.

"They look better today, less swollen," she said softly. "Um, there's a tube of medicine to put on the worst of them."

Cody rifled through the stuff he'd dumped on the bed. He found the tube and turned back to her.

Seeing the gashes triggered something primal inside her. One second, she was aware of the room, Cody, the pain inside her that never ceased. The next second, her mind shut off. It happened just that fast. She simply checked out. Lost in the fog of her mind, everything dull and quiet and blank.

Better than the images of the attack that tried to suck her back into a terror-filled nightmare.

Everything just went black.

Cody didn't know what happened. One second she was looking at him, then the grizzly gashes on her arm, and her eyes and face simply went blank. Nothing there. No movement. No emotion. Nothing.

Brooke was simply gone. Lost to wherever she went in her mind.

He bent at the waist and cupped her cheek, waving his other hand in front of her eyes.

Like a switch flicked, she came alive like she was ready to fight. She exploded, swatting and kicking and blocking. She screamed and tried to hit him again.

"Brooke!" Cody shouted right in her face.

She flinched and stilled, her gaze wide and finally focusing on him.

"Not Adam." The whispered words tore his heart to pieces and made him want to rage.

He was still tormenting her.

Cody brushed his fingertips softly along her cheek. "It's me, honey. It's Cody."

Her focus finally settled on him.

The tears came again.

His face was so close to hers, their noses nearly brushed. His breath mingled with hers as he breathed her in. "It's okay. You're okay. No one is going to hurt you. You're safe." He pressed his forehead to hers, while she sat staring up at him like she couldn't quite believe he was here and not Adam fucking Harris.

She touched her fingertips to his cheek. "You're real."

"That's my girl. Yes. It's me, Cody. You know me." He brushed his fingers down her hair, patiently waiting for her to really see him. "There. Now you see me. Let's fix your arm." He stood back and gently ran his fingertips up the backside of her arm until he slid his hand under her elbow. He held it up while he put the medicine on the worst of the cuts that covered her forearm.

Seeing them, her, like this, it gutted him.

"I'm sorry, Brooke. I should have known you weren't up for talking and moving around too much. We'll take things slow from now on. I promise."

She sat, blankly looking over his shoulder. Her whole body slumped in the chair. He had to hold her arm up for her. It was like she'd lost the strength to say anything or even move. She'd used up all her reserves and just needed to sit and not think or feel for a while.

He understood her desire to check out. But he'd have to watch her over the next few days and weeks to be sure she didn't fall too far into despair and away from him and living her life.

He finished putting the medicine on her wounds. "There we go, sweetheart. Did the doctor say to keep these covered?"

She dropped her gaze to her arm, then quickly turned away from it.

One of the cuts on her hand looked pretty bad. Two others farther up on her arm weren't in much better shape. The others were red but healing. Not so raw.

"Brooke, honey. Do we need to cover all of these again?"

"Hmm. Yes. No. What?"

"Look at me, honey." When she did, he asked, "Do we need to cover this like before?"

"No. The doctor said to cover the bad ones." She looked down at her arm again. "So, yeah, I guess that would be all of them, don't you think?"

He cupped her cheek. "We'll cover up the worst of them and leave the others alone. How long until the stitches come out?"

"I'm not sure. They gave me some papers with all the information. Mindy Sue put it in my bag. Some stay for a few more days. Others a week. Some more."

"Okay. When we get home, I'll make you an appointment with Dr. Nash. He can check you out and take out whatever stitches you don't need when it's time."

She grunted a noncommittal response.

He went ahead and put bandages over the worst cuts and rewound her arm in gauze to cover everything.

He ran his hands up and down her thighs until she looked at him. "I need to take the brace and bandages off your broken arm. I'm not sure I can do it without causing you severe pain."

"Just do it." She used her left hand to pull the straps free on the brace and winced, then gritted her teeth.

Cody took over, going slowly and methodically until he could lay the brace open with her arm on the desktop.

Every little jarring motion hurt her. The blood drained from her face and sweat broke out on her brow.

Cody tried to work quickly without jarring or moving her arm. He used the scissors on the desk to cut the gauze away. He tossed all the old bandages into the trash and quickly covered the cuts in medicine, re-covering them with new gauze pads.

His hands shook. He hated hurting her. He hated that Adam had done this to her and hadn't paid the price Brooke was paying now in pain and sorrow.

"Breathe, Brooke. I'm almost done." Instead of winding gauze around her arm again, he simply strapped the brace back on, trying his best not to move her wrist at all. "The brace will hold the bandages in place." He breathed a huge sigh of relief, then pulled her tank top strap down her shoulder and gently peeled the tape away from her skin, revealing the double scars where she'd been stabbed.

It shocked him to see the twin stitched cuts and bruising.

This could have been so much worse.

He tossed the bloody pads into the trash, slathered on a generous amount of medicine, then placed a new bandage over the wounds, taping it on all sides.

He breathed a huge sigh of relief to have one more task done.

But...now came the hardest one.

Cody sat and stared at her abdomen for a long moment, hesitating.

She gently pulled her top up, revealing the large bandage taped to her still-extended belly. She didn't look six months pregnant anymore, but her stomach wasn't flat either. Just deflated. Empty now.

His gaze rose to her engorged breasts. Soon her milk would dry up. She'd carried their daughter but never got to nurse her, hold her close and smell her, while she rocked and fed her.

That had been taken from her, too.

He'd never get to see that pretty picture in real life. Well, not with their daughter, but maybe with another child. One day. He hoped.

You're getting ahead of yourself.

He refocused on her belly, wondering how she had felt about sharing her body with their daughter. What a wonder that must have been for her. But now...she must feel so utterly alone and empty.

He wanted to say something to acknowledge that fact but didn't have words, because he felt an empty place in his heart now, too, and nothing would take away the ache and sorrow of losing another child for him.

But maybe being here for Brooke, helping her through this difficult time, would help him heal, too.

Cody rubbed his hands up and down her thighs to get her attention again, but all she did was stare at the wall, like she couldn't stand to look at her abdomen.

He sighed and gently peeled the bandage off her stomach, revealing the eight-inch, crescent-shaped line of stitches carved along the side of her belly button, disturbingly red and angry looking. He carefully dabbed on the medicine.

She hissed in a breath at his soft touch.

He stopped immediately and looked up at her.

Tears slid down her face, and one landed on her chest.

He brushed it away with the pad of his thumb, then brought it to his mouth and sucked it away, distracting her from the pain.

"Cody, please. It's too much. You have a fiancée waiting for you back home." She wasn't in any condition to hear what he had to say about that.

"We'll talk about Kristi when you're feeling better. Just know, everything has changed. I am here for you. So if you need me to tend your wounds, wipe away your tears, cry with you, hold you, love you, then I will do any and all of those things, anything to make you feel better. Or at least not worse. Because I understand your grief. I feel it, too."

Tears filled her eyes again. She didn't say anything about what he'd said, just gave the barest hint of a nod that she'd heard him, and kept staring at the wall.

He placed his hand on the outside of her abdomen, feeling the heat radiating from her skin. "This one looks really bad. I think it's infected. Did the doctor say anything about it?"

"He said it would be better in a few days and to make sure to keep taking the antibiotics they prescribed and using the medicine on it."

"Okay, I'll put more on later this afternoon and again tonight." He slathered on the medicine and bandaged the wound, taping it in place.

Others in the dorm were up and making noise in the hall and their rooms. A door slammed and she flinched, then immediately swiveled her head toward the door, like she expected *him* to walk through it any second. Her whole body trembled.

He put both hands on her thighs and squeezed, anchoring her to the here and now. "You need to get away from here and rest where it's quiet."

She needed someplace she could sleep without being disturbed, or thinking someone was coming after her.

"I want to take you back to the ranch. You need to rest. Your mother is frantic to see you."

She pressed her lips tight. "I have to turn in my paper and take one last test, so I can graduate. I can't let him take that away from me, too. The dean mentioned something about the press, too." Her breathing picked up after she said that last part.

Cody didn't like that she feared the press hounding her. He wouldn't let that happen. "You're not talking to the press, or giving them a statement. I don't want you to talk to anyone, including the governor and police, about what happened without me present."

Her gaze went back to the wall. "Okay."

"Okay? That's it? No argument? You wouldn't rather have Doug Wagner handling things for you?" Hurt tinged those bitter words.

"Doug was very helpful, but I don't want to take advantage, if you're willing to help me."

"I would have helped you through all of this if you'd said one single word that made me even suspect you were in trouble. I'm here, Brooke. I'm not going anywhere. I'll keep you safe and everyone you don't want to see away. I promise."

He needed her to trust him. He needed her to believe he wasn't going anywhere. He'd be right by her side. Forever if she'd have him.

"I don't really care what the press wants, what the governor wants, what the police and the school want. None of it matters. They can't bring her back." She stood from the desk chair and managed to lower herself onto the bed behind Cody. The heavy brace on her leg made it difficult to manage, but she settled on her side facing the wall, grabbed their daughter, brought her to her chest, and held tight. "I just want everyone to leave me alone."

She kept her back to him, her shoulders shaking as she cried.

He gave her some space, seeing the exhaustion on her face and in how hard every move seemed to be for her.

But he couldn't help offering comfort when she needed it so badly. He sifted his fingers through her soft hair and brushed it away from her cheek. "Get some rest, honey. Mindy Sue will be back soon with the food. You'll eat, and you'll feel a little better."

He hoped so anyway, because he couldn't stand to see her so broken and in pain, lost to her anguish and unable to really hear what he was trying tell her, let alone believe in a future for them.

He just needed to be patient.

And have that long-overdue talk with Kristi.

Chapter Nine

Cody's temper simmered beneath his grief as he thought about what Adam had done to Brooke and how the governor had swooped in to cover it all up. He wanted to know why Brooke went along with it, instead of calling for Adam's head on a fucking platter.

Maybe it was as simple as she just couldn't deal with it right now. As he'd seen, just breathing was all she could manage some moments. Her emotions seemed to be all over the place.

Not surprising given the hormones she was probably dealing with because of the pregnancy and birth, plus the trauma.

He remembered the way she'd drifted off while he tended her wounds, how the light literally went out of her. She wasn't in any frame of mind to make sound decisions right now.

He'd keep a close eye on her.

The governor had the advantage, took it, and ran with it.

Cody wouldn't allow him, or anyone else, to harm Brooke in any way.

Brooke was lost in overwhelming emotions and pain. Nothing would bring back their little girl. She needed time to grieve. To heal. To find her way out of this dark and devastating time.

Adam Harris was locked up—in a hospital for now, jail soon if Cody had anything to say about it.

Brooke wanted to be left alone. That might change, but right now, she needed time to sort out her feelings about what happened while mired under grief and depression. Soon, she'd get angry. It was an inevitable emotion and part of the grieving process.

As a lawyer, he'd seen enough tragedy hit his clients and their families. Sadness and depression gave way to not believing the event could have happened and bargaining with the universe to change things. Inescapably, somewhere in those stages came the anger. Brooke would go through all of that, and he would be there to help her through it until she came to accept what happened and find a way to move on with her life, absent their daughter.

He'd have to find a way to do the same. Again. He'd focus on Brooke, and in helping her, he'd help himself cope.

First he needed to know what information was out there, so he'd know how best to keep Brooke safe. He opened Brooke's laptop and logged in with the password she'd shared with him years ago. For the next twenty minutes, he mined the internet for information on the attacks on campus and Adam Harris's attempted suicide. It didn't surprise him that very little information made the news. Mostly the information gave a vague description of the attacker and an account of what happened to each of the unnamed women. Police and campus security were at a loss in identifying the attacker and most of the articles ended with warnings to women on campus to always stay in groups.

The articles about Brooke's attack didn't name her either, but gave the location and the general information of what happened.

If the press learned Adam Harris had been responsible for the attacks, they'd be unmerciful in uncovering the victims' names. They'd hound Brooke for her story. Cody would do everything in his power to shield her from having to talk about the murder of her baby and relive the attack and the loss over and over again.

As much as he wanted to yell to the rafters that Adam Harris tried to kill Brooke and had murdered his daughter, he wanted Brooke's privacy protected.

He wanted her to grieve in peace, while he found a way around the governor to the son who should rot in prison the rest of his life. There was no statute of limitations on murder. Let the governor think Adam was safe in the private, swanky hospital, getting well. All that meant was he'd be ready to stand trial.

Mindy Sue unlocked the door and walked in carrying coffee and breakfast. "Extra-large for you. Sorry, I could only get sugar." She pulled several packets out of her pocket.

He took them and set them on the desk. "No problem. I take it black. Thank you," he said, and took the large paper cup and the bag from Mindy Sue.

"How is she? Are the cuts healing?"

"All except the one on her abdomen. I'll keep an eye on it. Other than that, she seemed okay for a little while after you left, then she started drifting in and out. She jumps at things like he's coming for her."

Mindy Sue's eyes filled with concern and sadness. "That fucking piece of shit. It's like she can't get rid of him."

"It's over now. He'll never get close to her again."

Mindy Sue pressed her lips tight and stared at Brooke passed out on the bed. "She lost a lot of blood. The doctor said she'd be fatigued for weeks until her body recovered from the trauma."

Cody nodded and took a long sip of the hot coffee. He needed the caffeine kick. He'd think more clearly once it took effect. His gaze stayed on Brooke. "So many fucking scars."

"They'll remind her for the rest of her life of what he did and what she lost."

They both stayed silent and unmoving for a long moment before Mindy Sue dug through the bag of food and handed over two breakfast sandwiches to Cody. "She needs to eat. She needs to work on getting her strength back. And those are some heavy-duty meds they gave her."

"I'll wake her soon. She just settled down. Let her have a few minutes of good sleep. It'll help her get through the next couple of hours."

"Speaking of which... I went by her business management class and talked to her professor. He'll let her come in early to take the test alone. He said the dean told him she was going to take an incomplete, but I told him she wanted to finish the class and get her grade. She's got an A minus. If she can get through the test, she might keep it. I think it's best she finish for her own peace of mind. Adam has already taken so much from her, I'd hate to see him take away her graduation after all her hard work despite everything he's put her through all these months."

She bit into her sandwich and drank her coffee as they sat eating and watching Brooke sleep. "She can turn in her paper to her other class anytime today. She just needs to drop it by her professor's office. She planned to stay with me until after graduation and your honeymoon. I think she should go back to the ranch and spend some time with her mom. But if Kristi will be there..."

Cody could finish that sentence. Brooke had been through enough, especially this morning as he tended her wounds and she faced another day without their baby. "I will take care of Kristi as soon as I can. I'll take Brooke back to the ranch. I don't want her so far from home while she's in this condition. I want to take care of her, so that she sees I still care, that I need her as much as she needs me to get through this."

Mindy Sue eyed him, her father's tenacity glinting in her eyes. "I'm going to hold you to making Brooke happy again."

"That's all I want." He took another bite of his breakfast sandwich, chewed, swallowed, and changed the subject. "Tell me why Brooke agreed to keep things quiet."

"She didn't so much agree as she wasn't in any shape to do anything about it. That very private hospital the governor sent Adam to costs a fortune and specializes in mental health, but..."

"It's a country club psychiatric ward," Cody finished for her.

Mindy Sue scrunched her face. "He needs medical help, but he also needs to pay for what he's done, not live like he's spending time at a retreat and spa."

"He will." Cody would make sure of it.

Mindy Sue's eyes filled with regret and guilt. "We all hung out together several times. It was fun. Nothing stands out that came off creepy or weird. He just seemed...shy. He had a chance to ask her out the right way many times, but he didn't take it. Instead he..." Mindy Sue's gaze settled on Brooke.

All those bandages. All the harm *he* caused.

He killed their baby.

"Fuck," Cody barked and scrubbed a hand over his face, feeling the rough abrasion from his beard coming in.

Brooke rolled over with a wince and stared at him, concerned. "What's wrong?"

"I'm sorry, honey. I didn't mean to wake you."

"You woke up the children sleeping in China."

He smiled half-heartedly and unwrapped Brooke's breakfast sandwich. "Eat this, sweetheart. You need the energy. Want some coffee?"

"No. Water."

"Good. More coffee for me." He pulled a bottle of water out of the mini fridge and handed it to her.

"Sounds like you could use the whole pot."

"You're always looking out for me, sweetheart."

He helped her sit up and tucked a pillow behind her back so she could lean comfortably. Well, at least as comfortable as she could be. He took her hurt foot and propped it on his leg, ever watchful while she nibbled at her food.

"Mindy Sue spoke to your professor. After you eat, I'll take you over for your test if you're up for it. Then, I'll go and turn in your term paper. I'll come back here and pack whatever will fit in my car."

He turned to Mindy Sue. "Can you pack up the rest? I'll have a moving company come in the next few days and ship it home."

"Sure. No problem."

Cody glanced back at Brooke. "We can hit the road after your test if you're up to it."

Her head tipped down and she stared at her lap. "Cody, I don't know what I want to do yet. I have to—"

"You need to take care of yourself." He wouldn't take no for an answer. "There's only a week, maybe a little more of classes left before the entire campus goes home. I'm not leaving you here alone."

She finally looked at him again. "I'm not alone. I have Mindy Sue and Julie and all my other friends. They can help me." The tears spilled down her cheeks. She looked overwhelmed and exhausted.

"Honey, you can barely walk. You can barely stay awake for any decent amount of time. You can't tend to your wounds on your own. And judging by the fifty times you've looked at that door since you woke up this morning, I'm guessing you don't feel safe here. Let me take you home. I'll take care of you. Your mom will spoil you." He hoped that got her home. If she wouldn't come for him, which hurt to his soul, she'd do it for her mom.

"I don't know what to do." Her weak voice matched the uncertainty in her eyes.

He saw how hard she tried to think through her options.

She didn't have any, she just didn't want to admit it. He was taking her home.

She needed to remain in bed a few more days, or at least passed out on the couch in front of a TV, binge-watching something lighthearted and funny.

This wasn't the place for her. Soon, someone would leak that one of the victims was staying in the dorms. Reporters would camp outside for a chance to get to her. They might even sneak in to see her. Cody needed to get her out of here and back to the ranch, surrounded by familiar things and the ones who loved her most.

He needed to get her well enough and stable enough to listen to him and understand that everything was going to be different now.

Mindy Sue took his side. "Brooke, sweetie. Go home. See your mom. Cry on her shoulder and let her spoil you. Get away from here and everything that's happened. I'll come out to the ranch soon to see you. I promise."

Someone knocked on the door.

Brooke nearly jumped out of her skin.

Cody put his hand on her thigh. "You're okay, sweetheart. I won't let anyone hurt you."

Mindy Sue jumped up just as two girls peeked inside. "We're all set downstairs."

"Perfect timing." Mindy Sue turned to Brooke. "Sweetie, we have a little surprise for you. Come with me."

Brooke hesitated for a moment, all of them waiting for her to decide if she wanted to go.

Cody wanted to get Brooke up and out of the room and with her friends. He hoped it would boost her spirits and get her out of her head. "Let me help you up."

She reluctantly leaned forward and swung her legs off the side of the bed. He steadied her when she stood and swayed.

Mindy Sue tossed the trash from their breakfast. "You come, too, Cody. This is for both of you. Brooke, bring the baby," she said gently.

Brooke already cradled the silver vessel in her hand. She hadn't let it go for longer than it took to get changed and redo her bandages.

Cody didn't know what the girls had planned, but followed them without comment or questions. At the stairs, he carefully picked Brooke up and carried her down. She didn't say anything and tried her best not to let on how much everything hurt her, but he saw every wince and felt every time she tensed to ward off the pain.

They stepped out the back door into a small courtyard filled with the students from the dorm. They'd all come out to see Brooke after they'd been told Brooke had been in an accident and lost the baby. They gathered around the fountain. He set Brooke on her feet and stood behind her with his arms loosely wrapped around her waist. His hands clasped over hers, holding their daughter.

The circular fountain had a young girl standing in the center with an umbrella over her head. The water came out of the umbrella top and rained down into the surrounding pool. Everyone held a white rose and a small pink candle.

Mindy Sue took her rose and candle from Julie. They began the process of lighting the strawberry-scented candles everyone held. In all, more than thirty people attended the ceremony. Everyone had come to join Brooke in the informal memorial service.

"Everyone, this is Cody Jansen. He's the baby's father." Everyone stared at Cody standing with Brooke, his arms around her.

"We're all here to say goodbye to an angel that never got the chance to grace us with her presence." Mindy Sue swallowed hard. Her eyes glassed over with unshed tears, and she did her best to give Brooke and him sympathy and compassion for their loss.

"Brooke and Cody, there are no words that will make this time easier. Nothing we say or do will bring back your little girl. We'd all like you to know, we love you and are deeply sorry for your loss.

"Brooke, we spent the last six months dreaming with you about a little girl who'd have your brilliant smile and your sweet heart. I can only say, we're all sorry we never got to meet her. If she was anything like her mom, she was beautiful inside and out."

Mindy Sue gave Brooke the rose she held and set her candle in the fountain to float on the water. Julie did the same and both she and Mindy Sue stood beside Brooke as everyone came to her and gave her a rose and floated their own candle. Mindy Sue sang "Amazing Grace" and everyone joined in.

By the end of the ceremony, Brooke's arms were filled with roses and Cody stood with her, holding his daughter for the first time. The cool metal against his skin was startlingly in contrast to the warm little bundle he'd have liked to hold instead.

Completely overwhelmed, Brooke turned with all the roses in her arms and smashed them between her and Cody. She held on to him and buried her face in his chest and cried her heart out as everyone came and gave her a pat on the back and said goodbye.

Maybe this was too much too soon for her, but he understood Mindy Sue and Julie, her best friends, couldn't let her leave without acknowledging the loss and letting Brooke see how much everyone cared.

Cody held her until they were alone with Mindy Sue and Julie. He continued to hold Brooke when he addressed the other two women. "Thank you. I hadn't thought to...we haven't had time to..." He felt completely at a loss. He'd never seen such a display of friendship and love. Not like this. Brooke clung to him like she couldn't stand on her own. He was practically holding her up and thankful the roses had been de-thorned, or he'd have been stuck like a pincushion.

"It's okay, Cody. We did this for our friend. We did this for your daughter." Julie brushed her hand down Brooke's hair. "Brooke, look at the fountain. It's beautiful, don't you think? We wanted to do this for you tonight, but you'll be going home. We didn't want you to leave without our saying goodbye."

Brooke managed to turn around in Cody's arms and look at the little fountain. Lovely, the blue water against the white marble with all those pink candles sparkling, their sweet strawberry scent filling the courtyard. It reminded him of the lip balm Brooke used to always use when she was younger and still did in the summer.

Julie and Mindy Sue gathered the roses from her arms and tucked them into a huge vase. "We'll take these upstairs. You can get them along with some of your things after you take your test. My brother's friend works for a moving company. I'll call him tomorrow. We'll pack up your things and he'll bring them to the ranch."

Cody was touched. "Thank you."

Julie nodded and gave Brooke a hug. "Be well, my friend. I'll see you soon, I hope."

Mindy Sue hugged Brooke and looked over her shoulder at Cody. "I'll see you guys before you leave. Take care of her."

"I will. Always." Cody meant it with his whole heart. "We'll see you in a couple of weeks at the ranch." Meeting her gaze pointedly, he hoped Mindy Sue got the message. The next few weeks would be difficult for Brooke. Mindy Sue's visit would help.

Chapter Ten

Cody escorted Brooke to her class to take her test, even though she was wiped out. She insisted she needed to finish it before she left to keep her grade and graduate with honors. He begrudgingly left her to it and handed in her term paper to her other professor. Then, he went back to her dorm room and packed her suitcases and as much of her stuff as he could fit into his car.

Ready to take her back to the ranch, he called Susanne to let her know an approximate time to expect them.

"Cody, how is she? Are you on your way home?"

"Soon. She's finishing a test. We should be there by dinner."

Susanne let out a sigh of relief. "Okay. Good. Um, you should know, Kristi stayed at the house last night, waiting for you to return."

Kristi had started staying over more frequently after Christmas, but then it tapered off. She'd claim she was tired. That he was up too late working on cases or board stuff and he didn't spend time with her anyway. When they were in bed together...the sex lacked the kind of passion he'd gotten a taste of with Brooke. He'd tried harder to coax Kristi to be more...open. Uninhibited. Sometimes she even tried.

You can't compare her to Brooke. They're different.

Exactly. One fit him to a T. The other seemed to be a good match, but just wasn't.

Cody tried to focus. "I take it Kristi is still there."

"Yes." The bite in that word told him Susanne didn't want her there either.

"Do you mind handing her the phone? Or I could call her cell."

"She's camped out in the living room working on her laptop. Tell Brooke I love her and I can't wait to see her, okay?"

"I will."

Susanne huffed out a breath. "Hold on."

"Cody." Kristi's cheerful voice came over the line. "When will you be home?"

"Tonight." He needed to handle this delicately. "Brooke is...not doing well. I'm going to have to take care of her until she's feeling better." He hoped she got the hint.

"I'm sure Susanne will want to do that once Brooke is home. You have lots of other responsibilities and obligations." She wasn't giving up on having him all to herself.

He wasn't about to have this long-overdue conversation over the phone. "Brooke needs me. She can barely walk on her own."

"Once you have her here settled, she'll get all the rest and relaxation she needs." She sounded so reasonable, even though she was being heartless.

"Kristi."

"Yes?" Her voice hadn't changed at all during their discussion. It was like she was purposely avoiding the elephant in the room and the inevitable outcome coming her way.

"I think it would be best if you weren't there when I bring Brooke home. She doesn't want to see anyone right now. Your presence will only upset her."

"Cody. I'm your fiancée. I'm part of your life. Don't shut me out." The order came out clipped, with a heaping dose of frustration and anger.

Cody didn't have time or patience for either. "I'm asking you to think about Brooke and what she needs right now."

"All you do is think about her, isn't it?"

"Now is not the time to talk about this." He didn't want to do it over the phone. He wanted a clearer head.

"Great. We'll talk about it when you get home." She hung up on him.

Fuck!

He didn't want her there when he brought Brooke home, but he couldn't do anything about it now. Kristi had left him several messages on his cell phone since this morning. He'd ignored all of them. And now he was paying for it.

Double fuck.

He didn't want to put Brooke through any more stress or upset.

He hoped Kristi thought better of standing her ground and went home before he and Brooke arrived. He hoped that she'd understand that Brooke had lost something precious and didn't want to be around anyone right now.

After the loss she'd suffered, she should be more sympathetic. Kristi hadn't even asked if he was okay.

He didn't dwell on it or his other thoughts about Kristi right now. He'd get to that soon and used the extra half hour he had while Brooke took her test to call his office and take care of what he could over the phone.

When he walked into the classroom where Brooke sat taking her test almost two hours after she'd started, he expected to find her ready to leave and waiting for him. Instead, he found her sitting and staring into space, her test unfinished. She was far from done.

She didn't notice him. She held their daughter in her lap and zoned out.

"She's been like that on and off over the last hour. I've been able to talk her back and complete a few more questions. From what I can see, she's doing well on the exam." Professor Raymer set down the papers he'd graded and came forward. "Listen, if she can't finish, I can grade what she's done and base her grade on her coursework and the number of points accumulated on the test. Dean Fitzpatrick has already said she gets a break. She can have as long as she likes to take the test, but she's in no condition to do it."

"Let me see if I can get her to finish. It's important to her that she does."

"No problem. I understand." He went back to his desk and grading papers.

Cody approached Brooke slowly, not wanting to spook her. Although, she was the one who looked like a ghost. "Brooke, honey."

She flinched and raised her arms to protect herself.

He slowly kneeled in front of her.

Her gaze found his, but she still seemed out of it. "Hi, honey. How're you doing?"

"Fine," she said automatically.

"Yeah. Are you tired?"

Her eyes were half-closed. "Mmm hmm."

"How about we finish this test, so we can go home. You can sleep in the car. I have it all packed and ready to go. Your mom can't wait to see you."

"I'm still working on the test."

"Okay. You finish up, and I'll just sit here and wait, okay?"

"Okay." She looked down at the test, marked one of the multiple-choice answers, and went to the next.

Cody watched her. After about five minutes, she slowed down. She seemed to struggle over reading the questions, and then she just stared at the paper. All the while, she kept her hand on their daughter in her lap.

"Honey, I'll read the question, and you tell me the answer."

Her sad eyes found him again. "I'm confused. The words are jumbled."

"Okay. We'll do this together." He read the questions and answers to her for half an hour before she drifted again.

She slumped in the chair, her head down, too tired to do more than sit and listen, her face pale with a fine sheen of sweat covering her skin. He rubbed her leg and brought her back each time she spaced out. It took another twenty minutes, but she managed to finish. When they were done, the professor glanced over the test quickly and reassured Brooke, "You definitely passed with flying colors."

Cody shook the man's hand. "Thank you for giving her this chance to finish."

"She's smart. A great student. She deserves to pass the class and earn her credits."

Cody helped Brooke to the car, keeping his pace slow and easy, and gave her some meds to ease her pain. They drove over to the dorm. Brooke waited in the car and he texted Mindy Sue. Julie and a few of the other ladies came down to say goodbye. Brooke couldn't make it inside the building, let alone up to the third floor. All of the women cried as they said their goodbyes. Brooke was so wiped out, only a few tears came.

By the time he reached the interstate, she'd fallen asleep, laid out in the seat he'd leaned back flat. A combination of exhaustion and the medication. She slept fitfully the whole way home, and he was grateful.

The simplest things sapped her energy. Her face turned an awful gray, her cheeks hollow. The dark circles under her eyes and the way she moaned in her sleep worried him the most. She wasn't getting better and appeared worse as the hours passed. He seriously considered taking her directly to the hospital instead of the ranch. She'd done too much, too soon. At the ranch, she'd get the rest she needed.

Chapter Eleven

Cody breathed a huge sigh of relief when he took the turnoff for the ranch. Brooke squirmed in her seat for several miles, trying to get comfortable. A fine sheen of sweat broke out on her skin. He felt sick to his stomach every time he hit a bump in the road and she moaned in pain. Not really asleep or awake, fighting the pain and the long drive exhausted her.

The porch lights lit up the front of the house. He shut off the car and sat for a moment. Home, but still so much he needed to do.

Kristi's car sat in the driveway. A wave of anger and resentment swept through him.

Why was she being so selfish? Why couldn't she understand he and Brooke had lost a child and needed some time alone together? No. She had to stay and make it clear, he belonged to her and not Brooke.

That wasn't the case—never was. Not really. He belonged to Brooke—always had. Always would. He was too stupid to see it, or scared to admit it before. Brooke had gotten under his skin the moment she'd come to the ranch as a young girl. Over the years, she'd become so important to him, he couldn't live without her. That had never been more apparent than over the last six months, his thoughts always turning back to her.

He'd even been out to her favorite spot at the creek more times than he could count. He'd never tell anyone he'd gone there to think and feel close to her. He hadn't wanted to admit it to himself, just convinced himself he needed a quiet place to think.

He only ever thought about her when he was there.

He felt bad about not loving Kristi the way she deserved. He felt guilty for pretending the last six months that a life with Kristi and not Brooke was what he wanted. He'd fooled Kristi and himself. Not anymore. Never again.

Brooke had been hurt. He'd rushed to her side, seen her devastating condition, and let go of every reason why he shouldn't love her and be with her. The light in his life the last ten years. And now that she was living in the darkness of trauma and grief, he was determined to be a light in her life.

He would be a beacon for her and guide her back to him.

And that meant finishing old business and ending things with Kristi.

He scrubbed his hands over his face, got out, and went around the car, opening Brooke's door. He needed to carry her into the house. She'd never make it on her own, and lifting her meant more pain.

Her pain had become his, and he wanted it to stop. For both their sakes.

Leaning in, he cupped her face in his palm. "Brooke, honey, we're home. I need to pick you up and take you inside."

She opened her eyes, and they immediately filled with fresh tears. "Just leave me here. Leave me alone."

"Don't cry, sweetheart. Meds are just a few minutes away. Soon you'll feel better. I promise."

He slid his hands under her legs and around her back. He lifted her out of the car and stood. She clutched their daughter to her chest and gnashed her teeth to stave off the wave of pain. "You got her?" he asked.

She didn't answer, just laid her head on his shoulder, making his heart melt. He kissed her forehead and walked up the path to the porch. He managed to get the door open and walk into the foyer with minimal trouble. He kicked the door shut and slammed it.

Susanne and Kristi ran out of the dining room.

He felt for Susanne and her first glimpse of Brooke, who was devastating to look at. It had taken him some time to get used to seeing her in this condition.

Susanne stood shocked, her mouth agape and her breath held, like she'd turned to stone.

He didn't have time for her to recover. "Susanne, could you go up and turn down Brooke's bed?"

Janie walked in behind Susanne and gasped, her hand moving up over her mouth.

"Janie, could you please go out to my car and get the dark blue duffel bag? It's got her medicine and bandages in it."

Janie rushed to do as he asked.

Kristi stood across from him, anger in her eyes for him, and then a glare at Brooke in his arms.

It said a lot about Kristi, that she showed no compassion for Brooke in her time of need.

"Now is not the time," he warned her.

Susanne headed up the stairs, and he turned and followed. Susanne had the bed turned down and carefully took off Brooke's shoe and sock before Cody set her on the bed.

He cautiously moved her braced leg, keeping it from tangling in the sheets. "Susanne, she'll need a glass of water to take her meds." He brushed a strand of hair from Brooke's eye.

She could barely open them.

"You're okay, honey. I'll get your meds, and you'll feel better soon."

"Go away." She rolled to her side, careful not to hurt her broken arm or sprained ankle.

"I'm not going anywhere, and you better get used to it." Cody leaned over Brooke with his hands on both sides of her shoulders and stared right into her pain-filled eyes. "I mean it, Brooke. I'll be right here for you."

Janie brought in the bag, set it at the end of the bed, then placed the huge vase of roses on the side table.

"Janie, can you please find the plastic bag of pill bottles in that duffel." He turned back to Brooke and covered her hand on her stomach with his own. "Let me check the incision."

"It hurts."

"I know, sweetheart. Let me see."

He pulled her shirt up carefully and peeled back the bandage. Raw and red. He took the tube of medicine from Janie and put a generous amount over the long, stitched cut. He gently pressed the bandage back over the angry wound. He glanced at Brooke's pale face. Tears spilled down her cheeks and into her hair. He brushed them away with his thumbs and kissed her forehead. "How're the arms?"

"Fine."

"Sure?"

She nodded. He decided to leave her be. She hurt enough. But he did tuck the spare pillow under her broken wrist.

Susanne came back into the room and sidestepped Kristi, who simply stood there staring, not offering any help. Moving to her daughter, Susanne handed Cody the glass of water. He already had a handful of pills. "Brooke, are you okay?"

Brooke didn't answer, but looked to him with that horrible vacant look in her eyes.

Suanne's sad gaze held a thousand questions.

He stared down at Brooke, hoping she believed him when he said, "She's going to be fine. It's been a very hard day."

He put his hand over Brooke's on their daughter. "Her friends held a memorial service this morning for our daughter. As thoughtful and beautiful as it was, we weren't quite ready for it. Brooke had a difficult time taking her test, but we got through it. Didn't we, honey?" Brooke only stared. "The drive took a lot out of her. She's in a tremendous amount of pain."

He felt it echo through him. He didn't take his eyes off Brooke's. Sliding his arm under her shoulders, he held her up so she could take the pills, then slowly lowered her back down to the pillow.

"I'm going to give you some time with your mom. I'll come back and check on you in a little while."

He put his hand on Susanne's shoulder to reassure her everything would be all right. "She needs to eat and get some sleep."

Susanne nodded, then settled on the side of the bed.

He left her alone with Brooke and walked out of the room.

Kristi followed him. She wanted answers.

He was on the razor's edge of losing his shit. He didn't want to put all his fury on her.

She deserved to take the brunt of his wild emotions. But the scowl he shot her let her know he wasn't happy she was here, in Brooke's home, after he asked her to give Brooke some space.

If he could go back and change that morning after he'd been with Brooke and woke up happier than he'd ever been, clearer than he'd ever been about what he wanted, he'd have done everything differently.

He'd have chosen Brooke and the love they shared. He'd have promised to support Kristi through her pregnancy and to be the best father he could be to their child. He'd have made it clear that being with Brooke meant they could both be happy and that Kristi would find someone who loved her the way she deserved to be loved.

He'd have made the right decision for all of them.

But right now, he didn't have the strength or presence of mind to say all of that to her, because the rage and grief roiling inside him made him want to lash out.

And he wouldn't do that to her.

Exhausted, he felt empty like he'd never felt in his whole life. He didn't want to start a conversation with Kristi that he knew would turn ugly. He wanted to talk to her when he was rested and had his emotions under control.

He needed a stiff drink and a hot meal. Then, he wanted a shower and sleep.

What he really wanted to do was crawl in bed with Brooke and hold her while she slept. Maybe then, he'd be able to breathe without his chest hurting for her.

Maybe then he wouldn't be plotting all the ways he wanted to make Adam pay.

No. That was going to run in a loop in the back of his mind until Adam got what he deserved.

"Cody, we need to talk." Kristi dogged his heels.

He turned at the bottom of the stairs and stared into her eyes as she stood on the last step, looking at him with disapproval in her gaze. "I asked you not to be here, but you ignored me. I hope you'll heed what I have to say now: Not now. Not tonight. It's been a shitty couple of days. I'm tired and frustrated and very close to a rage I won't be able to control. I need a shower and a meal and to be left alone."

"Then we'll sit down together. Janie made a wonderful roast chicken with mashed potatoes. You can eat and explain to me what's going on."

"I plan on eating. As for the explanation, you know the result of what happened between me and Brooke. I want to tell you everything, explain it all...you deserve that. And I'll give it to you. Just not right now when my head is so messed up." He headed for the kitchen.

Kristi would be wise to heed his warning.

Susanne would be down soon. She'd want the details from last night and about what Brooke had been through over the last week. And the last six months.

He'd have to explain that everything was his fault.

All his fault.

The minute he walked into the kitchen, Janie set a plate of food at the breakfast table. He sat down, grateful for the hot cup of coffee she handed him.

Kristi took the seat across from him.

He didn't look up. He dug into the food, not really tasting any of it, but he needed the sustenance so he could stay strong for Brooke.

He bet Brooke could use a good meal. It had been nothing but fast food this morning. He glanced up to tell Janie to take a plate up to Brooke, but she was already walking out of the room with a plate and a bottle of water.

"Janie, if she won't eat that, try ice cream."

Janie smiled and headed up to Brooke's room.

"Ice cream?" Kristi asked.

"She loves ice cream. It was the one treat she allowed herself while she was pregnant."

He paused and thought about the fact that his daughter was gone. It hurt. It hurt so much.

Kristi placed her hand over his. "I'm sorry, Cody. I know it hurts."

His eyes glassed over, and he put his head down again, surprised by her compassion after the way she'd been acting, but grateful for it all the same.

He ate several more bites, but he'd lost his appetite. He let his fork fall to the plate with a clatter and picked up his coffee mug, taking a deep sip, hoping the hot brew warmed his cold insides.

Kristi sat back and watched him, waiting for him to say something.

He needed time to think. If they got into it now, he'd end up saying something he didn't mean. He wanted to do this right after he'd messed up so much over the last six months.

"I understand you're upset about whatever happened to Brooke."

Like she didn't know. She was just trying to distance herself from it. Maybe she was delusional.

More likely, she simply wished it weren't true.

"She's your friend. It's understandable you're upset."

"I'm beyond upset because our baby was murdered. Brooke is devastated and so am I," he snapped and took another sip of coffee, fisting his free hand on the tabletop. "Sorry. I told you I didn't want to get into this tonight."

"The Christmas party."

"Yes," he confirmed what she hadn't asked outright.

"Because we fought that night, you turned to her," she said furiously. "It's the same as always. Every time you have a problem, or need someone, you turn to her."

"I do." He couldn't deny it. Why lie or make excuses now? "You and I had been arguing about this or that for weeks. That night, *you* ended things and walked out the door. I was jealous as hell of all the attention Brooke got that night. I couldn't stop myself from wanting her." He finished off his coffee and set the cup down. "We'll leave it at that for tonight."

"You can't expect me to just leave it at that. You wanted her. You had her. You got her pregnant, and you didn't tell me."

"Yes. Yes. And yes and no. I didn't know she was pregnant. That's why she hasn't come home. She didn't want me to know."

"And you didn't think I deserved to know you'd slept with her."

"Let's be real, Kristi. You knew that morning you came over that something happened between me and Brooke the second you saw her and me in the same room. You didn't say anything, so neither did I because I was too devastated about letting her go. I didn't want to let her go," he snapped. "But I did it for *our* child. The one you didn't tell me you lost for weeks." If she wanted to push him to talk after he asked for space, then she deserved the cold hard truth, unvarnished or prettied up.

Though he couldn't blame Kristi for wanting to stick her head in the sand. He'd done the same the last several months. Not anymore.

Kristi slammed her hands down on the table, stood, and yelled at him, "This isn't over. We're getting married. You promised." She stormed out of the kitchen.

He let her go. He didn't want to make things worse.

She had to know the wedding was off. She just didn't want to face it.

What a fucking mess.

But he couldn't go on like this with her. Not when his heart belonged to Brooke.

She needed him right now, more than ever.

The door slammed on Kristi's way out.

It sounded as final as the night of the Christmas party, but Cody knew, just like then, she'd be back to try to talk him into staying with her.

Not going to happen. Not this time.

Chapter Twelve

Brooke's heart eased the second her mom took her hand, then she reached over and touched the silver vessel tucked against Brooke's side. "I'm so sorry, Brooke. I'm sorry he took her from you."

Janie brought in the plate of food and set it and a bottle of water on the side table. "To make you strong again."

Brooke couldn't even manage a smile but gave a nod before Janie left again.

"Honey, you should try to eat. You look so pale." Her mom brushed her hand over Brooke's cheek. "Please, honey."

Brooke couldn't speak. She let the tears fall and the pain fill her until she felt like she'd burst from the pressure building inside her body and especially her heart.

Brooke lay there while her mom took the plate and held a forkful of food to her mouth. She wasn't hungry and didn't want the food, but she ate because her mom looked so hopeful she would try.

After several bites, Brooke put her hand up to get her mom to stop. It took all her courage to face her. "I'm sorry. I didn't mean to hurt you by not telling you about the baby."

"I know that, sweetheart." Her mom brushed her hand over Brooke's hair. "I know you did it for Cody. You love him."

"I didn't want him to have to choose between Kristi and me because of a baby and an obligation."

"Love isn't an obligation. He loves you, honey. I saw him when he found out you'd been hurt. There was such pain in his eyes. I saw the fear, too. He knew he came close to losing you. He knew the baby was his, never questioned it. He just knew."

"She's gone now. And I'm...dead inside. I'm no good for anyone anymore."

Her mom frowned. "That's not true. You will get through this and be stronger for it, even if it doesn't feel that way right now. And Cody...he loves you. He wants you. He needs you like you need him right now."

"He doesn't," she cried. "He always told me we were just friends."

"That's the best place to start. Don't give up now."

"He let me go. He chose her. Twice."

"And he's paying for that now." Her mom gave her a look that said all too well that Brooke had to see the pain Cody tried to hide while he took care of her. "He lost a baby, too. You'll grieve for her together. It will bring you two closer together than you've ever been. But you have to let him in for that to happen."

"He's gone from being obligated to me because of our child, to pitying me because that maniac murdered her."

"You know Cody isn't like that. He'd never lie to you."

"No, but just because we both grieve for her doesn't mean it's something more. I've made so many things he's said or done into a love he never felt. I won't do that again. Give it up, Mom. I have."

"I don't think it's the grief. Something changed recently in him. And yesterday I saw how Cody distanced himself when Kristi arrived. I think they were headed for a very serious talk. I think he wanted you back and was planning on fixing things between you."

"That can't be right. The wedding is less than two weeks away. Why change his mind now? No. That can't be true." Brooke closed her eyes and held her daughter close. No more talking about things that would never be. She was home, and the first thing she'd seen coming through the door was Kristi looking like she owned the place.

"Well, I see you haven't lost your stubbornness. I know your heart is shattered after losing your beautiful daughter, but don't lose a chance at the kind of love you've always dreamed of having with Cody. Talk to him."

"I don't need or want his pity. That's all it is."

"Cody certainly has his work cut out for him convincing you he loves you."

Her mother leaned over, careful not to bump her, and kissed her on the forehead. "I'm here for you. I love you. We'll get through this."

Brooke just wanted everyone to leave her alone. So much so she wanted to scream it until she lost her voice and the rafters shook.

Why wouldn't they just go away?

Cody was still sitting in the kitchen at the table, staring out the window, when Susanne walked in and put her hand on his shoulder.

"Thank you for bringing my baby home."

He shocked her by wrapping his arms around her waist and laying his head against her.

She didn't hesitate to wrap her arms around his head and shoulders and hold him close.

He never thought of her as his mother, but tonight, right now, he felt the deep connection they'd forged over the years. "She has to get better. I can't stand it that she's so sad."

"Sometimes we hurt far more for the ones we love than for ourselves. It's okay to be sad about losing another child, Cody. It breaks my heart that you've suffered so much loss these last many months."

"She's suffered far more than I have. I hurt her. I let her leave when I really wanted her to stay. I just didn't know how to keep her and still take care of Kristi and the baby we were expecting."

She touched his chin and he looked up at her. "I saw the way you looked when you walked in with her. Is your heart clear now? Do you know what you want and what you have to do to get it?"

"Yes. I love her. I want a life with her. It's not going to be easy. She's in no mood to listen to me."

"She hears you, Cody, even if she's having a hard time accepting the truth." She squeezed his shoulders. "Go up to bed. Check on her, but get some sleep. You'll feel better for it. You'll be better for her tomorrow if you have a clear head."

"I haven't had a clear head since I found out she'd been attacked and my daughter was killed."

"She needs you to be strong for her, but that doesn't mean you don't get to feel the way you feel. Maybe if she sees it in you, it will allow her to feel it, too, and you'll both heal together."

She made a good point.

He stood and kissed her on the cheek, then dragged himself up the stairs and down the hall to Brooke's room. She slept fitfully in her bed, moaning in her sleep. Reluctant to disturb or scare her, he approached slowly and gave her a goodnight kiss on the forehead before he went to his own room. He didn't know how long he could wait until they shared a room and a bed. He wanted her in his arms and pressed along his body. He wanted her to feel his love while she slept, safe in his arms.

He wanted things back to the way they used to be, only better.

She belonged to him and he belonged to her.

He wanted her to know it in her soul, the way he did now.

After a hot shower, he fell naked into bed, thinking about Brooke. It seemed she was never far from his mind.

Images of her growing up on the ranch and all the time they'd spent together played like a documentary of their lives together. Every image and memory reminded him how close they'd always been. They were part of each other's lives, and he'd pushed her away. Because she was too young. Because it wasn't appropriate. Because he'd thought Kristi suited his life better. Because Kristi had been pregnant with his child. Because he'd been scared.

That last truth really hit hard, but it was a truth he had to face.

What if he didn't live up to the romantic version of him she'd imagined?

What if he lost her because he couldn't be what she thought him to be?

What if you don't try and you lose her anyway?

What if what you shared that night is what you share for the rest of your life?

God, he wanted that.

Because in the last six months, he hadn't felt right. Something had always been missing, and that something had always been Brooke. Without her, his life would always be lacking and incomplete.

I can't live like this anymore.

No matter what, he'd find a way to make things right with Brooke.

He'd find a way to make her believe in him again.

He'd prove to her how much he loved her.

Chapter Thirteen

C ody stood beside Brooke, looking into the stall at the gelding. He'd thought it might do her some good to come down to the stables and see the horses she loved. The chestnut, he hoped, would bring a smile to her face. She loved the horses and riding.

It wasn't working though. She had spent the last three days home, refusing to leave her bed. Every day she got worse. Her body needed the rest, but she barely ate, she didn't speak, and she stared blankly at the walls for hours. When she wasn't lying there with that vacant look, she cried.

He tried to be patient and understand how she felt. He was sad about his daughter and that sadness grew each day he didn't have her with them. It seemed that sadness grew exponentially every time he looked at Brooke and saw the emptiness in her eyes.

"What do you think, sweetheart? He's beautiful, right?"

As if the horse sensed her despair, he came to the gate and rubbed his nose against Brooke's cheek.

Brooke seemed to know what the horse wanted and gave him a rub. "You're sweet." Brooke took the carrot he'd brought down and held it out for the horse to take. She almost smiled.

Cody thought this was a good sign. She'd responded to the horses. Then, he saw the tears streaming down Brooke's face and had second thoughts. Maybe this wasn't such a good idea.

"Brooke..." His phone rang. He pulled it from his back pocket and glanced at the caller ID. "Honey, I have to take this. It's my office. A plea deal I've been working on with the ADA." He didn't know if she heard him or not.

She turned and walked away, unsteady on her feet. He kept an eye on her and answered his phone.

He followed as she made her way back toward the house. He thought she was going to go inside, back to her bed to hide. Instead, she veered to the rear of the house and the garden. The day was bright and clear; the sun would do her good. She'd kept herself cooped up in the house far too long.

He tried to keep an eye on Brooke and talk to his assistant on the phone. The last three days had been overwhelming, trying to balance being home with Brooke, checking in with the ranch manager, and going back and forth to his office and court. He'd never been busier. He'd never hated work so much because it took him away from her. But the ranch was doing well. Thank God. The children's hospital board didn't meet for a couple of weeks. And his brilliant assistant had already rescheduled client meetings and court dates for non-urgent matters. All he had to do was finish up the priority cases, so he could be home full-time with Brooke for the next few weeks.

She needed him. He needed to be with her. He wanted to show her he was all in. She could count on him.

He still had to take care of the wedding.

And he owed Kristi a proper conversation.

Kristi had come to the house the other day, but Susanne sent her away.

He wasn't ready to take on everything at once, but he'd realized he didn't have a choice. The wedding was scheduled to take place in ten days and he had to deal with it. His saint of an assistant was helping him do that, and Kristi would arrive at the house at any time for them to finally have their talk. He wasn't looking forward to it, but it couldn't be put off any longer.

"Honey."

Brooke stared out at the garden without really seeing it, lost in thoughts she refused to share with him.

"Honey." Cody bent down in front of her. He rubbed a hand up her thigh and waited for her eyes to focus on him. When they did, he smiled to reassure her he was there with her. "Hey sweetheart, I have to go into my office and look at some papers while I talk to my assistant. Will you be okay out here alone?"

He didn't know what set off the tears this time. Probably the word *alone* made her think of losing their little girl. But she nodded she'd be okay even if she didn't really look at him.

She pressed her hand to her shoulder, letting him know it ached.

He hoped the warm sun on her face and the birds chirping in the trees would bring her some peace, but she simply looked lost, and it tore at his battered heart.

He brushed his thumbs over her cheeks and wiped the tears, pressed a soft kiss to her forehead, then stood to walk back to the house.

"Cody."

He turned back the second she whispered his name.

He put the phone to his ear and asked his assistant, "Can you hold on another minute?" He took a step back to Brooke. "What is it, honey?"

She looked at him, confusion clouding her eyes along with fear.

"Brandy, I'll call you back. Brooke needs me."

Stuffing the phone in his pocket, he kneeled in front of her and cupped her cheek. She stared at him, unable to say anything.

"What is it, honey? Talk to me."

The pleading in his voice made her focus on his face and really look at him. She traced the lines on his forehead with her fingers, then brushed them along his jaw. "Are you okay?"

Exhaustion, frustration, sadness, so many different things weighed him down and made it hard to sleep or eat or function, but he forced himself to do what needed to be done and get through the day. For her.

"No, honey. I'm not okay." He leaned forward and pressed his forehead to her chest. His fingers dug into her hips where he held her.

She ran her fingers through his hair and held on to him. "I think she would have liked to play in the garden."

He looked up at her, his heart in his throat, as she stared at the flowers surrounding them. "I think so, too, sweetheart. She would have loved growing up on the ranch with us."

Her hands slipped off him and she settled them in her lap.

Everything in him missed her touch and the connection. He felt utterly empty. He'd lost her again. He didn't know what he'd said to put that look on her face, but he didn't like seeing it. "Honey, do you want to come up to the house with me?"

It took her a moment to turn her focus away from the garden and look at him. "Do you need something?"

He put his hand on her cheek and leaned in close, their noses a mere inch apart. Her breath washed over his face; he desperately wanted to lean in and kiss her. Not a quick stolen one, but one that meant something, everything. One that told her how much he loved her. He held back, hoping he could reach her with his simple plea. "I need you. Come back to me."

She leaned her cheek against his forehead, wrapped one arm around his head, and held on to him. He sighed out his relief, seeing this small show of affection.

"I'm here." She said the words, but she wasn't there. Not his Brooke. This wasn't the woman he knew and loved. This was just a small piece of her, and he wanted all of her back.

"No, baby. You're not. But I'm going to get you back. However long it takes, I'm going to find a way to get you back." He pulled away reluctantly and saw the confusion in her eyes.

She wasn't ready to hear him. She wasn't in any state of mind to believe him.

But he'd keep showing her. He'd make himself clear. Soon. He would make her understand just how serious he was about getting her back and keeping her. She just needed a little more time. "I have to go in and take care of some work. I'll come back out and get you in a few minutes. It's almost time for your meds. You'll feel better then."

She nodded, tilting her lips in a cynical smirk.

The meds took the edge off the pain and dulled her mind, but never actually made her feel better. He got it. Without her daughter, she felt like she'd never feel better.

He felt the same way.

Before he stood, she cupped his face in her hands, leaned forward, and kissed his forehead. "I'm sorry you lost both your babies."

Tears welled in his eyes. He looked at her sad, blood-shot eyes. "I miss them both, but I'm so glad I still have you." Tears slipped down his cheeks. He'd never hidden anything from Brooke, so he let his guard down now.

She saw through the mask anyway, down to the pain he tried to hide for her sake. "You'd have been a really great dad."

"I will be a great dad. And you're going to be the best mom any kid could ever have."

She didn't know it yet, but he was going to make sure they had another chance. They would have a family, and he'd have her. They'd have each other. And so much love, she'd be happy all the time.

Chapter Fourteen

Drawn back to Cody, Brooke walked into his study through the French doors. He sat at his desk, talking on his cell phone. His deep voice filled the room. So soothing. So familiar. Her heart fluttered at the sight of him smiling at her, his blue eyes focused on her. She could have gone through the patio doors and through the living room, but she'd come this way because she wanted to see him. She didn't analyze her thoughts or reasons.

She'd been working on instinct and survival since waking up in the hospital, and she didn't want to think Cody was part of that survival. She didn't want to need him in order to feel anything good.

But he did make her feel a spark of happiness every time she looked at him.

She felt even better when he stood and came to her. He carried on a conversation she didn't tune in to as he kissed her on the head and rubbed his hand up her good arm to her shoulder before going back to his desk and looking at some papers.

Feeling a bit better after the sunshine and Cody's attention and affection, she aimlessly walked out of the study and slowly worked her way up the stairs to her room.

"Brooke." Kristi walked from the kitchen into the living room. "I'd like to have a word with you, please."

Just the sound of Kristi's voice made her angry. Seeing Kristi in Brooke's home reminded her of Kristi's place in Cody's life.

Brooke ignored Kristi and continued to carefully make her way up the stairs. One step at a time, just the way she took every second of the day. Her ankle was stable in the brace, but sore, making it difficult to maneuver the stairs. Especially after the long walk to the stables and through the garden.

Kristie huffed out a breath of frustration. "Brooke. I'm talking to you."

Brooke ignored the peevish tone.

"Kristi. Let her be," Cody ordered. "You have nothing to say to her, unless it's to express your condolences on the loss of our daughter."

Not likely. Kristi didn't have any sympathy for Brooke. She wanted to fight over Cody.

Brooke didn't have it in her, and she'd already lost Cody, so why fight about it.

Kristi's silence spoke volumes.

"I have to finish this call, and then we'll talk." Brooke recognized the warning in Cody's voice that he was barely in command of his temper. "Leave her alone. She's having a rough day."

"Aren't we all?"

The snide tone set Cody off. "Was your daughter murdered while you carried her inside you?"

Cody's words hit Brooke hard.

Kristi pouted. "We lost a baby, too."

"And you were so upset about it you waited weeks to tell me about it, like it barely mattered to you, because, hey, we still had a wedding coming up."

Brooke felt the hurt in Cody's words wash through with another wave of grief for all he'd lost. She stared down at him from the top of the stairs.

He glanced up at her, an apology in his eyes for upsetting her and Kristi making a scene.

He turned back to Kristi, his phone still held against his chest. "I need a minute to finish this call. Then you and I are going to talk."

Brooke wouldn't want to be Kristi right now. Cody sounded like he'd reached his limit.

Still, they'd probably work it out. Kristi would get her way. She always did. And Cody would still be hers.

Another wave of sadness rolled over Brooke as she left the two of them behind to wallow in her grief and somehow get through the next minute.

And the one after that.

And the one after that.

She didn't want to think about how hard it was getting to live one moment to the next.

Cody finished his call in his office and walked back into the living room. Kristi stood by the windows, looking out at the pool and backyard, completely lost in thought. He just bet the wheels were turning. When she looked at him, eyes filled with sympathy, he didn't believe it for a second. Not after the way she'd acted when he brought Brooke home or a few minutes ago when she'd tried to confront Brooke.

In the last three days, she hadn't even attempted to talk to him about how he felt about losing his daughter. Brooke had known just by looking at him, he quietly suffered. She'd acknowledged both his losses and known how much he wanted to be a dad.

Kristi had skimmed over the miscarriage and focused on the wedding. Maybe that helped her cope, but it looked and felt like the loss didn't hit her the way it did him.

That never sat right with him.

He couldn't believe she'd chosen to confront Brooke about sleeping with him and had no compassion for all Brooke had suffered, physically and mentally.

He'd spent all his time with Brooke since he brought her home. Kristi saw what was coming and wanted to stake a claim and reel him back in.

But he didn't belong to her.

He didn't want to be with her.

He only wanted to make Brooke well and bring her back to him.

Kristi glided over to him and wrapped her arms around his neck.

He gently took her wrists, stepped back, and let her arms fall back to her sides as he analyzed everything she did. He thought back over their relationship and every time she'd approached him like this, trying to smooth over some upset between them.

Was any of it sincere? Ever?

His insides went cold.

She stared up at him, her blue eyes narrowed with concern. "Cody, honey. I'm so sorry you're hurting. The last several days have been tough for you. I can see Brooke is despondent. It must be hard dealing with her when she's being so difficult."

"She was attacked by a madman. Her baby was murdered. She's in more pain than any one person should have to endure. She's sadder than any person deserves to be. And your concern for me is that she's been difficult to deal with these last few days?"

She opened her mouth to say something, but he didn't want to hear it.

"She can't talk to me because she can't think of anything but the loss of our daughter. She can't move without being in pain and that only reminds her more of what happened. She jumps when anyone approaches her. She has nightmares that make her scream in the night. And you think I care that she's quiet and hurting and lost inside herself," he growled.

"I only meant to tell you that I'm here for you. I'm here for you to talk to and share some of the burden."

"Share the burden," he repeated in disbelief. "Are you going to share the burden of begging her to eat? Will you sit with her and watch her cry for hours, knowing there's nothing you can say or do to ease her pain? Will you tend to her many wounds? Would you be able to look at the eight-inch scar on her stomach and not remember a baby was inside her not two weeks ago? Can you look into her eyes knowing you can't give that back to her?"

His throat ached with all the sadness he held inside. "No. Probably not that last one, because you're glad the baby is gone. Then it won't come between you and me and the wedding you so desperately want."

The unconscious nod and pressing of her lips together told him he'd hit the mark. "I love you. More than anything. We're good together." She plastered on a soft smile and gazed up at him, her eyes soft with concern.

Probably for herself and everything she was about to lose.

"Cody, please. Don't make any rash decisions. You're upset. We can discuss this later. She's going to be fine. We'll get past this and move forward with our lives together."

He ignored the last part and glared at her harshly. "She'll be fine? Do you really think so? Because I wonder if she'll ever be anywhere close to fine again," he said, almost completely defeated. "I hope she'll be able to look at me someday and not blame me for what happened. I hope I'll be able to look in the mirror and not blame myself."

"It's not your fault." Kristi reached out to touch him, but he backed up a step. Her eyes went wide with surprise that he'd do such a thing. Again. "I hate seeing you this way. You didn't do anything wrong," she yelled at him.

"Didn't I? You knew something was up at the Christmas party between me and her. Is that why you chose the next morning to confirm you were pregnant? I mean, you had two weeks to take a test and share the news with me. And how exactly did you get pregnant? You swore you were on the pill. We used condoms as backup because it was my habit, a way to ensure no surprises. After the condom broke, you never said you'd forgotten to take the pill or something might happen. Why? Because you did it on purpose and a convenient accident happened?" He hadn't actually meant to accuse her of that, but then she looked away.

He'd seen too many people lie in his line of work not to spot the telltale signs of it now. "You..." He couldn't believe it. "You stopped taking it."

"Only for a few days, then I realized what I was doing and started it again, but I guess it was too late."

"Are you kidding me? You think that makes any difference?"

She huffed out a breath, arms rigid, hands fisted. "We talked about getting married, but you kept dragging your feet on actually proposing. I knew you wanted a family. We both did."

He hadn't thought he could be this angry. "Not that way. Not by deception. Not with you forcing a proposal and wedding. My God, Kristi, look what you've done."

"I've loved you. I've been by your side, building a life with you. And you wanted to ruin it all because you fucked your coed sister!"

That sent him back another step. He didn't know what to say, but he refused to defend himself after what she'd said and done.

Kristi held her hands out to him. "Cody, I'm sorry you're hurting."

"There is no end to the amount of hurt I feel, but it's nothing compared to the hurt I've caused her."

Kristi's ire rose again. "You didn't do anything to her."

"I spent the most amazing night of my life in the arms of a woman I love more than my own life."

Surprise and pain flashed in Kristi's glassy blue eyes.

He'd tried to do this the right way, hoping they could have a rational conversation without hurting each other more. He'd wanted to end things as close to friends as possible.

But she just didn't get it. She wanted what she wanted and to hell with everyone else.

He didn't work that way. He couldn't forget or ignore what he'd put Brooke through, what she'd suffered.

He couldn't let Kristi think there was any chance for them anymore.

He let all his anger and self-loathing spew out because he couldn't keep it inside, and Kristi had played a role in Brooke's destruction.

"I let Brooke walk out the door pregnant with my child. I made it impossible for her to tell me she was pregnant because she wanted me to be happy. She put my happiness above her own. I'd made my choice. You. Someone I thought was good and kind and would never lie or deceive me. Brooke sacrificed so she wouldn't take away my chance at happiness and being a father to *our* baby."

"Cody, it's not my fault I lost the baby."

"No, it's not. I don't blame you for that. I blame you for conceiving it in the first place and using it to get me to propose. You used our baby to tear me and Brooke apart. Then you convinced me she had her own life that didn't include me. And I let you because it was easier than trying to get her back and having her turn me down. If I'd tried, maybe I'd have at least gotten my friend back. Maybe she would have come home when she was scared for her life because of the bastard stalking her. Maybe I'd have been there to hold her hand in the hospital. Maybe she'd know how much I love her."

Kristi's eyes narrowed. "You don't have to feel obligated to her. It's not your fault."

"It is! Don't you get it? It's my fault she couldn't tell me she was pregnant in the first place. It's my fault I made

her think I don't love her by choosing *you* that morning
and again when I chose you after we lost the baby. It's my
fault she couldn't count on me to be there for her when
she needed me because she thought I'd turned my back on
her *twice*!"

Cody sucked in a deep breath and tried to contain the
rage building inside him. He never lost his temper. Not
like this. "It's my fault I ever trusted you when you lied to
my face and manipulated me to get what you wanted."

Kristi stared at him, wide-eyed, her hands clasped in
front of her. She pleaded with her eyes, but he just didn't
care anymore. She professed to love him, but she hurt
him at every turn, never seeing what he really needed and
wanted.

He'd tried to be a good man to her, but she'd used that
against him.

He'd never forgive her for that.

Kristi opened her mouth, ready for another round of
arguments, but she didn't get a word out.

Brooke flew down the stairs. Pure rage propelled her
down and across the room to him.

Stunned by her reckless actions, he stared at her in disbelief, filled with fear that she'd hurt herself.

"Give her back!" She shoved him with her bandaged
hands. "Is that why you took me down to the stables and
came back in without me?" She shoved him again. "You
just wanted to take her. Give her back. You can't take her
from me. Give her back!" She pounded on his chest with
her fists, completely oblivious to her injuries. "Give her
back!" She slapped his face with a resounding crack, the
brace on her arm scraping his skin.

It didn't even register. He stood there and let her pound on him and felt nothing but that he deserved it.

He didn't know what brought this on. He knew better than to grab her arms to try to stop her. He didn't want to send her into another nightmare of the attack like he'd done when he bandaged her arms in her dorm room. So he stood there and took the beating and everything she dished out. If she needed to do this to find a way to heal, he'd let her.

"Give her back." She grabbed fistfuls of his shirt and shook him. "You can't just take her from me. She's mine. She's mine," she said weakly. "Give her back," she begged and shattered his battered heart. "Please. Please. Give her back." She sobbed, all the energy she'd had moments ago vanished, and she leaned heavily against him.

Cody felt the tears slide down his own face. He didn't know what she was talking about. "I can't give her back to you, sweetheart. She's gone." He wished with everything inside him he could take it all away and have this madness be just a dream.

He briefly glanced at Kristi and saw the shock in her eyes and something else he didn't want to admit was guilt.

"Brooke." Susanne rushed into the room. Brooke's screams had echoed through the house, drawing Susanne out of the kitchen.

"Give her back, Cody. Please, please, give her back," Brooke sobbed. She had nothing left. Everything seemed to drain away and leave her blank. "Please, give her back." She pulled her arms back from his chest. Fresh blood stained the bandages.

She held her arms up in front of her in horror. She'd pounded on his chest so hard, she must have torn some of the stitches, or opened some of the more healed cuts. The blood drained out of her face, and her eyes rolled back in her head as she swayed.

He caught her before she fell.

"Brooke!" Susanne screamed and rushed over to help Cody lay her on the sofa. "What is going on in here?"

Cody gently laid Brooke on the sofa. He put her arm gently over her stomach and gazed up at Susanne. "I don't know. She ran down the stairs in a rage. She wants me to give her back our daughter. But I can't." He kneeled down beside Brooke and smoothed the hair out of her face. "Oh, baby, I'm sorry I can't give her back to you."

Susanne ran a shaky hand over her daughter's hair. "What do you think set her off?"

"I don't know." Cody touched a hand to Brooke's cheek and gently wiped some of the tears away, careful to avoid the stitched cut on her face. "I don't know," he said again absently.

Cody looked up and saw Janie standing by the kitchen door. "Janie, could you call Dr. Nash? He was due to come by in a couple of hours to check on Brooke, but we need him now. Tell him she's had some kind of breakdown and she's fainted. Tell him she's hurt her arms, and she's bleeding. Some of her cuts may need to be re-stitched. If he can't come, ask him if he'll meet me at the ER."

Janie left the room quickly to do what Cody asked.

Kristi came forward and stood at the end of the couch at Brooke's feet. She appeared hesitant and scared. "I didn't mean for this to happen."

A wave of anger rushed over him. "What do you mean? What did you do?"

"She wouldn't share her with you. I didn't think it was fair that she kept your daughter all to herself."

Cody stood. He was finally beginning to understand why Brooke had said to give her back. "What did you do, Kristi?"

"I know no one is supposed to know that Brooke was the victim of the campus stalker. But after I calmed down the other night, I remembered you saying that her classmates held a memorial of sorts for the baby. I thought we could do that here. Today. You and me. I brought flowers and candles and the ultrasound picture of our baby. I thought we could say something for the both of them, so I took the urn from upstairs and brought it down to your office."

Cody swore and fisted his hands, his whole body vibrating with rage.

Kristi implored him with her eyes to understand. "I just wanted to do something nice for you. For us to remember them."

"Cody!" Susanne took his hand. "Take a breath."

Nothing would calm the fury raging through him. "Susanne, please go get our daughter for Brooke. I don't want her to wake up without her."

He waited for Susanne to go into his study before he turned on Kristi. "Do you have any idea what Brooke has been through? She was stabbed in the belly. That six-inch knife went through my daughter's back and severed the umbilical cord, cutting off her blood supply. It literally left the baby and Brooke bleeding to death with every beat of her heart. Then, the doctors had to cut her open and take our daughter out of her. They didn't let her see her daughter. She never laid eyes on her. She never got to hold her own child. After all of that, *you* took her daughter away from her."

Kristi stood rooted to the floor, hearing the brutal truth, every one of his words laced with the hatred he couldn't hide. Tears shimmered in her sad, regretful eyes, but they had no effect on him. "I had no idea it was that bad. I'm sorry isn't enough," she began.

"You're damn right, I'm sorry isn't enough!" he bellowed. "You're jealous. You did this to manipulate me. You thought we'd have a little ceremony and grieve our losses and I'd change my mind about breaking up with you."

"I wanted you to see that I understand your losses and that as partners we could get through this together."

"Yet you came in here ready to confront Brooke the second you saw her. That wasn't about being kind or compassionate. That was you being selfish as usual. You can't stand it that you didn't get what you wanted this time."

"It doesn't have to be this way. We can work this out. You want the life we planned. I know you do. I got you that board seat. I can give you the family you want."

"I want a wife who cares about me. I want a family that supports and loves each other. A woman who puts me first when I need it. That woman is and will always be Brooke."

"You don't mean that."

"Stop telling me what I want and what I mean. I've made it perfectly clear. I'm hers. I was always hers. I will always be hers."

Tears fell over Kristi's pale cheeks. "I didn't mean for this to happen. Let me make it right."

Cody shook his head. "She needs rest. She needs time to heal. She needs a little fucking compassion. She needs to have her daughter with her!" he roared.

She clasped her hands tightly together in front of her. "I'm sorry, Cody. I'm so sorry."

Cody never raised his voice or shouted. At least now he had her attention.

"Cody. Give Brooke her daughter back," Susanne said from behind him.

Cody turned away from Kristi and carefully took the silver vessel from Susanne. He kneeled next to Brooke, wondering how long she'd been awake and how much she'd heard. Tears slipped out the side of her closed eyes. Gently brushing them away, he spoke quietly to her. "Brooke, honey. Look at me, baby."

"I can't. I hit you. I y-yelled at you. I accused y-you. I'm s-sorry." Her lips trembled and the tears flowed.

"Brooke, baby. Come on. Look at me. It's okay."

She finally opened her eyes.

He held up their daughter. "Here she is. She's right here." He put her on Brooke's stomach and pressed both of Brooke's hands over her. "You've got her now."

Brooke placed her hand on Cody's stinging cheek. "I'm sorry I hit you. I'm so sorry, Cody." She squeezed her eyes closed and cried harder.

"It's okay, sweetheart. I'm fine. You're the one who's hurt. Sshh. Baby, I'm okay." The harder she cried, the harder he tried to convince her. Finally, he kissed her. He fit his mouth over hers and kissed her again and again, until she realized he was insisting she kiss him back. When she did, he softened the kiss and let his lips linger over hers. He pulled away just enough to look into her eyes. "Are you okay?"

She shook her head no. "I hurt. My foot and arms, they're killing me."

"I bet. What the hell were you thinking running down the stairs on that leg like that? You could have fallen and cracked your skull open."

Her watery eyes pleaded with him to understand. "I wanted her back."

He brushed a kiss on her soft lips, then on her nose. "I know you did, sweetheart. I'm sorry she wasn't where you left her. I'm going to fix things right now. I promise."

Susanne cleared her throat to get Cody's attention. "Maybe we should get her upstairs before you and Kristi finish your talk." Susanne glared at Kristi as she stood there with tears in her eyes, staring at Cody leaning over Brooke.

Cody had other ideas. "I think Brooke deserves to hear this." He stood and turned to Kristi. "I'll never forgive you for doing this to her. I hope that whenever you do have a child you look at him every day and think about Brooke and the fact she doesn't have her daughter. I hope you look at your child and remember you took Brooke's daughter away from her for spite and to manipulate me."

"Cody. No. Don't do this."

He shook his head, trying to figure out how Kristi had turned into someone he didn't recognize anymore. "I wanted us to talk about this privately. I thought we could sit down the night I found out Brooke lost the baby and she was attacked and I could make you understand why I couldn't marry you."

She gasped. Maybe Brooke did, too, but he stayed focused on Kristi, who'd gone even paler. "You were going to dump me that night?"

"I had made the decision to end things days before that, but had to wait until your schedule cleared to meet with you."

"No." Kristi shook her head, in complete denial.

"I wanted to take the time to make you understand it wasn't that I didn't love you, but that I *couldn't* love you. I love Brooke. I always have. How could I love someone else? You? When I love her with my whole heart, but have been too stupid to see what was in front of me all this time?

"I thought we could end things amicably. I thought you'd understand now that I've lost my daughter, and it's tearing me up inside. I thought you'd have a little compassion and understanding for what happened to Brooke, and you'd see it's made me realize I belong to her, with her. I thought you'd bow out gracefully, and the good times we shared together would allow you to wish me well. But then, you had to pull this stunt.

"So, here's the deal. The phone call I was finishing was with my assistant. She spent the morning contacting the caterer, the florist, the band, everyone. It's all been canceled. I paid whatever it cost to stop all of it. Every single guest will receive an overnight delivery note telling them the wedding has been canceled. I was going to offer to go with you to your parents' home and explain. At this point, I don't care what the hell you tell them. Your behavior is deplorable. If you do anything further to hurt Brooke, I'll tell everyone who'll listen you purposely got pregnant to trap me into marrying you."

Kristi's eyes went wide with fear. "Cody, please. No. You can't."

"I will if you cause any further harm. The only woman I'll ever marry is Brooke, if she'll have me. I've wasted enough time with you. Get out."

"Cody," Brooke called to him and tried to get up, but couldn't even manage to raise her shoulders before she fell back into the cushion.

"Stop moving," he begged her.

She sighed. "Don't end things because of what happened to me."

"It should have, and would have, ended the night of the Christmas party if Kristi hadn't tried to manipulate me into marrying her. She stopped taking the pill on purpose without even discussing it with me. That's enough to end things. But what happened to you... I almost lost you forever."

"Come here, Cody." Brooke held out her hand.

He went to her and gently took her hand, concerned about all the blood soaking her bandages.

"We talked about this. Even if we'd been together, it wouldn't have changed what happened. *He* wanted me. He came for me. He would have found a way to get to me no matter what. This isn't your fault. You and Kristi have been together a long time. You love her."

He shook his head. "No. I don't. I thought I did, but then I found out what real love feels like. It's how I feel about you. I spent the last six months trying to convince myself letting you go was the right thing. So you could have an unfettered college experience. So you wouldn't be ridiculed about being with your stepbrother. So you wouldn't regret being with me because of my crazy busy life. But now I understand how you felt all this time. None of that matters as long as I'm with you. I love you. I want to be with you. That's how I feel. And I can't live without you anymore."

"Maybe you're not really in love with me. I'm not the Brooke you used to know anymore."

"Bullshit. You're so much more than the Brooke I used to know. And I love you, damnit."

All of a sudden the trauma caught up to her and her eyes drooped.

"Don't you dare fall asleep when I'm telling you I love you."

A hint of a smile tilted her lips. "I hear you. Australia heard you."

"Kristi heard you." Susanne pointed to the side table at the end of the couch.

Kristi had left her engagement ring on the table beside a picture of Cody and Brooke standing on either side of Cody's prize stallion. Sometime during Cody and Brooke's brief conversation, Kristi had quietly walked out the door.

Cody couldn't care less about the ring. He turned back to Brooke. "I love you. We're getting married."

"We are not," she said immediately.

"Yes we are. Don't argue with me. Don't fight me on this. Not tonight. I'm tired. I've had a shitty day. And you're bleeding again," he said miserably. "Please, honey. Just think about it. Let it sink in. Let yourself believe it because it's true. I love you. Maybe you can love me again, too."

Cody stood and greeted Dr. Nash as he walked in the living room after Janie showed him in. "Thanks for coming so quickly." He looked down at Brooke. She stared back at him, fear in her eyes. "You can trust me, Brooke. You know I would never lie to you." He leaned down and slipped his arms beneath her. "I'm sorry. This is going to hurt."

He carried Brooke up to her bed, trying desperately not to see the way her skin broke out in a fine sheen of sweat. She bit her lip to hide the pain. He hated hurting her. It clawed at his insides and left him raw.

He laid her gently on the bed.

Dr. Nash set his medical bag at her side and pulled out supplies.

Cody concentrated on Brooke's too-pale face. "You'll be okay, sweetheart."

He held her hand as Dr. Nash unwound the bloody bandages on her arm. He kept his focus on her.

Dr. Nash clamped a hand on his shoulder. "Why don't you go downstairs and give me a few minutes alone with my patient."

Brooke gave him a soft nod to go.

He didn't want to leave her, but the sight of all that blood, those long gashes and the reminder of how she'd gotten them, nearly undid him.

He kissed her swollen fingers as she held their daughter to her chest, then fled the room. He hated to leave her when she was in pain, but it was too much for him.

This whole day had been too much. Canceling one wedding. Deciding on another. Trying to help bring Brooke out of her funk and spend some time outdoors and not hiding in bed.

Kristi.

He really couldn't believe she'd admitted to getting pregnant on purpose. And that despicable stunt she pulled with Brooke.

When would they finally have some peace?

Chapter Fifteen

The strain on Dr. Nash's face mirrored Cody's when they met in his office.

"It's easy to see the toll Brooke's condition is taking on you. You need to take care of yourself, too."

Cody didn't respond. Brooke was and would always be his priority now.

"She's okay, Cody," Dr. Nash added.

Cody leaned back in his chair, turning his face up to the ceiling. Nash had been his doctor for a number of years. Cody had a lot of respect for the man. He found him easy to talk to and always ready to listen. When he'd decided to bring Brooke home, he knew Dr. Nash would take care of her with the empathy Brooke needed.

She needed more than her wounds tended to; she needed someone to understand all she'd been through.

"Is she?" Cody didn't think so.

Dr. Nash took a seat and sighed heavily. "I've treated a lot of patients, many of them hurt worse than Brooke. Sometimes it isn't the physical injuries that hurt the most." He stretched his neck, then settled again. "I fixed the cuts on her arms. Most of them are healing well. I took the stitches out of a couple and fixed the stitches on a few others. Janie helped me with some ice packs for the swelling in her arms and her ankle. Her broken wrist hurt her the most. She really banged it up good."

"She was upset. She pounded on me with every bit of strength she had." He had a couple bruises blooming on his chest.

"I didn't want to ask her about what happened." He eyed Cody, coaxing him to open up without pushing.

"She couldn't find our daughter's ashes. She thought I took her away from her." Cody ran a hand over his tight neck muscles and stared at the doctor. "She needs to talk to someone about what happened. Do you think it would be better for her to be somewhere other than the ranch? She's so lost and sad and..." He didn't know how to finish explaining how desolate Brooke could be at times.

"I think she needs to be here with her mom and you. I saw the way you kissed her. It's in the way you look at her. You're in love with her."

A statement of fact Cody didn't have to answer, but he did. "Yes. I love her."

"I thought you were getting married soon."

"I called it off. I love Brooke. I'm going to marry her."

"I see. That sounds...complicated."

"It's really not. And I don't give a shit about what people think."

Dr. Nash nodded with another quirky half smile. "What does it really matter if her mom married your dad? That was their love story. This is yours."

Cody had to agree. "We're family, but not blood. And the way we were when we were younger isn't how we are with each other now. We've both grown and changed. The closeness we share turned into more. I think even Brooke would say the crush she had on me changed into something deeper after she went away to college and she matured."

"That's what happens, right? We grow into ourselves with our experiences."

"Exactly. So who's to judge us for turning our amazing friendship into something more?"

"Not me. But some will."

"I only care about what she thinks and feels."

Dr. Nash motioned with his head. "Is that her ring?"

Cody glared at the diamond solitaire sitting on his desk. Even the sight of it set his blood to boil. It should have been Brooke's ring. "No. That one I gave to Kristi. If there was a volcano nearby, I'd toss it in."

Dr. Nash raised the corner of his mouth, finding a little humor in Cody's disgust with the ring. The situation wasn't funny, however. "You look wiped out, Cody. You should get some rest."

"Doctor's orders," Cody teased without much feeling.

"Something like that. Brooke needs you. You're no good to her if you aren't well and in your right mind."

Cody knew he was right. "Tell me what you think I should do. Everything I do doesn't seem to help her. I feel like she's out of my reach, and all I want to do is grab her and hold on. Sometimes I want to shake her to bring her back to me."

"Well, don't shake her."

He'd never hurt her. "Come on, Doc. How can I help her?"

"I've seen plenty of people like you, frustrated to the breaking point, trying to comfort someone who isn't ready to be comforted. Sometimes people need time to sit in their grief. That's where Brooke is right now. She wants to feel the pain of losing her daughter, even feels she has to feel it to prove to herself and everyone else that she hurts and her daughter is worth the pain."

Cody felt that deep in his soul.

"Love her."

That was easy.

"She needs time. She's grieving, just like you. You both lost a child. That's not easy. It's harder for her because she carried the child. She felt the baby move and kick and it's hard for her to fathom the child is gone when she was so real to her."

"That's just it, isn't it? For me, I grieve that she isn't here and for all the should-have-beens. But it must be so hard for Brooke not to have our daughter growing inside her anymore. She never gave birth. They didn't even let her see her."

"Comfort her. Show her she's loved. Talk to her about the baby. Believe it or not, I think it helps. Remind her there's still a lot of life left to live. It'll take time, but eventually she'll work through her grief and experience happiness again and not feel guilty for it."

"Guilty?"

"She thinks she should have been able to save the baby. I wouldn't be surprised if she feels like she should have died, too."

Cody hadn't thought of that. He hadn't thought she'd blame herself, or wish herself dead. He scrubbed his hands roughly over his face.

"Remind her this isn't her fault. Keep reaching out to her. She might bat you away, but deep inside she wants you to keep reaching for her. She needs you."

"I need her." He needed her more than anything.

"When she's ready, a grief counselor can be very helpful. For both of you."

Cody nodded. He wasn't ready for that yet either. "Listen, Doc, there are some things I need to know." He took a steadying breath and thought about what he wanted for his and Brooke's future. "Can she have more children?"

"I've looked over the copies of her medical records. According to the reports, there's no reason she can't carry another child, given maybe six months to truly heal."

"That'll be a relief to her. I know how much she wants to be a mom. Now I can tell her we'll have a family when she's ready. I want her to know that option is there whenever she wants it."

Dr. Nash nodded. "Right now, her abdomen is sore, but the infection has cleared up and it's healing well. The other injuries are far less serious. Her broken arm should be healed in a month or so, but that won't hinder her from all activities. She didn't give birth, so she can resume sexual activity whenever she feels like it."

Cody held up a hand. "Whoa, Doc. I wasn't planning on...you know...until she's better." They still had a lot to work out in addition to her wounds healing.

Dr. Nash settled back. "I'm just giving you the information you need."

Cody appreciated it. "How soon until she can walk on her foot without the brace?"

"At least another week, maybe more after today."

"Could I take her horseback riding?"

"Not until her abdomen is better. At least a couple of weeks."

"Okay. She loves to ride. I'd wanted to take her. I thought it might make her happy."

"Riding isn't a good idea at the moment, but getting her up and out of the house is. The more you get her engaged in life and out of her head, the better she'll be. The sooner she'll heal."

He'd take her over to the building she bought and show her all the renovations. He'd get her excited about opening the bookstore and café. A task, something to look forward to. It would help. He hoped.

"If you find her wallowing in her grief and sinking further into depression, let me know."

He frowned. "I don't want to have to medicate her."

"We'll help her any way we can to make sure she's safe." Dr. Nash didn't say it, but Brooke's depression could lead her to hurt herself. "I've contacted a colleague. Dr. Wick. He's a psychiatrist and specializes in trauma. He'll be by the house to check on her." Dr. Nash slid a card with the appointment information across Cody's desk.

"Thanks." He'd ask Dr. Wick about things he could do to help Brooke, too.

"I gave her a couple of shots for the pain and to help her sleep. That's all I can do right now. I'll be back in a few days to take out some of the other stitches. Until then, watch over her. Give her what she needs."

Cody would do anything to help her. He just wished he were confident in his ability to love her out of her grief and back to him.

Whatever it takes. I'm all in.

Chapter Sixteen

Cody dragged himself up the stairs and down the hall to Brooke's room. Susanne must have heard him coming and met him outside the door.

"I..."

"Don't, Susanne. Please don't tell me to go to bed and leave her alone. I can't. I just can't." He'd been down in his study working for hours, since the doctor left. Thanks to the drugs the doc gave her, Brooke had slept the last of the day away. He hoped she slept through the night, too. He'd eaten at his desk while he pored over his cases, trying to get as much work done as he possibly could, trying to free up his day to spend time with Brooke. He'd even managed to get a full update on the renovations in Brooke's building. Everything was running on time and on budget, which had to be because of the relationship between his dad and Danny, the owner of the construction company.

He'd have to call Danny soon and thank him for working so hard on the project and invite him to dinner.

Susanne leaned a shoulder against the doorframe. "I was only going to say I'm leaving her in your hands. She's sleeping well. I took the ice packs off about an hour ago. The swelling in her arms and ankle looks better."

Cody ran a hand over his hair and looked at Susanne. She smiled like she knew something he didn't. "Oh." He didn't know what else to say and shrugged. She wasn't going to bar him from seeing Brooke. As if he'd let her.

"It's been a long day. You're working too hard. After that fight with Kristi and what happened with Brooke, you need your rest."

"I'll rest when she's well again."

"Are you really going to marry Brooke?"

"Yes. I want to marry her more than anything. I love her, and I want to make her happy. I want to give her what she's always wanted. I want to be with her the rest of our lives."

Susanne smiled. "Your father and I were married here at the ranch. It was a huge celebration. Your father had a lot of friends and business associates."

"It was a beautiful wedding. Brooke was beautiful as your maid of honor."

"Yes. It pleased her a great deal when I married Harland. She loved him, too."

Brooke, the little girl Harland never thought he'd wanted, had claimed a very special place in his father's heart. Daughters were not Harland's idea of a family legacy. Brooke changed his mind.

Cody would kill to have his daughter here with him right now.

But Adam had taken her from them. And he'd pay for it. Because he and Brooke and the other victims shouldn't be the only ones suffering.

Susanne reached out and held his shoulder and gave him a soft squeeze. "I'm all for the two of you getting married. She's loved you practically her whole life. It took you a little longer to see she's the best thing that ever happened to you.

No one else understands you and accepts you the way she does. Sometimes we have to try different sizes before we find the best fit."

"She's the only one that fits. God, I've been such an idiot, and she's paid such a high price for my stupidity." He fisted his hand and resisted the overwhelming urge to punch something.

"Don't do that to yourself, or to her. Forget about how we got in this situation, and let's concentrate on making her well. Let that be the focus instead of what you did, what she did, and what Kristi did to get us here."

Cody tilted his head. "We can't change the past, so focus on the future?"

"Life is short. I don't think it's good to let her dwell in the past. Let's find a way to help her move forward. The baby is a huge loss. I'm not saying forget her, just learn to live without her."

"That's easier said than done. You saw Brooke tonight."

"She'll work her way out of this. I think having something like a wedding to look forward to will help settle her."

"She never said she'd marry me. In fact, she said she wouldn't."

"You surprised her. I think that's good. Keep her on her toes, but make it clear you really do love her. After all this time, Cody, it's hard for her to believe you mean it. It's what she's always wanted, but this isn't the ideal circumstance for her to get what she wants. She's going to have a hard time believing you aren't doing this because of what happened."

"I don't know how to convince her."

"You don't need to convince her. Just love her. She'll see it. She'll feel it. And soon, she'll respond to it. She won't be able to deny it. She loves you, and she wants to be loved by you. Give her what she wants. You know how."

He wished he had Susanne's confidence. Right now, he could use even a little of it. "I have no idea where to begin with her."

"You've been her best friend for the last ten years. That's a good place to start."

He looked past her at Brooke, sleeping peacefully in bed. Right where he wanted to be.

"I'll say goodnight. Sleep well, Cody."

He stepped into the room and sat on the bed next to Brooke as she whimpered in her sleep. "Hey, Brooke, you're okay," he whispered, hoping to soothe her without waking her.

"Cody," she called out, her eyes flying open.

"Yeah, baby, it's me. You're okay. You're safe."

She sucked in a ragged breath and let it out. "What time is it?"

"Nearly eleven. Go back to sleep."

She turned to him. "Lie with me. Just until I fall asleep."

"I'll stay as long as you like."

He shifted and settled in beside her on his side so he could see her beautiful face. "I've missed you so much, Brooke."

"I missed you, too." She bit her lip. "I'm sorry about what happened with Kristi."

"That's over. We don't have to talk about her ever again."

"But you loved her."

"Maybe once. It's hard to tell now. What I do know is that I love you more than anything or anyone. I knew it six months ago. I know it now. And I'll spend the rest of my life making up for letting you go. I won't make that mistake again, Brooke. I promise."

"What do you think she would have looked like?"

"When I think of her, I see you. A pretty little girl with your slightly up-tilted nose, green eyes, sweet smile, and dark hair."

She quirked her brow. "Not blonde?"

"Maybe light brown hair. A shade between yours and mine."

That earned him a soft grin. "And her eyes are blue, not green, and filled with your certainty and strength, with a little mischief mixed in."

He choked up at the thought and how much he loved lying here with her, talking about their little girl. "She's got your kind heart and laugh. She giggles like you did when you were young and laughed at all my jokes."

A tear slipped past her lashes and rolled down her cheek. "And she's smart as a whip, like you."

"Like her mother. And creative like you."

"Logical and passionate about helping others like you."

"What do you think she'd grow up to be?"

"If she's anything like me, she'll love you more than anything and want to follow in your footsteps. After she spends all your money riding horses and winning ribbons."

"Like her mom in high school."

"And she'd have loved books because we would have read to her every night."

"We'd have done everything to make her happy. We'd have loved her with our whole hearts."

"We still will."

"Yes, we will."

They fell quiet for a long time.

"Cody?"

"Yeah?"

"I'm scared. Will you stay?"

"Yes. But you don't have to be scared. You're safe here. I won't let anything happen to you."

"It's not him. Well, it's the nightmares. But also..."

"What?" He leaned up on his elbow and stared down at her. Waiting. He'd wait as long as she needed him to.

"I'm scared of the quiet and the thoughts that run through my head. Bad thoughts, Cody. So I need you to stay here with me. Okay?"

Cody tensed, even as he tried not to show his shock and fear. He put his hand on her shoulder and squeezed it gently. "Next to you is exactly where I want to be." He settled down next to her again, arranging his pillow right beside hers and his head close enough that his forehead nestled in the crook of her neck as he lay on his side, just an inch away from her hurt arm but close enough she could feel him next to her. "I love you," he whispered.

She didn't say it back, but she did put her hand over his and squeezed.

"You're going to be all right. Everything is going to be all right." He hoped she believed him.

Just being this close to her sent a wave of relief through his mind and body. He felt her relax next to him as her breathing evened out.

And finally, they slept.

Sometime in the night, she managed to scoot back into him, her rump snug against his crotch, back against his chest, her legs outlining his. His arm had found its way across her, nestled under her breasts with her arm over his, their fingers intertwined. He nuzzled his face into her hair, kissed her head, and settled back into the best sleep he'd had in months.

He came awake slowly the next morning, opening his eyes as he became aware of two things. Brooke was awake and she was still lying in his arms.

Brooke had woken up about twenty minutes ago, feeling calm and content because of the man snuggled up behind her.

He stayed.

And she'd slept the entire night without having a nightmare for the first time since the attack. She tried to dismiss it, reasoning it out that the sedative the doctor gave her had done its job. But in her heart, she knew it was Cody beside her, holding her in the night, keeping the nightmares away.

Cody nuzzled his nose into her hair. "This is how I want to wake up every morning."

She actually grinned. "Thank you for staying."

"No place I'd rather be." He held her a little closer, his breath feathering through her hair. "Are you in pain?"

"Always."

He pressed a kiss just behind her ear and whispered, "I'm sorry."

She didn't want apologies. "Maybe this was a mistake, us sleeping together."

He leaned up on his elbow and stared down at her. "This is the first morning you actually look rested. I slept better here with you than I have since you went back to school."

"Since you *sent* me back to school."

The light in his eyes dimmed. "What was I supposed to do?" He shook his head. "Maybe if I'd done what I wanted to do, none of this would have happened."

Brooke slowly shifted onto her back and looked up at him. "We can't keep doing this to each other. You're not to blame for what happened. I should have told you about the baby. About everything."

"It's because of me you couldn't come home or call when you needed help."

"My choice, Cody."

"You did it because you wanted me to be happy. So now I'm telling you, the only time I'm ever truly happy and just myself is when I'm with you."

His words sank into her hollowed-out heart. The weight of his words and their meaning washed against the bleeding walls and soothed them just as much as his arms around her in the dark had banished all the scary, ugly, and sad thoughts from her mind.

She opened her mouth. To say what, she didn't quite know.

But Cody put his finger over her lips. "You don't have to say anything." He'd read her mind. "You don't have to know what you want right now. You don't even have to trust me. But you will figure it all out. You will trust me again. Because I'll spend every second of every day from now on showing you that I love you, that I'm not going anywhere, that you—we—can have everything we want. I will love you, the way you always loved me. With my whole heart. Without any restraint. With everything I am."

A tear slipped past her lashes. "Cody...I do trust you. Everything you did is exactly who you are. You wanted to marry Kristi because you loved her and wanted your child to have two loving parents. A family. You let me go because you take care of your responsibilities."

"Maybe that's all true. But it's also true that I selfishly and desperately wanted to be with you. I loved you the whole time I was with her after our night together. Don't let last night and the night we shared back then be all we have. I want more. I want everything. And I think you do, too."

"I don't want it to be because we lost our child."

"It's not. I wish I could have told you that morning all the plans I woke up with in my head. I was so excited and anxious to build a life with you, one that was everything I ever wanted. A partner by my side who knew me better than I knew myself. A lover who gave herself to me completely. A friend who would always be by my side, willing to share the good, the bad, and everything in between. Someone willing to say not just what I needed to hear, but all the things I don't want to hear either." He cupped her cheek. "You are everything I ever wanted and was too stupid to see was right in front of me."

"It wasn't our time."

"It can be now." His eyes pleaded with her. "Or when you're ready. Because I'll wait as long as it takes. I'm not going anywhere, and I only want to be with you."

"I just..." She didn't know what to say. She didn't know how she felt. Yes, she loved him. She'd always love him. But

things were different now. She was different after what had
happened, and she didn't know if she'd ever feel like herself
again and not this empty shell.

Cody brushed his fingers over her cheek. "It's okay,
Brooke. I'm glad we had this talk. I wanted a chance to tell
you how I feel. It's deep and true, Brooke. And it's not going away. Ever. If you can try to believe that, that's enough
for now." He bent his head and pressed his forehead to
hers, his eyes closing, but not before she saw the raw love
in them.

She went still and held her breath, not wanting to give
any life to the hope that sparked inside her because it had
been extinguished too many times and it hurt too much to
lose it.

"Last night when you asked me to stay...it gave me
hope." His words echoed her thought. "I just wanted to
hold you, be there for you, so you'd know I was here in case
you needed me. For whatever you need from me."

She needed him more than ever, but was afraid to reach
for him.

"I didn't want you to be alone. And, frankly, I didn't
want to be alone. It's so damn hard to keep making myself
stay away from you when this is right where I want to be."

That tiny spark grew into a flame.

"I start thinking about what happened. I think about
her and all we've lost, and I need to see you and touch you
to know you're still here with me."

The flame spread through her heart.

"We can get through this as long as we have each other.
If you want me beside you every night to chase away the
nightmares, to hold you while you cry, to love you through
the darkness until the light comes back—it always comes

back. Please believe that—then I will be here. Because I need you as much as I hope you need me."

She did need him. And after all she and Kristi had put him through, she could understand he needed her comfort, even if he helped make a mess of things.

It was just so hard to believe he wanted to be with her.

Even more unbelievable, he loved her.

She squeezed his hand even though it hurt her broken arm. "I do need you. You're the only one who knows what it feels like to lose her."

He sighed heavily and held her tight, kissing her head again. "We're going to get through this, Brooke. I promise you. I'm going to make everything up to you. We're going to have what we've both wanted for so long."

"You said you wanted *her*." She couldn't help herself. It hurt that after what they'd shared, he'd let her leave without saying how he really felt about her.

Cody let out a ragged sigh. "Biggest mistake of my life, letting you go. I woke up that morning feeling like finally my whole world was perfect. I wanted to take you for a picnic by the creek you love so much. I'd make love to you in your favorite spot. I wanted to take you out to dinner that night at a quiet restaurant and hold your hand across the table and show you that I didn't care who saw us together. It didn't matter anymore because I loved you and I wanted everyone to see how happy we were together."

Cody buried his face in her hair. "You have no idea how much I hurt for you, seeing you standing in the doorway watching all that play out. I wanted to go to you and beg you to understand. I wanted to wrap you in my arms and tell you that you were the woman I loved with my whole heart. But I couldn't."

"Because you wanted to be all in for the baby."

"Yes. After you left, I did what I had to do. I tried to forget you and move on with my life. But there was something always missing. And honestly, I thought you hated me for what I'd done. I tried to make the best of things and appreciate what I had. Kristi. A baby on the way. Then she lost it and I thought of you. We could have a second chance." He rubbed his fingers over his forehead. "Then I misunderstood your text when I asked if we could talk. I thought you had someone new, someone you cared about. It wrecked me. I truly thought I'd lost you."

"You never lost me. I was just waiting until after you married her to come back and find a way for us to be friends again."

"And parents to our girl."

"Yes. I didn't know you loved me."

"I know. I'm sorry. I should have told you. I'm so damn sorry." He held her close and rested his cheek on her head.

It felt good to get it all out and clear the air.

Maybe they could start over. But not if they carried all this guilt with them. She held him tighter. "I just want to be here. Now. I don't want to think about it anymore. And I don't want it to be a wall between us again. I'm tired, Cody. I hurt from the inside out."

"I know you do, sweetheart. We'll find a way to heal."

"I'm trying. It's so damn hard." Some moments it was all she could do to take her next breath.

"I'm here. I'll help you."

"Stop blaming yourself. Stop feeling sorry for me. Stop feeling guilty. It makes me feel guilty, and I don't want to feel this way anymore."

"I'll try." He held her and let all they'd said settle.

She needed time, the quiet, and him.

Cody nuzzled his nose into her hair, then kissed her softly behind her ear. "Do you want to go down and get something to eat?"

She nearly smiled. "Are you desperate for coffee?"

He pressed his lips to her ear. "I'm desperate for you."

She felt the same way because she felt a tiny bit like her old self lying this close to him. "Cody..."

"Don't worry, honey. We're going to work our way back to each other. I know you need time to heal and to learn to trust me again."

"I do trust you. I was only going to ask you to kiss me." Because when he did, she forgot everything but how good it was to be lost in him.

"Sweetheart, you never have to ask." To prove it, he ran his hand through the side of her hair and waited for her to turn to him and nestle close again. He brushed his lips over her mouth in a soft caress, more of a whisper than an actual touch of lips. He increased the pressure.

She felt lighter than she'd felt in months with his lips warm against hers. His thick erection pressed to her hip. She instinctively moved against him, unable to stop her response. She wanted to touch him, feel him pressed against her. Hampered by her injuries, she focused on his mouth connected to hers and savored the taste and texture of him. God, she'd missed him.

The memory of their night together, all the fantasies she'd had over the last six month of his hands on her, his lips, his tongue, his cock deep inside her, making her feel wanted and cherished like he did that night, had built up in her mind and body. She ached with wanting him and what they'd shared. She dreamed of having him back in her arms. This was just a taste of what it had been like, but it was also a release of the daunting past six months and a renewal of all the feelings and untamed desire that still burned between them even if they were still being careful not to hurt any of her wounds.

She wanted more.

She wanted him.

Her breasts tingled and felt heavy. "Cody, I need your hands on me."

He slid his hand around her ribs. She took it and planted it over her breast. His thumb brushed over her hard nipple. She arched into him.

She wanted more.

He gave her everything.

More kisses. More touches. More loving, keeping her awash in his love and blocking out the grief.

This wasn't a distraction. This was a reminder that life and love could feel good. Oh, so good.

He kissed her again and again like he could do it all day. The more she relaxed and lost herself in him, the deeper and longer the kisses, the softer and more tender the caresses.

She loved it.

Any apprehension or negative thoughts that this wasn't real disappeared as he showered her with his patience and enjoyment and the need rolling off him that he was right there with her, feeling everything she felt, connected like they'd been once and needed again now.

Overwhelmed with emotion, tears welled in her eyes.

He rested his forehead to hers and stared into her eyes. "I know just how you feel. I've missed you, too, sweetheart.

I've missed you so damn much." He kissed her again, then just held her.

For a little while, everything went away. Their world stood still.

She felt safe and loved in his arms.

But this couldn't last.

He had responsibilities and obligations.

She needed to figure out what to do next. "We should get up." She brushed her fingers along his arm, loving being able to touch him like this.

Cody snuggled closer. "I'm happy to stay right here with you all day."

"I'm sure you have other things to do."

"Whatever they are, they can wait. You are my priority."

She loved hearing that, but also felt like a burden. "How about we get breakfast. I'm actually hungry." She'd barely eaten since coming home.

Cody rose up on his elbow and stared down at her. "You are?" The hope and surprise in his eyes made her feel like shit that she'd made him worry so much about her.

"Yeah."

He slipped from the bed and stood beside it, looking down at her. She let her gaze roam over his body, wrinkled clothes, and the impressive bulge against his zipper, memorizing every line and curve of muscled body and expanse of tanned skin. His eyes remained hot on her.

"Like what you see?"

"I can't believe you're real." *And here with me.*

"I'm very real. And so is this." He leaned over to kiss her again, but the knock at the door stopped him inches from her lips.

"Cody, your office called. They need to talk to you. I told them you'd call back."

Brooke gasped, startled her mother would come to her room looking for him.

"Give me a few minutes," he called back without turning away from her. "Your mom knows I'm here and there's no use keeping me from you. She wants you to be happy, and she believes I can make you happy. I'm going to do everything I can not to disappoint her. Or you." He stole a quick kiss. "Get used to it, because the only place I'm sleeping from now on is next to you." He kissed her again. "I need a cold shower. As you can plainly see." He kept it light, teasing, no hint of expectation that she couldn't fulfill in her condition. Just understanding and patience. "Do you need help getting up?"

She appreciated that he didn't put any pressure on her but still managed to bring them closer together by putting her needs first.

"Everything is sore and tight and uncomfortable first thing in the morning, but I'll loosen up the more I move."

Cody took the pills from the side table and handed her four with a bottle of water. He helped her lean up to take them.

"Rest a little longer? Maybe try a little stretching if you feel up to it. When I get out of the shower, I'll help you up. We'll have breakfast together."

"But you have a call to return."

"I'll take care of it later. I'll work from home as much as possible over the next few days. I've got to go to court a couple of times, but otherwise I'll be here with you."

He walked away like it was settled and it was okay he'd changed his whole schedule to be with her because she was such a basket case she couldn't be left alone.

She wanted him, but she didn't want to be a burden.

She needed to find a way through her grief. She just didn't know how.

Today felt like a better day, because she'd slept and woken up with him. For the first time in a long time, she felt safe. And sharing the loss of their daughter helped ease some of her pain.

"Brooke, you okay?"

"Yeah." She met his concerned gaze. "I think I'm going to be."

He sighed out his relief. "That makes me feel a lot better."

She really hoped this was the start of their new life together. She hoped she could hold on to this feeling instead of getting sucked under by the crushing pain and sorrow.

She'd try.

For Cody.

For her daughter. She'd live in honor of her.

For herself, because second chances didn't come often and she didn't want to waste this opportunity and what could be a really happy life if she let herself accept it and believe in it.

That was easier said than done. Because she wasn't sure how real or how serious Cody was about being with her. Not that he'd lie. But maybe he was just caught up in his grief and almost losing her.

Was that all this was? His reaction to the circumstances? Or did he really see a life together for them?

Chapter Seventeen

Adam sat in one of the common rooms made to look like a living room in someone's home. This room was for guests to meet with patients. To make visitors feel comfortable. So they didn't have to be confronted with the fact they'd locked their family members away for their own good.

The doctors had stitched him up and put him on several medications. They helped him see things more clearly, but that didn't alleviate the remorse that consumed him.

Somehow, in the last year, his desperate need to have someone understand him, to see him as his own person, and that he was spiraling in his loneliness had turned into a fixation with Brooke that turned deadly.

He didn't know how he'd gone from wanting to have coffee with her to obsessing over their brief conversations and creating a fantasy world in which he was her secret admirer. A delusion in which she knew all too well it was him and loved that they had a secret relationship.

He'd had other bouts of depression, but not this kind of total mental meltdown.

Even now, thinking about it, wondering how he'd duped himself into believing she wanted him to buy her those gifts, to watch over her on campus, to learn to be the man she needed him to be so he could go to her and show her how much he loved her... It was crazy.

It wasn't real.

Yes, she'd been his friend. But nothing more.

And he'd ruined even that.

He'd rationalized it all in his mind with irrational excuses for what he'd done.

She hadn't known he was the one doing those things.

She'd reported his activities to the police and told them she was scared.

He'd thought she'd loved the attention. He'd done it to please her, so that she knew she wasn't ever alone.

And that freaked her out.

Because it was crazy for him to think she wanted someone to stalk her every move and send her things that were personal and that she liked without ever approaching her and telling her it was him, and that he just wanted to make her happy if she'd let him.

And that was the lie he had told himself again and again.

She wanted me to do it.

She wanted me.

But now he knew better. Now he had a clear head. Now he knew what he'd done. To her.

To those other girls.

Oh God. What have I done?

Right and wrong got crossed in his haywire brain.

In the moment, he'd thought everything he'd done leading up to confronting Brooke was just him experimenting like college kids did all the time. But it had been dark and twisted.

And Brooke and the others paid the price for his obsession.

He stared at his mom's perfectly done up face and saw the lie there mixed with the truth in her eyes. She was embarrassed, ashamed, and a little scared of him now. "Did you give her my letter? What did she say? Will she come? I need to see her." He had no right to ask her to come. But he hoped. And he needed. He couldn't shut it off. It's all he thought about now.

Yes, he knew it was what got him into this trouble, but he couldn't seem to help himself.

His mother pressed her lips tight and looked to his father for the answer she didn't want to say to him.

His father sighed and gave him that *you're so exasperating* look. "I've told you a dozen times, she doesn't want to see you. We came today to find out how you are and if you're progressing with your treatment."

Adam ignored all that. "But you gave her my letters. She read them."

His mother leaned over and reached out to touch his knee but pulled her hand back at the last second. "Adam, honey, Brooke is upset. She's grieving. She's traumatized. You understand that, right?" She didn't wait for him to answer. "She lost her child."

Of course he knew that. They didn't need to tell him. He'd seen what he'd done. It was bad. So bad. But he couldn't help it. It had just come over him. He'd lost it.

He had to make her understand.

"Adam." His mom snapped out his name to get his attention again. "We haven't been able to talk to her."

He leaned toward her, and she leaned back. "That's why I asked you to give her the letters. I need to see her," he demanded.

"It's never going to happen." His father rested his forearms on his thighs and hung his head. "You need to focus on *you* and getting better."

"I need to see *her*."

"She doesn't want to see you. I can't even get a meeting with her. And if she goes to the police and tells them you are the one who attacked her... Well, you can kiss this hospital goodbye, because you'll spend the rest of your life in prison. Stop thinking about her and think about yourself. So far I've been able to keep any connection between your attempted suicide and the campus stalker attacking Brooke from creeping into the police investigation or reporters' questions. If Brooke comes here...if you contact her...I won't be able to keep that a secret. Someone will leak something. I hope you've been careful with what you tell the doctors and nurses here."

Adam sighed. His father didn't get it. Adam didn't care what happened to him. "I just want to talk to her. Can you set up a phone call? Something. You're the fucking governor. Make her do it." He stomped his foot, earning him another glare from his parents.

His father's stern gaze held his. "Make her. Like you tried to make her be your girlfriend. I couldn't make her talk to me in the hospital because she was so broken and grief-stricken she couldn't stop crying long enough to hear what I had to say. Make her! I won't make her do anything she doesn't want to do for you. Not after what you've done. Not after you ruined your life and could quite possibly destroy my life's work."

Adam tried to be contrite, even though he wanted to rage at his father for making him this way. "Please. Can't you try? If she read my letter, then she knows I'm sorry."

"What good is sorry to her after what you did? The best we can hope for is that she never utters your name ever again. That is the only thing I am willing to do for you."

Adam eyed his father, seeing the calculation and resignation. "What does that mean?"

"I will talk to her again. When she's feeling better and has had time to think. Hopefully she'll come to the same conclusion she silently agreed to in the hospital, that you're better off here than in a jail cell." His father fell back in his seat and stared up at the ceiling. "If people knew..." He pressed the back of his fist to his forehead.

Adam leaned in and let his hatred show. "That's the only thing you care about. What people will say. What will happen to you. I need to see her! I can make this right!"

His dad sprung up from his seat and towered over Adam. "No you can't! Nothing will make this right! Her baby is dead!"

His dad walked out and slammed the door behind him, leaving Adam flinching and alone with his mom.

He turned to her. "Please. Won't you do this one thing for me?"

"No," she snapped. "I will not push your needs on a grieving mother."

"He didn't send her my letters, did he?"

"Adam..."

"Right. Of course he didn't."

Her stern face softened. "If you really care about Brooke, you'll leave her alone and let her recuperate in private."

"I want to help her heal." Adam pulled the paper out of the back of his pants. "Please, give her this."

His mother took it, then stood. "I better go find your father. Please listen to the doctors. Do what they say. Take your meds. And remember that your father and I are only trying to protect you." She walked out on him then, too.

He stood, went to the door, and looked out at the two of them, standing with his doctor. His mom said something to his father, then handed the letter over to him. He crushed it in his hand and stuffed it in his inside coat pocket.

Ever the gentleman, he shook the doctor's hand and walked to the elevator with his mom.

Adam wondered if they planned to ever come back and see him again, or if they'd just leave him here for the rest of his life, out of sight, out of mind like always.

Well, if they wouldn't do what he needed them to do, he'd have to find a way to do it himself.

He owed Brooke.

He'd see her again.

Chapter Eighteen

C ody had to swing by his office today to pick up some files and deliver a surprise to his assistant, Brandy. She loved the box of honey almond shortbread cookies he'd picked up from her favorite bakery downtown. She'd gone above and beyond helping him with canceling the wedding plans and notifying guests. Which was why he'd also given her a gift card to her favorite restaurant, so she and her husband could have a nice night out together on him.

He was just about ready to leave when Brandy popped her head into his office. "Heads up. Kirk Randall is in Parker Beecham's office."

Cody rolled his eyes, knowing they were probably discussing him.

Kirk wanted to ruin him.

Brandy sneered. "They're having lunch together at Pandora's."

Of course Kirk would take Beecham to the most exclusive restaurant in town. He was surprised they weren't meeting there, but he guessed that Kirk hoped to find Cody in his office for a little face-to-face chat.

He stood and headed for the door.

Brandy's eyes went wide. "You're not going in there, are you?"

"I have no reason to hide."

Brandy moved out of his way and went to sit back at her desk as he walked past all the cubicles that separated his office from Beecham's much larger one.

The door was open as Kirk stood facing Beecham's desk. "And how is our little project going? Is he feeling the pain and his career slipping away?"

Cody tempered his initial wave of anger and dealt with Kirk like he did all hostile witnesses. With composed professionalism. "I'm actually enjoying having more time to spend at home with Brooke." Cody leaned against the doorframe, enjoying Beecham's stuttered, surprised gasp and Kirk's embarrassed blush at getting caught, though the flush quickly turned to one of fury.

"You have some nerve sneaking up on us like that."

"No sneaking required. The door was open. I saw you standing here and thought I'd say hello to a colleague, since we both work on the board for the children's hospital."

"After what you did to my daughter, you won't be working anywhere in this town ever again when I'm done with you."

Cody knew Kirk meant the threat. It simply didn't bother him. He knew his own worth. "You and I both know the board is never going to fire me. They have no cause to, because I'm the best thing that ever happened to that hospital. Up until recently, you enjoyed taking credit for bringing me on. As for this vendetta you're using Beecham to carry out for you...well, he knows as well as I do that he's indulging you for now."

Kirk took a quick glance at Beecham's pale and regretful face.

Cody explained why Beecham looked that way. "At the end of the month, when the managing partner sees that my billable hours are down because *he's* not assigning new cases to me, he's going to ask why. With no apparent reason for not keeping me working as I have in the past, Beecham is going to get the order to load me up again, so this firm earns the money they know I bring in. This will look bad on Beecham, but he doesn't care because it gets you off his back about whatever he owed you for, and his father won't do anything about it because he wants his son up on the top floor with him, named as the next partner. Minor infractions like this don't trump family. Beecham will be fine. So will I."

Kirk's neck and face flamed red with rage. "You broke her heart and you just get away with it. No. I don't think so. Not after you fucked your stepsister and knocked her up while you were seeing Kristi."

Cody shook his head. "I'm not surprised she lied to you about what happened. Not after the treachery she pulled on me to get me to marry her."

Beecham sat up, intrigued by that bit of news.

Kirk seemed to take that in and hesitate. "You just want to blame her and not take responsibility for what you did."

"I did take responsibility. She counted on me doing that. And her deceit cost me six months of not knowing I was going to be a father and being with Brooke when she needed me, all the while I was trying to make *your* daughter happy."

"Kristi is better off without you." Kirk's rage had turned to a simmer now that he knew Kristi wasn't so innocent in their breakup, even if he didn't know exactly what Kristi had done.

"I'm glad it's over. Now we can both move on. But don't for a second believe the breakup was all my fault. She was selfish and deceitful with me and cruel to Brooke, causing her great pain. I won't forgive her for that."

Confusion filled Kirk's eyes. "I don't know what you're talking about."

"Ask your daughter, though I doubt she'll confess. I have nothing more to say about it. If you'll excuse me, I'm going to take advantage of my lack of work and go home." Cody looked past Kirk to Beecham. "Unless you need me to stay."

Embarrassed and resigned, Beecham shook his head. "Um. No. Enjoy the rest of your day. I'll have something for you tomorrow."

"Can't wait." Cody left the two men and walked away like nothing was bothering him and he didn't care that several people in the office had overheard that conversation.

Let them talk.

Maybe now Kirk would shut up and stop trying to retaliate against him.

Cody understood it came from a place of love for his daughter.

He didn't want to disparage Kristi in Kirk's eyes. That's why he'd left off the details about a broken condom, Kristi stopping her birth control and not telling him, so she could use a pregnancy to trap him into marriage. Or that she'd been pregnant and lost the baby, also without telling Cody right away. She wasn't innocent.

Neither was he.

Kirk had taken things too far.

If it stopped here, Cody would let it go.

If Kirk took things further, well, then Cody would have to do something about that, too.

Chapter Nineteen

Brooke was tired of staring at the walls and everyone in the house staring at her, wondering if she was okay. She wanted to feel normal again. She wanted to get out of the house and do something. So she asked Cody if he'd take her to see her new building and storefronts. He'd suggested the trip a couple of times over the last few days.

Today when she approached him, it had made him happier than something so small should, and she knew she'd made the right choice. She couldn't wallow forever.

Though she had her reservations about being in public with her injuries and her head not in a great place, the thought of seeing all her plans for the building coming together actually excited her.

But she couldn't stop fidgeting, hyperaware of how many people were out on the sidewalks downtown.

She knew Adam was locked up in a hospital, but that didn't mean her body knew it. Adrenaline pumped through her veins. At least it was light out. She didn't know if she could take being out at night.

Cody opened the car door and held out his hand to assist her to her feet. She didn't remember them stopping and him getting out of the car while her mind raced.

She sucked in a deep breath, concentrated on the feel of the warm sunshine on her face, and that she'd worn a long-sleeved shirt to cover her sliced up and bandaged arms. She couldn't hide the brace, but no one would think anything but that she'd sprained her wrist or something.

"You okay?"

She nodded at Cody, biting her bottom lip. "Fine."

"No one knows anything. No one is staring. It's just you and me."

She appreciated the reminder. She feared being ambushed by the press. But so far, all anyone knew was that the campus stalker's unnamed victim had gone home just before the semester ended and he remained at large.

She'd have to do something about that soon.

But not right now.

Today was to look toward her future, and he had no place in it.

She squeezed Cody's hand and he squeezed back, letting her know he was there and she was safe. It settled her nerves like his kiss grounded her, even as it made her heart soar, and she appreciated his understanding and not saying anything about her sweaty palm.

This was the first time she was seeing the renovations in person and she wanted to take it all in and enjoy it. Cody and Danny Quinn from Quinn Construction had sent her extensive pictures and videos of the progress. But nothing beat seeing the improvements in person.

They were parked right outside the old bookstore. The front windows had been cleaned, the trim painted in black. A sign hung over the door. Brooke's Book Nook Café.

He'd gotten all of that done over the last week while she was at home grieving and just trying to breathe through each agonizing day. He somehow found the strength to take care of her, grieve, work to satisfy his obligations, hold her through each night to keep the monster away. How did he do all of that and help her to make her dreams come true?

"Cody?"

"Yeah." He stared down at her, expectant and ready to answer or give her whatever she needed.

"Thank you."

"For what?"

She held her hand out toward the building. "This. Everything. Taking care of me. Being you."

He put his arm around her shoulders, drew her close to his chest, and kissed her forehead. "You don't have to thank me for anything. It's my pleasure to do anything, everything for you."

She went up on tiptoe and lightly kissed him. "Thank you." She wanted him to know she meant it.

He cupped her cheek and brushed his nose against hers. "You're welcome."

She gave him a smile and got one back. "I love the sign's design with the shelf of books all lined up under the shop name."

Cody squeezed her hand and turned to look at it with her. "Did it turn out the way you hoped?"

"It's even better in person."

"You've been in the bookstore a bunch. Let's start in the café space." Cody held her hand as they walked next door. The front of the storefront matched the bookstore's

whitewashed painted brick exterior to brighten up the
façade with black-trimmed windows.

"I think I'll get some large pots to put out front and
fill with flowers. Maybe a few café tables, so people can sit
outside."

"Sounds good to me." Cody unlocked the café and
guided her in before he stepped back and let her take it in.

"Last I saw the space, there was just a big empty room."
Now, a twenty-foot counter spanned the right side of the
area, with counters and mirrors against the wall. The far
side of the counter had space for two cash registers, where
customers would order their drinks and purchase food.
Next to that space, a glass case beneath the countertop
would show off all the baked goods they'd sell. To the right,
customers could sit at the counter, or wander to the cozy
chairs and love seats with tables to sit and enjoy their food
and beverages while reading or chatting with friends.

The furniture was covered in plastic to protect it until
opening, but she loved all the colors of the items she'd
picked out in jewel tones of purple, blue, green, and pink.

"That little blue sofa by the window is my favorite."
Cody pointed to it. "I love the Brooke's Book Nook Café
logo on the wall above the sofa. It is the perfect little spot to
curl up and read." His praise boosted her confidence and
pride.

"Thank you. It means a lot that you like it." She'd
worked really hard on all the details, wanting this space to
feel light and airy and comfortable. She wanted people to
feel like they could sit a spell and get lost in a book.

"I don't just like it, Brooke. I think it's fucking amazing
what you've done here."

That took her aback. "You oversaw all the work."

"But this is your design and vision. I liked the idea when you presented it to me. I expected that you'd do well. But people are really going to love this place. It's going to be packed all the time. There's nothing else like it downtown."

She grinned again. This time it came easier. "Did you match all the chairs at the tables?"

"Yeah. Well, me and your mom. Why?"

"It looks great. It's just..."

"What?" His gaze roamed the room, looking for anything out of place from her detailed plans.

"Everything is exactly where it should be," she assured him. "It's just that I thought I'd mix and match the chair colors at each table." She'd bought the chairs in four different but complementary styles and thought it would be kind of cool to have different chairs at different tables.

"I'll rearrange them if you want." He let her loose and stepped toward the first table.

She grabbed his arm. "Cody, no. It's fine. I actually think keeping the colors together makes the place look more polished and soothing." Everything in her head felt chaotic. Order made her feel more relaxed. She wanted that for her customers.

"I don't mind changing it if that's what you want, sweetheart."

She stared at the beautiful space. "No. This is perfect." Except... "I think I'll buy a few plants to spread around the place in pretty vibrant pots to match with the furniture material."

"That would look really nice," Cody agreed. "We'll add a trip to the nursery for the week before opening."

Brooke's hand pressed to her belly the second she heard the word nursery. Yes, it was a different kind than the one she'd planned to decorate for her little girl. Still, it hit her right in the heart.

Her spirits dropped at the thought of postponing the opening. Even if it was only a couple of weeks. But she just wasn't ready to take that on in her condition.

"It's okay, Brooke. You need time."

"I don't know how you've held it together this long." The two weeks she'd been home felt like they dragged on forever.

"I do it because I have to."

"For me?"

"Yes. I wasn't there when you needed me. I'm here now. I won't let you down."

"But that's not fair. You lost her, too."

"And I grieve right alongside you. I just..."

"What?"

"I need you to get better. That's all I think about. I just want you to be happy again. I know that probably feels like a lot of pressure. I know it will take time. And I see the steps you're taking, like the walks you and your mom have taken the last few mornings together. You always look...relaxed when you come back."

"We talk about her, you, life. The past. The future."

"That's good. And you can talk to me anytime you want. You know that, right?"

She nodded. "I am trying, Cody." But it was hard to find her way out of the pit she'd fallen into after the attack. Cody was always there when she reached for the light. When she reached for him.

"I know you are, baby, I just miss the way things used to be. The way they were for that split second when you and I were happy together before it all went to shit." He turned away from her. "I know you've changed because of everything that's happened. So have I. But I still think we can get back that magic we had when our love shone the brightest."

She pulled him back around to her. "I know you want that. I'm just..."

"Not ready. I know. And I'm trying to be patient and not push you for something you aren't ready to give. I'm just..." He repeated her words. "Lonely without you."

She cupped his face, drawn in by his sadness. "I'm here."

He shook his head. "Right now...yes. But then I lose you when you sink into that place where I can't reach you. And it makes me feel desperate."

"And alone."

"Yes. I'm sorry. I know you're going through a lot. You deserve your time and space to cope and heal in your own way and time."

"You're hurting, too, and you need me, too."

He held her face, the way she held his. "I always need you. Always. Forever, if you'll have me." His earnest and love-filled gaze held hers.

She couldn't find the words to tell him she wanted that but she was afraid. That glimpse of sheer joy they'd shared had been taken away. She didn't know if she could have him and lose him again.

And if they went there, he'd want to have children.

The thought of losing another child scared her. But she didn't want fear to deprive her of feeling the way she felt when she was pregnant. Happy. Expectant. Joyful as she dreamed of her daughter's life.

Her arms ached to hold her baby.

Maybe one day she would hold another baby.

And maybe then she'd get to see the wonder and happiness in Cody's eyes as her body changed and their child came safely into this world and their arms.

It would be such a blessing.

Cody kissed her forehead, drawing her out of her daydreaming, then stepped back and took her hand. "Come. Let me show you upstairs." He didn't say anything about her not answering him. He just led the way.

Maybe that was his plan for them getting back together. He'd simply lead her right into a relationship with him.

It wasn't that long ago that she followed him everywhere.

Maybe it was that simple. That easy.

So she didn't hesitate to walk out of the café and wait while Cody locked up.

"So this is how it is? I lose everything and Little Miss Magic Cunt gets you and is the talk of the town."

Brooke nearly jumped out of her skin as she spun to face the woman spewing those angry words.

"Kristi," she gasped, though she shouldn't be surprised at all.

Chapter Twenty

Cody gently pushed Brooke behind his back and faced off with his ex. "Watch your mouth."

She raised a brow, seething. "Seriously. You ruin my life and think you can tell me what to do."

"We both said and did things we shouldn't have, but that's no reason to attack Brooke on the street. In public."

"Why not? It's very public now that you called off the wedding. You seriously told all those people that you realized you loved someone else more and couldn't go through with the wedding because it would have ultimately hurt me."

Brooke gasped behind me. "You did what?"

He shifted so he could see both women, though he could block Brooke easily again if Kristi got any ideas about going after her. "I told the truth. And most of the people said they thought it was a difficult but wise decision."

"You could have said it was a mutual decision."

"I did, because why the fuck would you want to stay with me when I love someone else?"

Her whole body went rigid, her arms locked at her sides, hands fisted. "You humiliated me."

Cody shook his head. "There was no way out of telling everyone the wedding was off without giving an explanation. They'd all start speculating and making shit up. This way, I took the brunt of the load by saying it was me. At worst, I thought people would speculate I cheated on you."

"You did. The whole time we were together."

Brooke took a step forward. "That's a lie. You broke up with him."

"Because he kissed *you*, you selfish bitch." Kristi glowered.

Cody checked out the few people walking down the sidewalks, who were now giving them looks. "You're right. I did do that. And that's when you and I both knew I was in love with her, even if it took me a little while longer to really let myself believe it."

Her eyes glassed over with unshed tears. "How could you?"

He shrugged and implored her with his gaze. "I couldn't help it. This is how it was meant to be. She's the one."

Kristi's blue eyes turned stormy. "I was the one you asked to marry you."

He and Brooke didn't say anything to that, because the truth was, he'd never actually proposed.

The second that dawned on Kristi, she glared at Brooke. "Another thing you took from me."

"You set yourself up for that when you got pregnant under dubious circumstances," Brooke snapped back.

Kristi's eyes went wide. "You told her that."

"I don't keep secrets from her." They'd shared a lot of whispers in the dark each night. Mostly daydreams about what their daughter would have been like as she grew up.

The things she'd love to do. The way she'd be. The mile-stones she'd reach. Birthdays. Each new school year. Grad-uations. Boys. The talk they'd each have with her about dating and sex. What they'd say to her on her wedding day, when she had her first child.

Whenever one of them started with the, "She'll never..." the other stopped that by replacing it with, "She would have..."

It worked most of the time to keep them from drowning in sorrow for all she'd never do. But not all the time.

Kristi's glare finally stayed on him and away from Brooke when she said, "My father can't believe you did this to him after he got you the board position at the children's hospital. You owe him, and this is how you repay him?"

"First, those words sound like his, and it must really piss you off that his concern is that he did something for me and thinks I owe him, not that your heart is broken. Second, I didn't do shit to him. I appreciate the opportunity he gave me. I thanked him for it many times. But I also cul-tivated relationships with the other board members and came up with a lot of cost-cutting services while imple-menting others for the staff and patients. I've made myself useful and necessary, while your father uses his position to throw around his perceived power because of the people he knows and uses. I bet he even thinks he can get me kicked off the board for hurting you. I mean, that must feel nice, but you know, and I know, it's just his ego that can't take it. He wants me gone because I showed him up in the nine months I've been there. There's no way the board will vote against me. I made sure of that by doing exactly what he wanted me to do. I showed all of them that I deserve that spot."

He gave her a smug look. "That's exactly why you loved being with me. Because I'm ambitious and good at what I do, and people notice. You loved standing beside me and flaunting it that I was yours. I didn't mind. It made me feel good. You made me feel that way because you're intelligent and strong and capable all on your own. You don't need me, your father, or anyone else for people to see those things and more in you. I get this has been hard on you. I get that you're angry. But we were never going to work, not after the things we did to each other. It was always coming to a destructive end."

She still simmered with anger. "It didn't have to be this way."

He could see it in her eyes. She couldn't let it go. Not yet. She was too caught up in the pain and anger.

Kristi huffed out a frustrated breath and turned a spiteful gaze on Brooke, even though it should be directed at him. "You'll get what's coming to you." She stormed away.

Cody ushered Brooke into the other door that led into the small lobby of her building. Two elevators up ahead, the door to the stairs on their right. On the left, a board that they'd use to tell visitors which businesses were upstairs and in which suite.

He stopped Brooke before she hit the elevator call button to go upstairs. "I'm sorry."

She turned to him, her eyes narrowed. "For what?"

"That? Whatever that was." He'd thought Kristi would stay away after she left her engagement ring and walked out. He should have known better. She seemed to always come back after doing her dramatic exits.

"She's angry and embarrassed. It's not your fault." She tilted her head and stared up at him. "Is her father trying to get you kicked off the board?"

"No."

Brooke eyed him, looking for what he wasn't saying. "Cody?"

"Just leave it alone, Brooke."

She took a step closer to him.

He breathed in her familiar scent and all he wanted to do was pull her into his arms and kiss her. "It's nothing."

She took another step, her breasts an inch away from brushing his chest. Her eyes were all-knowing and filled with determination to get him to talk.

So he did. "Her father is very good friends with Beecham."

"As in the founding partner at your law firm?"

"His son, who has a lot of pull because of his family connection."

"And what is Kristi's father asking his friend Beecham to do?"

"What do you think?"

She gaped. "He wants you fired."

"Oh, it won't be that simple. I bring in too much revenue. I win a higher percentage of cases than my counterparts."

"Is he pulling cases from you?"

He leaned in and rubbed his nose against hers because he needed to touch her. "You're so fucking smart."

"Cody! You can't let him get away with this."

"What do you want me to do? Go to Beecham and plead my case? He knows I'm a valuable asset and is still doing what his friend asked. There's a rumor that Beecham owed Kirk a favor. He's called in his marker. Sometimes this is the way the world works. Sometimes, a guy does you a favor because you're dating his daughter. Sometimes that same guy uses another favor to fuck you because you dumped his daughter."

She put her hands on his chest. "How can you be so calm about this?"

"Because it doesn't matter. Nothing matters but you."

"You can't mean that. This is your career we're talking about. You've worked so hard to get to where you are right now."

"And I'll keep working hard for my clients. I'll find another law firm if I have to. But be clear, Brooke, after nearly losing you...nothing, not my job, not any fucking thing is more important than you." He cupped her face. "Can I please kiss you? I need you so fucking bad."

She went up on tiptoe and kissed him.

He tried to keep it tame, to just get a taste of her, but she had wonderfully amazing other ideas and swept her tongue along his bottom lip, then deep into his mouth when he opened up. He took the kiss deeper, sliding his tongue along hers, pouring every bit of the love he had for her into the kiss, even as he told the rest of his body—mostly his achingly hard dick—to calm the fuck down, because this was all he could have right now.

He'd take it, whatever she was willing to give, and be happy and grateful for it.

The elevator dinged and the doors opened.

Cody didn't pay it any mind, until Brooke broke their kiss and her eyes went wide with terror as he shifted his weight to protect her from whatever threat she saw coming.

All he saw was a blond guy dressed in black jeans and a black hoodie coming out of the elevator, a hammer in his fist and tool belt slung over his shoulder.

But that was obviously not what Brooke saw...

One minute Brooke was in total bliss, kissing Cody, and the next she saw a man in black coming at her and she was right back in the dark outside the library, Adam coming at her with that knife.

Brooke screamed and scrambled backward, trying to get away without turning her back on the guy.

Cody planted his hand on Adam's chest and pushed him to a stop. "Don't move." He stepped between her and her nightmare.

"L-look out. He's g-going to get you."

Cody glanced back at Adam, then to her again. "It's not him, Brooke. It's not him. It's one of Danny's guys. A construction worker. He's not going to hurt you."

Her back hit the wall and she stared from him to the guy by the elevator and back again.

Cody's voice softened. "He's on Danny's crew. One of the construction workers. That's all. He's not going to hurt you."

The guy peeked around Cody. "I'm not, lady. Swear it."

Brooke's eyes filled with tears. "I-I'm sorry."

"Nothing to be sorry about." Cody kept walking toward her slowly, like he didn't want to spook her again. "You got scared. That's all." He was only two steps away now. "No worries, baby." One more step. "Everything is okay." He wrapped her up in his arms and kissed her on the head and she breathed again. "That's it. You're safe."

The construction worker held his hand up. "Hey, man, I'm really sorry. I didn't mean to scare your girl."

"She's okay. You just reminded her of someone, that's all." He kissed her head again. "You're okay, right, Brooke?"

Not really. Not with her nails biting into his back as she held on tight to him.

She didn't answer, she just kept holding on.

He didn't seem to mind and glanced over his shoulder. "Did you need something?"

The guy shook his head. "No, man. I was just leaving for the day. Dentist appointment. I'll be back tomorrow. Danny's upstairs. Knows all about it."

"Okay. If you don't mind keeping this to yourself?"

"Sure thing, man. No sweat." He smiled at Brooke. He had kind eyes.

"Thank you." Cody watched the guy leave, then stared down at her. "Baby, tell me what you need?"

Her fingers clutched at him tighter. "You."

He held her close and pressed his cheek to her forehead. "You got me. I'm not going anywhere."

Her whole body trembled in his arms. "When will this stop?"

"I don't know. But I think you need to talk to someone. Dr. Nash left me a referral for when you're ready."

Her gaze fell to the floor. "I thought it was going to be a good day."

He put his finger beneath her chin and gently pushed up until his gaze could meet her watery green eyes. "It is a good day, sweetheart. We're spending it together. That's all that matters."

Chapter Twenty-One

Brooke tried really hard to focus during the rest of the walkthrough of the second and third floor, but it was hard to get the incident in the lobby out of her head. Maybe she did need therapy.

Maybe it was too soon to be out in the world instead of under the covers in her bed, avoiding everything and everyone.

That place of numbness she both craved and hated protected her in a way. She didn't embarrass herself in front of strangers. Or Cody.

He had to think she was losing her mind.

Cody squeezed her hand. "Stay with me, Brooke." He led her into the third-floor apartment that was meant to be hers. The light blue walls were soothing. The massive amount of light coming in from the tall windows made the place feel open and airy. She'd imagined herself here. In her mind's eye, she saw the furniture she had sitting in online carts, just waiting for her to click buy. The crib and changing table she and Mindy Sue both found at different times and texted to each other, saying, "This is the one."

"Brooke, honey, what is it?" Cody swept his thumb under her eye, catching the falling tear.

"I imagined us here. Me and her. All the furniture I planned to buy. All the memories we'd make. I'd be on my own, but with her. Our first place." She looked around the empty space and felt it echo inside her empty womb. "She's not here." *She's not coming. She'll never be here.*

Cody pressed his forehead to hers and looked deep into her eyes. "Can you please try to imagine a new future? With me. We can redecorate the house. It's due for a refresh. We'll pick things out together."

She looked into his earnest eyes and asked about the one thing that had been circling her mind with everything else. "Did you really decide to end things with Kristi before you brought me home?"

He cupped her face and never stopped staring into her eyes. "Yes. I couldn't pretend that I was happy settling when I really loved you. I'm happiest when I'm with you. No one compares to you."

"But I'm not that Brooke anymore."

"You're her. More than and a little less than you used to be. And that's okay. You've changed. I've changed. But this remains the same: you're still the only woman I love more than anything."

Something in her heart clicked back into place and eased her worries. "I'll make a lot of money on this place. Someone's going to love it."

Cody's palpable relief told her she'd eased his mind and heart, too. "I guess that means you're staying home with me."

Home. It had always been that to her. But right now...the way he said it...like it was their home...it hit differently. And she imagined that they really were a couple, living in the big house, loving each other. The way she'd always dreamed it would be.

"I always want to be with you."

He sucked in a breath and stood back from her. "Do you mean that?"

She went up on tiptoe, wrapped her arms around his neck, and pulled him close. "Yes. I mean it. I'm just..."

"Scared," he finished for her. "Like it will be taken away again. I know. I've felt that, too. But I won't let it happen. Never again, Brooke. You're mine. I'm yours. I promise."

She loved the feel of his arms around her. "I need some time."

"We have all the time in the world." Cody stared down at her for a moment, then slowly bent his head, giving her time to ease away from the kiss he intended. She met him halfway, hoping to find the peace and intimacy his lips offered.

The kiss was slow and sensual. A renewal of what they'd missed while apart. A tempting prelude to the passion they once shared. Cody kept it soft, light, a reminder that they did in fact have time to take things slow and let them build. Mend. And turn into something new and lasting.

They didn't have to rush.

Tell her heart that. It pounded in her chest as Cody took the kiss deeper, his tongue sliding along hers. Slow. Easy. Like he could kiss her all day and not get tired of her taste or her lips pressed to his.

It was a reclaiming.

Brooke had to admit, it felt so good to be held and loved like this. She wanted more. She wanted forever.

She'd lost that fear of losing him, knowing he'd finally chosen her. Not because of the baby, or because he'd almost lost her. He'd made the decision before he knew anything about the pregnancy or her attack.

Her continued grief made it hard to be joyful, even though right now, in this moment, she was happier than she'd been in a long time to be back in his arms, knowing they had a future together. She'd work her way through her grief eventually. She'd get help, because she wanted to move on. With Cody.

"Get out of your head, baby, and just feel me. Us. I kiss you and everything seems possible. I hope you feel that, too."

"I do." She went down to her flat feet and rested her forehead to his chin. "I still melt when you touch me. I still want you like I've never wanted anyone else."

Cody tipped her chin up again with a finger beneath her chin. "You make me feel that way, too. I love you."

"I love you, too. I'm just not all here yet."

"I know. And that's okay."

She raised a brow. "Is it?"

"Yes. You need time and distance from what happened. You need to feel safe again. With me."

She cocked a brow. "I'm not afraid of you. You would never hurt me."

He looked her in the eye like before. "I did hurt you. And it's okay to hold yourself back until you're sure. Because I will prove it to you that when I say I love you, I mean it. When I say I want to marry you, I mean it. When I say I can't live without you, I mean it."

"I know you do." She needed him to believe her, too.

"Maybe in your heart. But your head needs some convincing."

"Only because it's really hard for me to think right now."

"I know. But you'll get better. Your physical injuries are healing nicely. Your mind is going to take longer."

"The nightmares have tapered off."

"I hope that's because you feel safe sleeping next to me."

"I do. My head just keeps spinning."

"What worries you the most?"

"That everyone still thinks he's out there. Those other women don't know what I know."

"I have a call with Doug later. He's been in contact with the governor."

"You don't want to speak to him yourself?"

"I'm trying to keep a buffer between him and you, and I can't be civil with him right now."

"He isn't the one who hurt me."

Cody's eyes burned with rage. "No, he's the one letting his son get away with murder."

"Adam is disturbed and will probably get better help in the hospital than in prison." As much as she wanted Adam to suffer the way she was suffering, she still had enough compassion to understand the governor's desire to help his child.

"Is that what you want? For him to get help? Or to pay for what he did to you and our little girl?"

She took a step back and slid her fingers through her hair on both sides of her hair. "I don't know. Thinking about him makes me...insane." She dropped her hands. "I want him to hurt like I hurt. I want him to feel the loss I feel." She put her fist to her broken heart. "I want to rage at him and claw at him." She brushed her fingertips over her bandaged arm. "I want him to bleed like I bled. I want him to know what it's like to fall so deep into despair that death seems like an embrace and life feels like a brutal fight you can't win."

"Brooke." Her name fell from Cody's lips on a ragged sigh filled with sorrow.

"I want him to want her back as desperately as I do, so he'll know the rawness of it and the biting emptiness of her absence." She cupped his cheek in her hand. "I want him to take all your pain and mine, and still it won't be punishment enough for what he took from us." A tear slipped down her cheek. "But I can't have what I want."

"You can have me."

"That is the only reason I'm still standing. And if it's taken away, then what will I have left to live for?"

Cody wrapped her in his arms and crushed her to his chest. "Please, Brooke. Stay with me."

"I would never leave you like that, Cody. But without you...I wouldn't be able to breathe." She could barely get a breath with how hard he held her, but she didn't care. She needed to feel his strength, to know that what happened hadn't broken him. And that's when it dawned on her, she'd been so caught up in her pain, she hadn't checked in with him on how he was feeling. He seemed capable of handling everything. But maybe he needed...something, some way to release it, too. "Cody?"

"Yes?"

"Are you okay?"

"You know I'm not."

"I mean..." She looked up at him. "What do *you* need?"

"You. More of this. More of you talking to me, sharing with me everything that's spinning in your head."

"You can tell me how you feel, too. I can take it. I want to be there for you, too."

"Just having you back, being able to touch you, that helps me. Taking care of you, knowing I'm able to ease your discomfort or your heart helps me. I feel like this all happened because I let it. I let you go. I—"

"You save me every day." She hugged him harder, not caring that it pulled at some of her stitches. Most of them were getting better, but there were a few still-tender spots.

Cody kissed her again.

This time the brush of his lips didn't feel so new. She didn't hesitate to return the kiss. She leaned into it, him, this step closer to what they used to be. Or at least what they were fighting to be to each other again.

Cody was all in. She knew it. She felt it. She was the one holding back. He'd been right about that. So right here, right now, she made the decision to be open to the possibility that the worst was behind them and this was the beginning of something better. Happier. Forever.

And all of the good vibes she was feeling when Cody walked her out of the building and to his car died when she spotted the slip of paper tucked under the windshield wiper on the passenger side of the car.

"What's that?" Her heart pounded in her chest for no reason.

"Probably a flyer for one of the local stores or something."

She shook her head. "I don't think so."

Cody pulled it from the wiper and opened it, stepping back the second she tried to read it.

"What does it say?"

"Nothing. Get in the car. We're leaving." He stepped around her and opened the car door.

She stood her ground. "Let me see it."

"It's not for you. It's for me."

Her eyes went wide. "Now we're keeping secrets?"

He stared at her, unbending.

"I kept secrets from you and look what happened. Please don't shut me out. Not now. I can't take it if you do."

"It's nothing, Brooke."

"Then show it to me." She held out her hand.

He simply turned the paper around so she could read the note.

WE'RE NOT OVER.

"Kristi?"

"Maybe." The fury in his eyes said he knew more.

"What aren't you saying?"

"It's not her handwriting."

The blocky letters could be anyone trying to disguise the handwriting.

"Are you sure? Have you seen her handwriting a lot?" Most people texted or emailed. They didn't send each other notes.

Cody huffed out an exasperated breath. "She used to leave notes in the case folders I'd bring home to work on at night. This isn't from her."

"But she was here just a little while ago. And..." She glanced down the street one way, and then the next. "What if it was him?"

Cody took her by the shoulders. "He's not here, Brooke. He's locked up."

"How do you know? Maybe his father let him out."

Cody shook his head. "No. Not possible. He wouldn't do that, knowing you'd go to the police."

"Maybe that's exactly what I should do. Tell the police everything."

"And lose your privacy? Let everyone come after you for details? The cops. The press. Strangers who have nothing better to do than feel better by victim blaming and shaming."

"Who the hell would take his side in this?"

"Shitty people do. I won't let that happen to you." Cody pulled out his phone.

"Who are you calling?"

"Doug, I'm out with Brooke. I just found a note on my car. It says, *we're not over*. Can you confirm, right now, that Adam fucking Harris is still locked up?" Cody listened for a couple seconds, then hung up. "He's calling the governor." Cody waved his hand toward the open car door. "Please, get in." His voice still held all the pissed-off vibes of a thousand angry hornets rousted from their nest.

She slipped into the car and buckled her seat belt.

Cody closed her door and got in behind the wheel. His phone rang the second they pulled away from the curb and headed home. Cody put the call on speaker again. "Well?"

Brooke said *Be nice* with her eyes.

"Governor Harris assures me he is still in the hospital, locked in a private room. He received an update two hours ago. Adam was still agitated and insisting on seeing Brooke."

"What?" Brooke eyed Cody.

"Shit. Sorry." Doug sucked in a breath. "I didn't know you could hear the call."

"My bad," Cody said. "But Brooke and I aren't keeping secrets from each other. And that fucker can beg to see her all he wants. It's not happening. Ever."

"Brooke, I'm sorry if I upset you."

"You didn't." She tried to slow down her breathing and the fear that somehow she'd be forced to see that murderer again. "I was just surprised."

"How are you?" Doug's soft voice conveyed his concern and caring. He'd been so kind to her.

"I'm...getting better a little at a time."

"It's so good to hear your voice. You were so quiet in the hospital. You scared me, sweetheart. I know you and Mindy Sue have exchanged a few texts. She'd love to hear from you when you're up for it."

"I'll call her soon. Cody and I are headed back to the ranch. I'm tired. I think I need a nap."

Cody put his hand on her thigh. "I took her to see the building today and her new businesses. Kristi showed up, then we saw the note."

"Could it have been from her?"

"Maybe. Probably," Cody conceded. "How would he even know where to find her?"

Brooke sighed. "Adam was the one who actually encouraged me to buy the bookstore after I told him how Harland used to help those in the community when they fell on hard times." She had a hard time reconciling the guy who'd encouraged her and hung out with her with the man who'd obsessed over her, attacked several women on campus, raped one of them, then killed her daughter in a fit of rage because Brooke had been with someone else.

How had she not seen that ugly side of him all the times they were together?

She sank into the seat and stared out the side window.

"Doug, thanks for checking things out and running interference with the governor."

"Anything for you and Brooke. In fact, now probably isn't the best time to talk about it, but I've heard some rumors about you and your law firm."

Cody raised a brow. "What rumors?"

"That Kirk Wagner is trying to get you fired."

"He can try, but they'd be stupid to let me go. My billable hours are higher than some of their partners and I win my cases."

"I know. I've been keeping tabs on your career like everyone else who knows your family. Which is why I want to make sure no one else scoops you up if they're stupid enough to give in to Kirk Wagner and offer you a partnership."

Brooke sat up and turned toward Cody, her mouth agape.

Cody's stunned gaze stayed on the road as he took a left and stopped in a grocery store parking lot. "Are you serious?"

"You're young and hungry. You've proven yourself over the last few years. I'm surprised your firm hasn't fast-tracked you for partnership. Their loss will be my gain. We're so busy, we're turning away potential clients. We've hired a new crop of lawyers, but none with your potential. The ones I've got in the pipeline to partner don't have what you have. Drive. Ambition. The innate ability to read people and cases the way you do. Quite frankly, you remind me of myself. So are you interested in leaving someplace that hasn't fast-tracked you and is willing to let you go to repay a debt to a guy who uses favors as fuck-yous?"

Cody rubbed his finger over his forehead. "Has Mindy Sue filled you in about me and Brooke?"

"She told me that you and Brooke have the epic kind of love that people rarely find, that Brooke's loss was your loss, and that when Kristi told you she was pregnant, you did what you thought was right for your child, at the expense of your own happiness. And Brooke's. That about sum it up?"

"Yes."

"While I think what you did was honorable, you should have used that brilliant mind to figure out a way to keep the love of your life. But I get that you didn't know all the facts. And that's how we lose cases and you lost Brooke."

"Biggest mistake of my life."

"One you won't make again."

"Never."

"So about my offer. Interested?"

"I'm not stupid enough to make a second mistake by turning you down."

"Good to hear. We can talk details and compensation tomorrow, and then I'll have my assistant draw up an official offer letter if we come to terms."

"Sounds great. Thank you, Doug. I really don't know what to say. I never expected this."

"You know, you could have used the connection between us because of our girls to get a job here in the first place."

"I wanted to earn it."

"You did. And then some. I really hope to see you here soon. Brooke?"

"Yes?"

"I love you. I just wanted you to know that you've been such a bright light in Mindy Sue's life and mine and Rochelle's. You're like a daughter to us. If Cody makes you happy, the way Mindy Sue says he does, don't ever let that go."

"I won't. And I love you, too. Thank you for everything you did for me, for coming when I needed you."

"Anytime. Talk soon." He hung up.

Cody turned to her and a smile spread across his face, so big and bright and joyous. "Fuck! Can you believe that?"

"Yes. I can. Because you deserve it. Let's go home and celebrate."

"Really?"

"Yes." She smiled at him, so happy and excited for him.

"God, you're so beautiful. I've missed that smile so much."

She gave him another grin. "You're going to be partner. I'm so proud of you."

"Are you going to be mad at me for working insane hours still?"

"Are you still going to be in bed with me every night?"

"That's my every dream and fantasy come true."

"Then the rest we'll work out, won't we?" For the first time since the attack, she felt like maybe that was true. Everything would work out.

But first they had some old business to take care of and healing to do before they settled into their new lives.

Chapter Twenty-Two

The morning bloomed with vibrant colors streaming through the windows. Happier than he ever thought possible, Cody woke with Brooke lying on his chest, her leg thrown over his thighs. He felt as if she were holding him down, so that he couldn't get away. Like he'd ever want to leave her now.

He smiled to himself and brushed his fingertips up and down her back in soft caresses that made her snuggle in closer.

Dr. Nash had stopped by last night to check on her again. He'd taken out the last of her stitches, though the pink scars reminded them all of what happened. He'd switched out the bulky ankle brace for a smaller, slimmer version. She was walking much better on it. Even the pain in her broken wrist had subsided to a dull ache.

Physically, she was getting better. What a difference a few good days made.

Dr. Wick, the psychiatrist Dr. Nash recommended, had come to see her the last four days. Their talks remained private, but Brooke's initial upset after each session turned to quiet contemplation and an easing in her grief and fears.

Each day, she walked with her mom in the morning, and she got a little better. She didn't stare into space for long periods of time as often as she had those first few days. When she did lose herself, all he had to do was say her name, or touch her softly, and she came right back to him. She spent time in the garden reading. She went to the stables and visited her beloved horses.

It did his heart good to see her doing the things she loved.

She'd even started slowly moving forward with her plans to open the bookshop and café with her mom's help.

She spent time with him, even if that meant sitting on the sofa in his study and watching him work. He loved looking up from his papers and seeing her looking at him with those intense green eyes.

She smiled more easily and cried less often.

All good signs, indicating she was recovering.

He didn't worry about leaving her alone for short periods of time anymore.

They hadn't talked about the note they found on his car.

If it was Adam, he was locked up, unable to get to her. If it had been Kristi, then he'd made it clear, they were definitely over.

He kissed Brooke on the head and brushed his hands up and down her back, whispering, "Good morning, sweetheart," waking her gently. "I love you, and I wish I could stay right here with you in my arms, but unfortunately I need to get up. I have an eight o'clock call."

She surprised him by hugging him close, kissing his chest, then sleepily slipping off him with a disgruntled grumble that made him chuckle.

He'd kept things tame these last many days, only kissing her when she looked up at him with that very desire in her eyes. He kissed her every night before they went to sleep, too. He was giving her time to settle in to their relationship. He was waiting for her to tell him she wanted more intimacy between them.

They had it in the way they spent all the time they could with each other, in the quiet talks they shared. And he loved it.

Yes, he wanted more. He hoped their physical relationship would heat up in time. On Brooke's terms. He thought it would bring them even closer, but not if he pushed her too far, too fast, even if he desperately wanted to be as close as possible to her in every way.

Since she seemed open to affection, he slid out of bed, kissed her shoulder, and laid a trail of kisses all the way down her arm, not missing a single scar as she reached out to try to pull him back into bed with her.

"Stay," she grumbled, not even opening her eyes.

Nothing made him feel better than to have her wanting him next to her in the nest of sheets. "I want to, baby, but I can't miss this call. I'll make it up to you."

"Promise."

He kissed her on the head. "Promise."

He left Brooke in bed and went down to his room to shower and dress for working at home again. He didn't have to go to court today. Janie had coffee and his breakfast ready. He took both into his office and worked until he had lunch with Brooke, then took several more calls while she read a book on the sofa.

After dinner with Susanne, where they discussed inviting some local authors to do book signings at the grand opening, Brooke went upstairs to relax and watch TV.

He spent the evening at his desk, preparing his opening arguments for an upcoming case. He'd accepted Doug's offer as partner and signed off on his offer letter. He'd given his notice at work, getting a counteroffer from the firm, but ultimately deciding that he didn't want to work for someone who put his career on the line because of a favor owed.

He'd finish this one case, then start at Wagner & Mitchell. Scratch that. Wagner, Mitchell, and now Jansen in two weeks. He wanted to spend a week with Brooke at the ranch with no distractions.

Maybe they'd take a short trip somewhere for a change of scenery.

His cell phone rang. He checked caller ID, hoping Doug wanted to talk about him coming on board and not anything about Adam or the fact that the governor remained resistant to letting Adam's other victims know they were safe. Brooke wanted them to have the same peace she did knowing he was locked up.

The last few days had been quiet at the ranch and Brooke was responding to him and being home and safe. She was finally starting to feel like her old self in many ways, she'd confessed last night.

This call threatened to ruin everything, and he didn't want to pick up, but couldn't ignore Doug after all he'd done for them.

"Hi, Doug. I hope you're calling to check on Brooke and not deliver bad news."

"I wish. How is she?"

"Incrementally better every day but far from being herself. Tell me you aren't going to say something that will set her back."

"I'm sorry, Cody, but you are definitely not going to like this. Did you catch the evening news?"

"No. We're keeping Brooke away from anything that might trigger her."

"Understandable. You don't want her to see this. Click the news link I sent to your email."

Cody clicked his email tab on his laptop, clicked the link, and waited for the news banner and intro to end before the reporter announced, *"The University of Texas at San Antonio campus security, in conjunction with the San Antonio police department, are asking for the public's help in identifying the unknown subject who has attacked five women and raped one of them. With the spring semester over and most of the students returning home for the summer, and no new attacks since the fifth victim was hospitalized with life-threatening injuries and later released, it's feared that the campus stalker may remain unidentified if he's also left campus. The police remain dedicated to apprehending this dangerous individual and have set up a tip line, hoping someone will come forward with new information about the perpetrator or any information about what they may have witnessed or know about the specific attacks. The number appears on the bottom of the screen."*

Cody sighed. "Of course the police are still looking for a suspect and keeping the story relevant to the public. They still think he's out there." The governor had done a damn fine job of keeping the police and press from linking the campus stalker and Adam's attempted suicide together.

"He's the reason I'm calling. Governor Harris contacted me after he heard about the news report."

"Why? He got what he wanted. Brooke's silence and his son hidden away, not having to face the consequences of what he did."

"He knows Brooke's silence has only been because she's not able to face everything yet. He suspects she'll get stronger and come out fighting. Especially after I let him know that she wanted the other victims notified that the perpetrator is no longer a threat."

"Tell that to Brooke after she saw that note someone left on my car. If it was him, that means he's still able to torment her."

"The governor has made assurances that Adam has no contact with anyone outside the hospital."

Maybe that was true.

Kristi could have left that note. He wouldn't put it past her after the way she'd acted when Brooke came home.

"The governor wants a meeting with Brooke. In person."

Cody shook his head even though Doug couldn't see him. "Not going to happen."

"He wants to know what she's planning to do. He's scared. He thinks at any moment she's going to go to the police or press."

Cody smacked his hand on the desk. "Brooke spent six months terrified Adam was going to come after her."

"My daughter was in the same room with Brooke. So I get how you feel." Pent-up anger filled Doug's words. "The governor's already spun things well enough that the police don't even suspect Adam Harris. At this point, he's gotten rid of any evidence in Adam's place that could be used against his son. She's the only one who can point the finger at Adam for stalking and attacking her. The press would connect him to the other victims simply from their obvious physical similarities to Brooke. If she names Adam, his suicide attempt pretty much confirms his guilt. Governor Harris can kiss his career goodbye."

"Unless he spins all that and makes Brooke look like a broken victim who lost her baby and is grieving so hard she's not thinking straight and trying to blame him for everything."

"She can tell a fucking compelling story. People will believe her."

Not all of them. Because the governor would start a smear campaign to discredit her. Cody didn't want to see that happen.

Brooke didn't deserve that after everything she'd been through.

How far was the governor willing to go?

Cody didn't know.

Would he do anything to protect his son?

His position and power? His name at the expense of Brooke?

Cody seethed. "My father helped put his ass in the governor's chair. He's been invited to my house countless times over the years, and this is how his family fucking repays mine."

"History doesn't matter when things get personal. He wants to see her again, Cody. He wants to settle things with her. She has the power to destroy him. He can't let that go."

"She's in no condition to meet with him and relive what that bastard did to her. She's grieving for our child. Doesn't he get that? For God's sake, his own son tried to kill himself. He should have some fucking sympathy. He should understand she isn't ready or willing to see him."

"He's a politician. Nothing trumps him holding on to his power and position."

Cody fisted his hand. "He wants to shut her up."

"That's my take on it, yes. He hasn't come right out and said what he plans to say or do. At the bare minimum, expect an NDA. He'll want her legally gagged. Also, he's careful not to include you, despite my objections and adamant assertion that he won't see her without you by her side."

"He's afraid of me. I hold sway over the ranchers' association and can influence them to go a different way in who they back for the next election."

"Then I'd watch your back, because he's going to be looking for leverage to hold you to his side."

"Fuck him. He knows how I feel. He knows what I'm capable of, and I am and will always be standing between him and Brooke."

"The last time he met with Brooke, she was mostly unresponsive. I think he's concerned her silence didn't actually mean she agreed."

Cody fisted his hand on the desk. "Her doctor advised us not to push her to talk about what happened. Right now, she's satisfied with Adam locked up and away from her. But she wants the other victims to know that he can't hurt them either. If she doesn't get that, I'm not sure what she'll say or do."

The governor wanted a sit-down. He wasn't used to being denied. Eventually, he'd force the meeting.

Cody didn't want Brooke blindsided. "Hold him off as long as you can. She's not ready. I need more time with her." Cody rubbed his fingers over his aching forehead. "Listen, Doug. I appreciate all you've done for Brooke and me. I don't think I can deal with the governor rationally. I have a lot of undirected rage over what happened to Brooke and our daughter. Every time I look at her injuries, or see her crying, I want to kill someone."

"Yeah, well, if you let that rage out, you've got a defense attorney if you need one."

No telling what he'd do if he had Adam in his sights, but he'd try to hold it together with the governor when the time came. Some things were inevitable. He wouldn't hold the governor off forever. Men like him always thought they'd get what they wanted. They either made it happen, or took it by force. Cody would hold him off as long as possible and find a way to prepare Brooke.

"I was there with her in the hospital," Doug continued. "I never want to go through something like that again. I kept thinking it could have been Mindy Sue." Doug sighed. "I'll tell the governor Brooke needs more time."

"Thank you."

"You got it. You do realize she's going to have to decide what she's going to do about this situation. If she lets it go, it'll disappear and those other girls will never know who attacked them. People will think the man simply left school after the semester like they're reporting."

"I know. I'm not sure how to handle this. Adam is locked up, probably where he belongs, because he truly does need psychological help. I keep telling myself the governor isn't responsible for his son's actions, but he is responsible for the cover-up and trying to protect his own reputation. I'm pissed about all of it."

"I hear you. I'll hold off the governor until you tell me otherwise."

"Thanks, Doug. I really owe you for this."

"You don't owe me anything. We're partners now. Take care of Brooke. I'd like to see her well. Mindy Sue's worried about her. She took it hard, trying to help Brooke and knowing there was nothing she could do to make it better."

"I know just how she feels. But let her know, Brooke is getting help. She's slowly getting better." Cody leaned back heavily in his chair, happy about Brooke's progress but exhausted from another long day. It was almost seven, and the morning had wilted to a black night as dark as his mood.

"Take it easy, Cody. I'll let you know if anything else comes up."

Cody said goodbye with a heavy heart. He didn't want to deal with the governor and bring all the bad back into Brooke's life. He didn't want to see her go five steps back when he'd only gotten her to take one step forward.

The time they spent holding each other every night in the dark helped ease them into a more intimate relationship and rebuilt the trust he'd lost. She was slowly beginning to believe how much he loved her and wanted to make a life with her.

He wanted her to be his wife. He'd wait as long as she needed to make the commitment to him that he'd already made in his heart to her.

But first he needed to figure out who sent that damn note and a way to deal with the governor and make sure Adam paid for what he'd done without destroying Brooke in the process.

Chapter Twenty-Three

B rooke stood in the doorway, staring at Cody, high-lighted by the single lamp on his desk, casting the rest of the room in shadows. She remembered a lot of other nights she'd found him just like this. She remembered the night they made love.

Deep in thought, he stared at nothing. She walked into the room and around the desk. She didn't think he noticed her, then he reached out, took her hand, and pulled her gently down into his lap. She went willingly, sinking into his warmth. His arms wrapped around her. He pressed his cheek to her head and held her close. She sighed and snuggled in closer, her heart glowing warm with the love he made her feel more and more each day instead of the cold emptiness inside her.

"Hey, sweetheart. I was just thinking about you." His deep voice resonated through her.

She traced her fingers along the vein running over his muscled forearm. "I hope I'm not the one who put that dark look in your eyes."

His hand rested on her thigh and squeezed. "Never. I've just got a lot on my mind."

His other hand held her bare arm. His fingertips traced the scars. The stark reminder of what happened would fade over time. But right now they stood out just like the nightmare in her mind. She wondered how long it would take them to fade.

Cody didn't hesitate to take her hand and kiss each scar with openmouthed kisses. Each brush of his lips countered the grim sight of them with the warmth and desire he spread through her system.

He held something back from her despite his efforts to distract her from seeing it.

"What's wrong, Cody?" The words were soft and coaxing.

The strain of whatever weighed on him left lines in his forehead and bracketed around his sad eyes. He leaned his forehead to hers and stared at her. He sighed his frustration. His breath washed over her face.

She placed her hand on his cheek. "Please, Cody, talk to me."

"I love you." He put his hand over hers on his face and looked her right in the eye. "I love you so much."

The flutter in her heart made it feel like it could soar right out of her chest, yet she went still at the joy his words brought. After all she'd been through, she didn't quite know what to do with the vibrant, light feeling inside her but stand still and bask in it.

Cody frowned. "If it takes a hundred million times to see you light up with happiness when I tell you I love you, I'll do it. I won't stop. I'll never stop. Not until you really believe that everything you hoped for and dreamed about with me is yours. And no one is going to take it away from you or me or us. I love you." His solemn eyes pleaded with her to hear him.

His head fell heavy against the seat back. His gaze fell away from her, so filled with regret and remorse it made her stomach sink and her heart ache.

Something inside her shifted.

How could she guard her heart and have the relationship she wanted with Cody? It wouldn't work. Not like this. Not while she was holding back, holding him at arm's length so she didn't get hurt again.

Cody would never hurt her. He wanted to love her.

She wanted to love him. All she had to do was show him her heart might be broken, but it still beat for him.

Brooke closed the distance between them and kissed him softly, letting her lips linger over his in a kiss so achingly tender it brought tears to her eyes. She ended the kiss, rolling her head until their lips broke apart and her forehead touched his. She opened her eyes and stared into the blue depths of his, so filled with love for her it couldn't be denied.

"'I love you' doesn't cover how deeply, irrevocably I *LOVE* you." She pressed her hand to the side of his face, her fingers softly caressing his temple, her thumb pressed to his soft lips. "I never stopped. I never will." She kissed him again. Longer. Deeper. Lost in him and the love she felt him pour into the kiss to match her love for him.

"Say it again." He grabbed fistfuls of her long hair and held her close.

"I love you. I've always loved you. I'll love you until the day I die."

"Will you marry me? Will you be mine forever?"

"I always have been. I always will be," she answered without answering.

She hadn't said she'd marry him, but she had told him what had always been true, and he'd never taken seriously. In fact, he'd taken it for granted.

Like he read her mind, he gave her what she needed. "I'm sorry I never accepted that, or realized the same is true of me. I'm yours, Brooke. I hope you know that."

"I do. Everything has been so...overwhelming. Over the last few days, I feel like the postpartum depression, trauma, and my pregnancy hormones have eased off and I can breathe and think. I feel steadier. And a lot of that has to do with you."

"I'll do whatever it takes to help you heal and be happy and healthy again. I need you in my life. I need you by my side. I love you."

"I want to be a real partner to you. So, please, tell me what upset you tonight."

He barely hesitated before he confessed, "Doug called about the governor again." Cody had been trying desperately to hold back the world and give her the time she needed to recover. She hadn't really thought about how Cody had been dealing with his own grief, a full-time job, a breakup, a canceled wedding, the ranch, and now this. "I told him you're not ready to talk about it."

"Good. I didn't get a say in whether or not Adam went to jail or that hospital. He doesn't get a say in when I see him. Or how long it will take for me to be ready without it all crashing down on me again." She shook off her rising ire and focused on him and the grin on his face. "What?"

"I love it that some of your spunk is back."

She smiled for him, then kissed him tenderly, knowing that he'd noticed she'd initiated the kisses. "Let's hold off the world for a little while longer." She kissed him again.

"Take me to bed, Cody. I need you as much as you need me."

It was all getting to be too much, and she wanted to make him—both of them—feel better. She knew one way to do that.

"Are you saying what I hope you're saying?"

"Yes. Make love to me, Cody. I need to be close to you. I think you need that, too."

"I do. It's just...as much as I want you, I'm afraid I'm going to hurt you, and the thought of that makes me sick."

"I really am feeling better. No aches in my shoulder, arms, or abdomen. Just watch the wrist and ankle. Those I can keep out of the way. So, take me to bed. Love me."

"I do. I will. Anytime. Always." He stood with her in his arms and walked across the library with her pressed to his chest. She wrapped her arms around his neck, bent her head, and kissed a path up his neck to the back of his ear. Her fingers brushed through his hair. Her tongue swept along his earlobe a second before her lips closed softly around it.

He growled and took the stairs two at a time, kicked her bedroom door shut, set her on her feet by the bed, then sat and pulled her between his legs, his hands on her hips.

He placed one hand on her stomach and stared up at her, a question in his eyes.

"You won't hurt me. Just love me." She leaned in and kissed him again.

He swept his hands up inside her top and pushed it until he had to break the kiss to peel it over her head and down her arms. Her bra disappeared in a fraction of a second. Her breasts ached for his mouth. His lips pressed to the scars above her breast, then clamped onto her tight nipple.

He swept his warm tongue over the peak, then sucked her into his mouth again and everything inside her turned molten.

"Yes, Cody. That's what I want. You make me feel so good." She moaned as he took her other nipple into his mouth, sucking hard, his teeth grazing the tight bud.

She let him know how much she liked it with another soft moan. She slid her fingers through his hair, arched her back and offered her breasts up for his thorough attention, and held him to her as he took his time and savored her.

With him distracted by her, she reached down, grabbed fistfuls of his shirt, and dragged it up and over his head, tossing it to the floor. She put her hands on his bare shoulders, felt the heat of him, and the rippling muscles beneath her palms.

"I think about that night all the time," she admitted, sliding her fingers through his hair, holding him close. "How you touched me. How free I felt to be with you. It was all I ever wanted."

Cody looked up at her, his palm over her breast. "*You* are all I want."

"Show me again." She begged with her eyes.

He hooked his arm around her waist and pulled her close, taking her mouth in a deep kiss. He fell back on the bed and she lay on top of him, her legs dangling until she levered herself up and straddled his lap. His hard cock pressed against her soft folds. She rocked her hips and rubbed against him, needing the sweet agony of the contact that was just not enough.

His hands tightened on her hips. "Are you sure you're up for this?"

She rubbed her aching center along his full length and hoped that answered his question. She wanted this. She needed it, to take back her body in this way after every-thing. Now she wanted to feel all the pleasure and share it with Cody. So she gave him the words to reassure him she was more than ready. "I want to feel you inside me and all around me. I want this to be a new start for us."

He dipped his hands down the back of her leggings and panties and squeezed her ass, then pushed her along his length again. "I won't let you go this time. Ever."

"I know."

He shifted her off of him and onto her back at his side and somehow pulled her pants and panties off all in one move, even with the small ankle brace. She lay there naked and desperate for his touch. The last of his clothes dis-appeared, but all she paid attention to was the revealing of all that skin and muscle. The way he moved, slow and deliberate as he leaned down and kissed her thigh, it built the anticipation and her need for him all at once. One kiss turned into two as he shifted between her legs and kissed his way up her thigh to her hip, then planted an openmouthed kiss just under her belly button.

His gaze shot up to hers, then he looked down at her mound and settled his big body between her thighs, pushed her legs wide, knees out so she was bared to him. His head dipped and his flat tongue licked her soft folds all the way up until the tip of his tongue teased her clit.

"Oh God, Cody, yes."

He did it again and she melted into the mattress. He circled her clit with the tip of his tongue again and slid one finger deep into her. She rocked her hips as he slowly finger fucked her, his tongue teasing her clit and making her crazy for him.

She was nearly there. "Oh God, Cody, yes. Right there."

To push her over the edge, he thrust two fingers deep and sucked her clit. She rode his fingers and shattered, her body spasming around his fingers and against his mouth.

His fingers worked her with a slow push and pull as her orgasm faded and he stared up at her. He pulled his fingers free, then stuck them in his mouth and sucked them clean. "You taste so damn sweet." He licked his lips to get another taste.

And he wasn't done with her yet. He kissed his way up her body, stopping to nip, lick, and suck her breasts. She slid her hands over his head, shoulders, and down his back. She dragged her fingers back up both sides of his spine, pulling him closer and up to her. He gave her a quick kiss on the lips, but didn't settle on top of her, instead leaning over to open the bedside table drawer to pull out a condom and tear it open with his teeth.

She eyed him. "When did you put those there?"

"The day after I was back in your bed. The doctor said you can't get pregnant again for at least six months. Your body needs time to heal. I won't risk your health or the baby's.

Her eyes glassed over just thinking about the baby they'd lost and if they'd ever try again. She wanted to. Someday. Maybe sooner than later, because she'd been so excited to be a mom. She loved being pregnant. The anticipation. The excitement of it all.

And she wanted to share it with Cody.

But maybe after losing two babies, Cody didn't want to risk another heartbreak like that at all. "Do you still want to have children?"

"Yes," he answered immediately. "I want a family with you. But not until you're ready." He cocked his head. "Unless you don't want to—"

"I do. I want you to be part of all of it next time."

"I do, too. When you're ready. However long it takes. I'm in." He kissed her softly. "Until then, we can spend this time reconnecting and loving each other. We will have a family, Brooke. I promise. Until then, let's enjoy this." Cody kissed her, distracting her from the past and showing her what they could have for their future. Each other.

She lost herself in the feel of him moving over her, kissing her lips, then trailing kisses down her neck and chest until he reached her breast and licked her tight nipple, then took it into his mouth, heating things up between them all over again in such a delicious, sexy way.

He kissed his way back up to her mouth and slid his tongue along hers in a deep, sensual kiss that only made her want more.

He kept most of his weight off her, but she loved the feel of his legs along hers, his hips nestled between her thighs, his hard cock pressed intimately against her wet folds as he gently rocked his length back and forth along her slit.

She brushed her hands up his back and down his spine to his hips. The head of his cock nudged her entrance but barely sank inside, even as she raised her hips to take him in deep.

Cody broke the kiss and stared down at her. "I love you." With that, he slowly slid into her channel, joining their bodies and burying his cock to the hilt, stretching her deliciously.

Her body responded to the fullness and heat of him inside her. She pulled her knees back and he sank deeper.

"Fuck, yes, Brooke. You feel so perfect." He pulled out in one long, deliberately slow glide, then sank back into her.

She squeezed his ass and rocked against him. His dick hit that spot deep inside her and she shivered with pleasure.

That's all it took to get him to stop treating her like she would break. He pulled out and thrust deep again. She let him know how much she liked that by matching his toe-curling pace.

They lost themselves in each other, just like they did the first time, only this time they knew nothing would tear them apart.

They took their time, savoring every kiss, caress, and glide of their bodies moving together, joined in the magic they created until they were both overcome with desire, their hearts thundering, and they both came with their lips and hands joined, eyes locked on each other.

Cody's breath panted in and out against her cheek. "Am I hurting you?" He tried to move off her, but she liked his weight and the feel of him surrounding her. She kept him where she wanted him with her good leg hooked over his ass.

She slid her hands down his spine to his lower back. "Stay. I'm good. This is perfect."

He rose above her on his forearms and stared down at her, his blue eyes filled with such deep emotion her throat went tight. He slipped one hand behind her neck and into her hair and leaned down and pressed his lips to hers. He kissed her with so much love and longing, the emotions behind it welled up inside her heart and overflowed, bringing tears to her eyes. He brushed his thumb along her cheek and held her close as the kiss slowed to just their lips pressed together.

The kiss had rocked her to the core because of its simple demand that she give all her love along with the press of their lips. And she did. He had her heart. He was her everything.

"I love you so damn much, Brooke. Nothing will ever change that. No one will ever come between us again."

She believed him with her whole heart. "I love you, too."

Cody brushed his lips against hers one more time, then shifted to her side and rolled out of bed to do the condom cleanup. He was back in seconds, pulling her close.

She laid her head on his shoulder and snuggled into his big, warm body. He kept his solid arms banded around her. She felt protected and safe. The steady beat of his heart hypnotized her into that relaxed space between awake and sleep. She sighed, rubbing her cheek against his warm skin, and kissed his chest because he was there and she could. She sighed again and whispered, "I feel better."

Cody hugged her tighter and kissed her head. "I'm glad. I know you miss her. So do I. We will always miss her, but we'll be together, and I think she'd like that."

Tears clogged her throat and choked off her words. "If I can't have her, I'm happy I have you."

"I wish you could have both of us. But I know how you feel. I'm so happy you've come home to me. This is only the beginning for us." His arms tightened around her.

She believed him, and finally allowed herself to dream of a future with him again. She drifted off to sleep with that happy thought in her head and blossoming in her heart.

Chapter Twenty-Four

C ody woke up feeling on top of the world. And it all came crashing down when he received a text from Doug two hours after he'd seen Brooke and her mom having coffee in the garden and laughing together.

There was no way he could give this terrible news to Brooke.

DOUG: The young woman Adam raped committed suicide last night.

Fuck!

Chapter Twenty-Five

Adam sat in the chair opposite Dr. Green. He hated these mandatory therapy sessions. Even worse, the group ones.

Everyone stared at him.

Word had spread that the governor's son was here. He had no privacy. He couldn't make a phone call, send a text or email, go outside without an escort, let alone leave this fucking place. He couldn't do anything without permission.

And right now, they'd placed restrictions on everything.

He hated the food, the constant supervision, the bare-bones room they gave him, the drugs they fed him that made him groggy, his head in a fog.

"How have you been sleeping?" Dr. Green sat across from him, his attention solely on Adam.

He hated the patient look in his eyes. "Fine."

Dr. Green frowned. "Your chart states that you spend three to five hours a night pacing your room."

Because they wouldn't let him out to see her. They'd locked him in a cage. Didn't they know he had to finish what he started? "When I sleep, it's fine."

"Any thoughts of harming yourself?"

Yes. Kill me now and save me from this incessant prying.
"No."

"What are you thinking about when you're alone in your room at night, pacing?"

I think about her. "Nothing."

"This process only works if you open up to it."

"To you." He eyed the doctor with disdain.

"Yes. I want to help you, so that one day you can go back to your life."

Adam guffawed at that. "There's no going back."

"Why do you say that?" Dr. Green held his stare, one eyebrow raised. He didn't know what had really happened. He thought Adam had tried to take his life. He didn't know why.

The why mattered.

She mattered.

Adam couldn't tell him what he'd done. Not that it would do any good. There was no taking it back. Saying I'm sorry wouldn't fix anything. If he wasn't here, he'd be in jail. At least here he had a chance to make things right. He needed to make things right. He needed to see her.

"Adam. Why can't you go back to your life? You've graduated college. Aren't you looking forward to getting a job after all the hard work you put into finishing your degree?"

"Sure. Whatever. Are we done?"

Dr. Green leaned in. "I'd like to talk about that night and what you were feeling before you tried to take your life."

"Take it? It's mine. I decide what to do with it." That didn't sound exactly right to his ears because up until he met Brooke, he'd still been trying to please his parents, doing everything they wanted him to do. He'd even taken a major that, yes, he was good at, but didn't thrill him. He'd caved to pressure. So it would look good when his father talked about him.

Adam couldn't give a shit what anyone thought. Except for Brooke. He needed to show her that she mattered. He was sorry. "When can I make a call?"

"Who do you want to call?"

"Her."

"A girlfriend?"

"I thought she was." In a way. This was as close as he could get to saying anything about Brooke without explaining what happened. "I need to talk to her."

Dr. Green nodded like he understood, then crushed Adam's hopes. "Now is the time to focus on yourself. She'll be there when you're better and able to communicate your feelings once you've reconciled what you did and why."

"I know why."

"Then let's talk about it," Dr. Green pushed.

"I did something terrible. I didn't realize how bad, when I started. But now I know. I have to make it right."

"You need to understand what led you to that dark place, how you ended up there, and what you can do to prevent yourself from ending up in that place again."

"I know what I need to do, but no one will let me fucking do it." He grabbed fistfuls of his sweats at his thighs in frustration as his right knee bounced up and down like a piston.

Dr. Green noted the nervous action. "What do you feel like you need to do?"

He gripped the arms of the chair so tight his knuckles went white. "You don't understand."

Dr. Green leaned forward, his forearms on his knees. "Help me understand by explaining it to me."

"I hurt her. I need to make it right."

"Do you think your loved ones are upset or angry about what you did?"

Of course they are. I'm a monster. One that needs to be put down.

But all I want is her.

He rocked back and forth in his chair. *Please. I need her.*

She had to have gotten his note.

She knew he was coming to see her.

His parents had refused to send her his letters, so he'd had to find another way. The cute young nurse who was so eager to help, so enamored with the fact that she got to take care of the governor's son, the one who didn't want to get into trouble by upsetting him and possibly getting fired for not taking care of him.

She didn't know what he'd done. No one here did.

So he had a cute little nurse who was eager to please. And yes, he fucking used it. Her.

He begged her to get the note to Brooke with a simple story of how he loved Brooke and wanted her to know that after everything that had happened, he still loved her. They weren't over.

Little Nurse Nell ate that shit up, and because the facility was close to downtown and Brooke's bookstore, she agreed to drop the note off there, refusing to take it to Brooke's house. She didn't want to get caught as his go-between.

What-the-fuck-ever.

She'd reported back that not only did she deliver the note, but she'd put it on Brooke's car so she wouldn't miss it.

He knew he was taking risks, but it was the only way to let Brooke know he'd fix this. Them.

Which gave him another idea. Her store was soon to open. He'd send her a gift to let her know he was thinking about her.

He was always thinking about her.

Adam stood. "I'm done. I want to go back to my room now."

Nurse Nell would be there soon with his next round of meds. He'd take them because he had to, then send her off on another errand.

She wouldn't deny him.

He was the governor's son.

Chapter Twenty-Six

Brooke was just finishing up the last of the three romance bookcases in the bookstore when a wave of excitement overtook her. The upcoming opening loomed, and she couldn't wait. Butterflies swarmed her belly. She really wanted this to be successful. A new start for the new her. And she had Cody and her mom to thank for overseeing everything while she was away at school and when she returned home, broken and lost.

She wasn't completely healed. Her body was mostly there, but her heart and mind still needed time. And that was okay. She'd get there. She wanted to make her dreams come true. And she had the support she needed from her doctors, friends, her mom, and especially Cody.

She shelved the last of the books, sat back, and grinned. Done. Ready.

The light, happy feeling disappeared when she heard someone at the door and froze.

Keys jangling, the lock turning. The door opening. The lock turned once again, sealing her inside with whoever had come in.

She held her breath, listening for another sound. Anything to tell her who it was. She wanted to call out, but couldn't find the breath.

"Brooke, honey, where are you?" Cody called out to her.

She let out a relieved sigh and clasped her trembling hands together in front of her. She didn't want Cody to see her like this. "I'm here." She calmed herself with steadying breath, walked around the long double-sided bookcase, and found Cody standing just inside the door, dressed in a black suit with a dark gray shirt and turquoise tie that made his blue eyes stand out beneath his golden hair. The suit fit him to perfection. Though he was starting to look a bit uncomfortable with the bulge thickening along the front of his slacks.

"You're so beautiful."

She smiled. It came easier these days. Especially when she was with him. It had been a week since they made love again for the first time. It changed everything. They couldn't keep their hands off each other now. The second they woke up, the day started with a kiss. Every night it ended with one. And if Cody needed a fix, because he'd become addicted to her taste, she found herself with his head between her legs at least once a day, sometimes as many as three or four. And that didn't include how often they fucked because she got one look at his sexy smile and that strong body and she was after his belt and his hard cock.

It felt freeing to dive into those moments of bliss in his arms. And it drew them ever closer together, sharing that intimacy, letting her guard down, being in the moment, lost to the passion and belonging she only felt with him.

"I know that look, sweetheart. We have a reservation. Don't tempt me."

She flew into his arms, wrapped hers around the back of his neck, and kissed him, long and deep, like she hadn't seen him in forever. His thick erection pressed to her belly. He groaned deep in his throat and sank his tongue into her mouth, mimicking what they both wanted him to do with his cock.

She pulled back and looked him in the eye. "How was your day, dear?" She'd never get tired of seeing his smile.

Today was his last day at his old firm. They'd spend the next week together without all the distractions from his job. The board at the children's hospital didn't meet for another two weeks, too, so she had him all to herself for the next seven days. She had a few minor things to finish at the bookstore, but otherwise she was ready to open.

Cody wanted to celebrate a new beginning for both of them. He wanted to go out. He wanted her to stop hiding at home. "They threw me a small going-away party at lunch."

"Nice. And is your assistant ready to move over to Wagner, Mitchell, and Jansen?"

His cheeks went a bit ruddy at the new name of the firm he was a partner at now. "She's going to start next Thursday, organizing my office and her cubicle before I hit the ground running the following Monday."

"Should I be worried that you can't leave your assistant behind?" She quirked an eyebrow at him.

"What? No. Besides, her girlfriend is a spitfire who would probably come after me for any kind of untoward move on her girlfriend."

Brooke chuckled. "Well, then I won't have to drop by the office to stake my claim."

"Baby, that isn't even necessary. I'm not stupid enough to make the same mistake twice and lose you." He held her tighter and ground his dick against her belly. "You know

I'm completely, irrevocably in love with you. But please, come to my office any time you need a reminder. I'll be happy to lay you out on my desk and prove it to you again." He kissed her softly. "And again." He took the kiss a bit deeper this time. "And again." He practically devoured her with his kiss as he walked her backward toward the little sofa in the romance section and laid her down on it. As he pressed her down into the cushions, his hand gathered her long skirt up to her knee, then he pulled it up to her hips.

She broke the kiss and raised a brow. "I thought we had a reservation?"

"We have time for this…" He slid down her body until he was on his knees next to the couch. He kissed her thigh as he pulled down her panties. "These are really wet, Brooke."

"Have you seen you in a suit?" The kiss he pressed to her clit made her moan.

"Glad you like it." His cocky smirk turned devilish as he teased her with the tip of his finger, stroking her seam.

"I know what you look like under that suit." She groaned as his tongue swept up along her slit and flicked her clit again. "Stop teasing. I need you."

"I need you, too." He sank his tongue into her core and strummed her clit with his thumb, back and forth as she writhed on the couch, her fingers buried in his thick golden hair.

One finger, then two filled her wet channel, and he stroked her as he sucked on her clit.

She rocked against his fingers, finding that perfect rhythm between them as he licked and circled her clit with his tongue, taking her up and holding her at the precipice of release. "Cody, please."

"Please, what?"

"Make me come."

He thrust three fingers deep, hitting that spot that sent her over the edge as his tongue swept over her clit. He slowly thrust his fingers in and out as she rode out the orgasm, then he pulled free, stuffed them in his mouth, and sucked her off his fingers. "Mmm. So good."

So fucking sexy.

"How did I get this lucky?"

Cody stilled and stared down at her. "Not you, Brooke. I'm the lucky one to have this second chance with you."

"We're both lucky." She sat up and reached for his belt buckle. "Now give me what I want."

"We don't have time."

"You know you want my mouth devouring—"

A knock on the door stopped them both.

Cody stood and put the end of his belt back through the loop to secure it. "Are you expecting someone?"

She shook her head and pushed her skirt down over her legs. "No." She snatched her panties off the floor and wadded them in her hand.

"Stay here. I'll get it."

She let him go so she could slip back into her panties.

Cody unlocked the door and opened it again. Almost immediately, he closed it without saying anything.

She walked around the bookshelves and spotted him holding a box of her favorite chocolates and a note on a piece of paper. "Who is it from?"

"They didn't sign it." Something in his voice told her she didn't want to see it.

We aren't over.

"Was it her? Or him?" she asked, though neither answer would sit well with her.

"I don't know. I didn't see anyone. But my car is parked right out front again, just like last time."

"Has Kristi tried to contact you at all?"

Guilt clouded Cody's eyes.

"What? Seriously? You've been talking to her."

"No." He dumped the box and note on the checkout counter and took her by the shoulders before she could back away from him. "I didn't want to say anything because it's just her venting. I don't respond to any of her texts."

"Then why keep it from me?"

"Because I didn't want to put that on you. She's angry with me. I can take it."

"It's not like she's blameless in your relationship. She manipulated you. She purposely stopped taking the pill to get pregnant and a marriage proposal. If not for the broken condom, it wouldn't have happened. Still...what is she saying to you?"

Cody pulled out his phone, tapped to get to the text string, then handed his phone to her without hesitation.

KRISTI: All of my friends are whispering behind my back about you and Brooke

KRISTI: I can't believe you chose fucking your sister over me!!!!!!!!!!!!!!!!!!

KRISTI: My boss made a comment in a meeting today about how I can help with a project since I won't be taking my honeymoon and everyone went quiet and looked at me with pity.

KRISTI: I bet no one is saying shit to you, because you're the golden boy lawyer with poor broken Brooke to take care of.

That one ended with a vomiting puke face.

There were more. All of them the same vitriol, about someone commenting about the breakup or canceled wedding and her taking it not just badly, but in a way that read into others' comments in a way that maybe they didn't mean.

Brooke handed the phone back to him. She didn't want to read any more of that venom. "Why the fuck don't you block her?"

"If she needs to vent, then let her do it that way, instead of some other destructive way. She blames me. Fine. I choose to take the high road and focus on what's important to me. And that's you. I hope she moves on the way we're doing."

"Maybe you should set her up with a friend?" She considered her words, then shook her head. "Forget what I said. You don't want to lose a friend, too."

Cody hooked his arm around her shoulders. "You're bad. And I like it, because it means you're back to your teasing, and that's a good sign."

She met his gaze and her smile fell with her next words. "What you're not saying is that this could be him again."

"We don't know that."

"Maybe I should talk to him. Or at least his parents."

"I don't want you anywhere near him." Cody's hand fisted at his side.

She put her hand over his and brushed her fingers back and forth over the back of his hand. "I just want it to go away."

"Are you ready to talk to them? Because more than likely, the only thing you're going to hear is about them."

She shook her head. "My mind is finally starting to clear of all those dark thoughts and nightmares. I don't want to bring it all back. I can't. Not yet. Not now. In therapy it's easier. I can take it one piece at a time and as slow as I want."

"You don't owe them anything."

"Don't I owe it to myself to find a way to put it to rest?"

"Isn't that what you're doing by going to therapy, opening up your businesses, being with me, planning the future you want, learning to be happy again? That's what you owe yourself. You did nothing wrong. He killed your joy, your desire to really live. It's coming back. Don't let anyone ever take that from you again, because they're selfish and only concerned about themselves."

"You're right. But you know I can't put them off forever."

"If you want to, that's exactly what we'll do."

She glanced at the box of chocolates and the note. "After reading her texts...I think this was him."

Cody sighed and confessed, "I do, too."

"How?"

"Someone had to help him."

"Will it ever end?"

"Yes. I'll make sure it does. But there's one way to ensure he never contacts you again."

"If I go to the police, my whole life will blow up. Everyone will know what happened. I don't want that for us, Cody. I don't want a public spectacle made out of our tragedy. I've come to terms that he'll have a decent life locked up in that fancy hospital. I've come to terms with the fact he'll have a cushier life than if he were in prison. Some days, I still wish him dead. Others, I find enough compassion to hope he gets the help he needs. But my true feelings lie somewhere in the middle where I want him to just be miserable the rest of his life, knowing he can't have me. Ever. And the best revenge I have is being happy with the man I truly love."

Cody pulled her into his arms and held her close. "I don't know how you do it. I'm still stuck on killing the bastard."

She was so glad he shared his feelings. "That's okay. My best friend's dad is a really great defense attorney who can probably get you off."

Cody chuckled. "Yeah. My partner already said he'd defend me."

"Doug is a good guy." She frowned. "And I miss Mindy Sue."

"She offered to come out last week but you said no."

"Because her boyfriend invited her on a family trip with his parents. That's a big deal. I couldn't ask her to miss meeting the parents for the first time."

"You'll see her next week at the picnic. If you're up for attending."

"I will be. It's going to be our closest friends."

Cody checked his watch. "We need to go. We're going to be late for our reservation."

"Well, that was your fault."

"No. It was my pleasure. And I'm coming back for seconds the moment I get you home."

She put her hands on his chest, went up on tiptoe, and kissed him softly. "I like the sound of that."

Chapter Twenty-Seven

A dam hated it here. It didn't matter how nice the place, it was still a prison keeping him from Brooke. Fourth of July.

His parents hadn't come to visit in over a week. Today they were probably hobnobbing at some picnic, fair, or charity benefit. Maybe all three. He wouldn't put it past his father to use this day and Adam's hospitalization for everything he could squeeze out of them.

Was Brooke at home with her family?

Were they holding their annual event?

Was she thinking about him?

He was always thinking about her.

One year ago today was the day everything changed for him.

For her too, he guessed.

God, he wished he could be there with her. It would be perfect.

But he was stuck in this hell, desperate to get out and do what he needed to do.

He needed to be with her.

Soon.

He'd find a way.

Chapter Twenty-Eight

Eight days after the chocolates and note incident, Brooke sat on the bench at the edge of the garden, staring at all the people who'd come for the Fourth of July party.

Last year's picnic had been a much bigger event.

She couldn't handle that many people at the ranch this year, so they'd kept the guest list small. Intimate.

Still, everything reminded her of how she'd spent time with Mindy Sue and all their friends, including Adam. More than likely, that time they spent together had sparked his obsession for her. Everything about this day and the picnic reminded her of him, how she'd thought she saw someone in her room that night.

It was him. Had to be.

The memories flooded her mind and threatened to send her over the edge.

This was why Cody had wanted to forego the party this year. She'd insisted they carry on tradition.

She didn't want one more thing taken away from her.

She wanted to stand up to him in this small way and prove to herself that she was getting stronger.

She loved the parties Harland and now Cody threw at the ranch. She loved having their family and closest friends gathered together, even if it sparked whispers and sad looks.

Even though it overwhelmed her, she needed that right now.

Her anxiety had sent her to the outskirts of things a few minutes ago. She needed a minute to gather herself again. But she had a view of Cody standing at the bar with a group of their ranch hands. They smiled, joked, and laughed together. Cody seemed so at ease, just like he'd always been at these parties.

The perfect host. A great boss. Everyone loved him.

His gaze never strayed from hers too long. He wanted her to know he was there if she needed him.

She wanted to go over and join him, to be the woman he deserved by his side. But anxiety and fear held her back. Too many people all at once. She was afraid someone would come up behind her and send her into one of her panic attacks.

Better to play it safe. For now.

Cody wasn't the only one who glanced her way. It seemed everyone stared at her, understanding why she isolated herself and wondering if she'd ever be the girl they used to know. Not likely. She'd broken into a million pieces when her baby died. Brooke didn't know exactly who she'd become, but she was a survivor and she'd find her way eventually.

She tried to give herself a break, like her therapist told her she deserved.

"Hey, stranger."

Brooke jumped up from the bench and caught Mindy Sue in a tight hug. "You came."

Mindy Sue hugged her back just as fiercely. "I promised I'd be here."

Brooke stepped back. "I'm so happy to see you." She waved at Mindy Sue's boyfriend, Tony, at the bar.

Mindy Sue's gaze swept over her. "You look good. How are you?"

"Better." Brooke sank back down to the bench and pulled Mindy Sue's hand to tug her down beside her.

Brooke stared across the courtyard at Cody. He held up his beer to her and Mindy Sue.

"You two can't stop looking at each other. How are things between you? As hot as they sound?"

Brooke blushed. She didn't hide things from her best friend. That didn't mean she gave every detail either. "At first, it hurt to look at him. But he wouldn't go away. He stayed with me, no matter how hard I tried to push him away. Every time I came out of my funk and fog, there he was, waiting for me."

He spent his days trying to make her smile, telling her jokes to make her laugh, rearranging his schedule to spend more time with her. They slept together every night. He made love to her like every time might be the last. He told her he loved her at least five times a day.

"Now...it's everything I ever wanted and more."

"Back when you first came home and Cody was calling and updating me, he said you two were going to get married." Mindy Sue pointedly looked at her left hand, still in the brace for her broken wrist. "Is that what you still want?"

"At first, I didn't believe it. But now that I'm really with him, like spending every day and night together and living like we are a couple and partners and everything to each other...yeah. I want it."

"I'm glad you guys are taking some time to settle into it."

She smiled. "I haven't been all here for some of it, but I'm getting better."

"You look better. You sound better. I know you still have some difficult moments and days, but that's okay."

"I'm trying to be okay with my darker thoughts and emotions taking over sometimes."

"It's just your brain's way of processing all you've been through."

She set aside thoughts of the past and focused on the future and the man still staring at her with so much love in his eyes. "I can't believe he wants to marry me."

Mindy Sue squeezed her hand. "It's real, Brooke. I've spoken to him several times over the last few weeks. Believe me, if I thought for a second he wasn't all in, I'd tell you. He is one hundred percent, dead set on marrying you."

"Yes, I am." Cody smiled down at her.

Mindy Sue took the beer he offered her. Brooke took the sangria he held out to her.

Cody bent in front of her. His hand settled on her thigh and slid up to her hip. "Happy your best friend is back?"

Brooke smiled from him to Mindy Sue and back. "Yes." She confessed to Mindy Sue, "I was kind of afraid to see you again."

Mindy Sue's eyes went wide. "Why?"

"Because you were there that night and after. I thought seeing you would bring it all back. But instead, I'm just so happy you're here." She hugged Mindy Sue and both of them wiped away a tear.

Once they separated, Cody brushed his hand over her hair. "I'm so glad you're happy, sweetheart."

"You make me happy, Cody."

"I'm trying." He squeezed her hip. "Did you tell her about the counselor?"

Mindy Sue glanced at her.

Brooke filled her in. "Cody and I went to see a grief counselor yesterday. We talked about our daughter."

"It helped me," Cody said.

She laid her hand on his arm. "It helped me, too. We have a few more appointments with her over the next several weeks. The psychiatrist helps me with what happened with Adam, but the counselor is a way for Cody and me to grieve together." She'd needed to deal with her fear and trauma to get to a place to talk about her grief and the pain of the loss.

"It's a great first step to learning to live without her," Mindy Sue encouraged.

Cody stole a quick kiss to distract her from thinking about all they'd lost. "Everyone wants to say hi and talk to you. Feel up to joining the party? Mindy Sue and I will stay beside you. If you get overwhelmed and need some space, no problem. We'll come back and hang out here."

She was scared. Scared to be around so many people, even though she knew them all. Scared of what they would say or ask her.

She needed to be brave and daring like she used to be.

She took Cody's outstretched hand. He pulled her up and they walked to the patio where everyone was gathered. Mindy Sue followed along.

Cody stopped on the edge of the small crowd, released her hand, wrapped his arm around her shoulders, and pulled her into his side. "These are the people who love you most, Brooke. I want you to feel that." He waved his free arm. "Everyone, may I have your attention." The much smaller crowd than past celebrations quit their conversations and turned to Cody and her. "I'd like to thank you all for coming tonight. In addition to our annual Fourth of July barbecue, we're here to welcome Brooke home. No one is happier than I am to have her return to the ranch. Of course, I have my selfish reasons. I love her." Cody leaned down and kissed her softly on the lips. The crowd cheered. Cody smiled down at her, then at the crowd. "Your friends and family love you. Welcome home, Brooke."

"Welcome home," the crowd echoed.

Cody tipped back his beer. She took a sip of her wine and smiled at him and everyone around them. "Thank you."

Cody cupped her cheek and locked eyes with her. "This is your home. This is your place. Right beside me." He sealed those words with another soft kiss.

Brooke settled into his side and the rest of the evening. Cody walked her from one group of friends to the next, starting the conversation and letting her join in when she felt like it. Mindy Sue flirted with Tony and kept Brooke's mind occupied with silly jokes and reminders of all the other good times they shared, making it easier to keep the dark thoughts at bay.

Cody pulled her onto the patio and into his arms. Others were already dancing to the soft music coming from the garden speakers. She settled in against him and swayed to the music. She held him tight, comforted by his familiar scent and the heat of his body against hers.

"All I want to do is take you upstairs to bed," he whispered in her ear.

"I want to always be this close to you."

Cody pulled her tight against his body. They barely moved to the music. "How are you?"

"Tired of everyone asking me that and staring at the scars on my arms."

The Texas heat didn't allow her to cover up the way she desperately wanted to do to keep everyone from seeing the scars. She'd nearly told Cody she couldn't attend the party because every dress in her closet was either short-sleeved or sleeveless. In the end, she realized she couldn't hide what Adam did to her—it was still written on her face and in her eyes as well as on her body.

She'd settled on a raspberry-colored, sleeveless dress with a pretty, sheer ruffled edge at the bottom of the skirt. She'd picked a pair of silver sandals and a silver and crystal beaded necklace to complement the outfit.

The people who were here were the people they knew and trusted to keep Brooke's secret that she'd been attacked on campus.

"Maybe they look for a moment, but then they remember you're still the Brooke they've always known. The scars don't matter, honey. That you're safe and home with all of us matters more than anything else."

"You always know the right thing to say."

"I didn't always. I wish telling you I love you was enough to..."

She pressed her thumb to his lips and her hand to his cheek. "It's enough, Cody. I feel how much you love me."

The song ended and Cody stared down at her. She went up on tiptoe and kissed him in front of everyone. They ended the kiss to another round of applause.

Feeling lighter than she had in weeks, she smiled and buried her face in Cody's chest, embarrassed to be caught in such an intimate moment.

Cody looked ridiculously happy, and that made everything better. Cody took her hand and led her away from the crowd.

Her mom stopped them and pulled Brooke into a hug. "Everyone is so happy for you and Cody, Brooke. I'm so glad you're home."

Her mother had done a wonderful job planning and setting up the picnic. She'd been invaluable helping Brooke get ready to open up her bookstore and café. She owed her mom so much.

She smiled for her mom, knowing how much it made her happy to see it. "It's been a really great party."

"We're not done yet, sweetheart." Cody pointed to the pasture across the way.

"Why is there a fire truck here?"

"I know how much you love fireworks."

"You didn't." She'd done that as something special last year, but didn't think they'd do it again because it cost a fortune.

Cody tipped her chin up and kissed her softly. "For you, I'd do anything." He walked her to the stone wall, clamped his hands on her waist, and hoisted her up.

Mindy Sue sat on her left beside Tony, Cody on her right, and her mom on the other side of Cody. The other guests gathered around just as the first set of rockets lifted off and burst in the air.

She leaned her head back and stared up at the night sky and the sparkling stars. The fear came when she remembered another starlit night she'd stared up and wished for Cody to save her. This time, the night lit up with bursts of color, and twinkling lights danced back to earth from the sky like sparkling gems raining down.

Cody wrapped his arm around her and held her close to his side. "Do you like it?"

"I love it." She pushed the fear away.

Adam couldn't hurt her anymore. He was locked up.

She never had to see him again.

With Cody by her side, she'd find her way back to always being happy. How could she not when she had him to show her the way?

Chapter Twenty-Nine

C ody caught himself singing along to the radio. Finally happy again, he could barely stand it. Brooke was better. Since the Fourth of July party, she became more and more herself each day. They seemed to have left the worst of the bad behind them in June and found a little bit more joy in July.

And now they were ten days away from opening her store.

Time had allowed Brooke to let her reservations go and actually believe in a happy ending for the two of them.

All he wanted to do was marry her. Make a life with her. Have a family.

He wanted to give her everything.

He had the ring in his pocket, a plan to make some new happy memories with Brooke, and an expectation and excitement that she'd say yes and they'd take this next step, both of them excited and looking forward to the future.

He pulled into the driveway and scowled at the two black SUVs parked in the driveway, complete with drivers, security, and the official state seal on the door. All the good feelings filling him up evaporated under his fury.

The governor had ignored his command to stay away from Brooke.

Cody parked in his usual spot, slammed the car into park, and killed the engine. He wanted to kill something else entirely, and hopefully with the last name Harris.

He rushed to the front door hoping Susanne headed off the governor before Brooke saw him.

Chapter Thirty

B rooke walked down the stairs to answer the knock at the door. Her mom stepped out of the kitchen with a cup of tea.

"I've got it, Mom." She hopped down the last two steps and smiled. No more brace on her ankle. No more pain in her leg. Six weeks at the ranch had done wonders for her recovery. The days she spent in the sun had given her skin a warm glow. The cuts on her hands and arms were completely healed. She still wore the brace for her broken wrist. The scars and the way others stared at her would take more time to get used to completely.

She opened the door and froze. Fear and a desperate need to run rushed through her system. Two weeks working with a grief counselor and even longer with a psychiatrist went out the door along with her breath. She couldn't remember a single thing the doctors told her about living in the moment and trying to avoid triggers that sent her into quiet depressions that smothered her ability to see the joy in anything.

The suffocating darkness opened up under her feet and swallowed her whole.

"You aren't welcome here," her mom snapped, rushing up beside her. "Leave. Leave now before you cause any more harm to my daughter." Her mom wrapped a protective arm around Brooke's waist to draw her away from the door.

Brooke's whole body trembled with fear and anger and a misery so deep it hurt her heart to beat.

Why did Cody have to work late tonight? She needed him desperately to hold the world at bay and keep her safe. She needed him so she could breathe through the pain and find the peace that he gave her.

"We've only come to talk," Mrs. Harris said, stepping forward. "Please, Brooke. Give us just a few minutes of your time."

"She doesn't owe you anything." Her mother seethed. "Can't you see you've upset her?"

"We aren't here to hurt her, only to talk. Please," the governor pleaded.

Her mom glared daggers at him. "Your being here hurts her. Seeing you brings it all back when she's done so well these last weeks to put it behind her."

Brooke snapped back into herself with her mother's fierce words. The truth was, she'd never put what happened behind her. She'd been hiding on the ranch, biding her time, waiting for something that would never come.

She'd never magically erase what happened.

She'd made some strides out of spending her whole day and night wallowing in pain and misery. She'd found enough focus and drive to slowly get her bookstore and café ready to open, with a lot of help from her mom and Cody. She'd even settled into her relationship with Cody and loved that they'd found their way back to each other.

But none of that meant that she'd fully dealt with and healed from the attack and the loss of her daughter.

Focused and driven in everything she did, she used to know exactly what she wanted and who she was. Now she was finding her way through her new normal, allowing herself to still sit in those dark moments knowing there were good things in her life waiting for her. But there were still some mornings that Cody had to remind her to eat, that even a kiss from him didn't bring a smile.

So maybe she did need to stop putting this off and face it. Them.

If they wanted to talk, then she was going to finally have her say.

She reached out and touched her mom's hand. "Mom, it's okay."

"Brooke." Her mom pleaded with her eyes.

She needed to do this. "Governor, Mrs. Harris, please come into the study. We can talk there." She didn't wait for them to come in, simply turned on her heel and headed for Cody's office. If they wanted to talk to her, they'd follow.

She walked into the study, saw the rug by the couch, and stopped short. Poor choice for this discussion. Her daughter could very well have been conceived in this room.

Instinct backed her out of the room and straight into the governor's chest. He gripped her arms to steady her. She stifled a scream and tore herself away from his grasp, taking several steps away. "We can't use this room. I'm sorry. The living room will have to do."

She rushed past the wide-eyed and curious couple and crossed the room to the fireplace, not giving them an explanation about her seemingly irrational reaction. They had to know it was because of their son.

She paced back and forth a few times, trying to compose her swirling thoughts. She wrapped her arms around her middle, holding herself tight, trying to pull herself together.

She didn't care if she looked unhinged. She felt that way.

They'd opened up her festering wound.

Mrs. Harris took a seat on the sofa and the governor stood beside his wife, giving Brooke space.

The governor took the lead this time. "Brooke, we're so sorry to barge in on you like this. We've tried to reach you through Cody and your lawyer, Mr. Wagner. They've made it clear you aren't ready to talk to us about this situation, but we simply wanted to tell you face-to-face how sorry we are for what happened."

The sharp retort that flashed through her mind caught in her throat.

Cody ran through the front door and slammed it in the governor's security guard's face with a resounding thud. He stopped for a second in the foyer and stared at everyone in the living room. Her mother stood sentry just behind Mrs. Harris. Brooke suspected she was ready to pounce like a mama lion if her cub was in any danger. Cody stood rigid, his hands fisted at his sides. He looked ready to kill.

Cody's gaze swept over her, a moment of relief in his eyes before his much sharper gaze fell on the governor. "I told you not to come here. I told you she wasn't ready to talk. Get out of my house."

The barely controlled rage in Cody's words registered as resignation in the governor's eyes.

"How dare you come here, knowing you're not welcome. She's the victim. And you should respect her wishes and needs. And the last thing she needs is you in her face with your agenda and demands. Now get out!"

Brooke rushed to him and took his fisted hands in hers. His chest rose and fell heavily with each heaving breath he took. Angrier than she'd ever seen him, he was trying to protect her. It made all the difference. She could take care of this because she had him on her side, ready to shield her and defend her to the bitter end.

She took his face in her trembling hands and made him look at her.

When he finally met her gaze, he softly touched her cheek and pleaded with her, "Please, honey, don't do this. Go upstairs. Let me take care of it. I don't want to see you hurting, not like that, not ever again."

"I have to. I was his victim. Now I'm a survivor. I can't hide forever."

"If this gets out, that he came here to see you and why, the media will never stop hounding you. You'll never be able to let it fade into the past."

"That's just it, Cody. I live with it every day. Nothing will change that. It's in my head and affects everything I do and think. I look at you and I ache inside because I wonder if our daughter had your blue eyes and the same dimple in her left cheek that only comes out when you try not to smile. I look at the scars on my body, and I remember the knife slashing through my skin. I can feel how tight my chest gets as I remember my desperation to protect myself and her. I walk around the ranch and every little thing reminds me she isn't here. She'll never run through the garden, splash in the pond, learn to ride a horse, or play hide-and-seek in the hayloft."

Cody's eyes shone with unshed tears.

She brushed one of her own away. "You want me to put it behind me. So do I. The counselor told us it takes a lot of little steps to finally put some distance between yesterday and today. This is one of those steps I have to take."

Cody cupped her face, much like she held his, and stared into her eyes. "Everything inside me tells me not to let you do this. To protect you no matter what. I didn't protect you from him but I can protect you now." He sighed and looked her up and down. "But I know you, Brooke. You're strong. So fucking fierce. If you say you can, then I know you will. If this is what you need..."

"It is."

His words, his confidence in her, it gave her the courage to speak for herself and their daughter.

"Then I'm here for you." Cody stole a kiss and released her. He stood beside her, his arms folded over his chest, and eyed the governor. No mistaking his unspoken threat. *Make a wrong move, say the wrong thing, and you'll answer to me.*

Brooke took a deep breath and turned to face the governor. "Why are you really here, Governor Harris? You made yourself clear in the hospital about what you really want. Seems to me the cover-up is well in effect. No one knows what your son did. His pampered ass is sitting in a swanky hospital instead of a cell. And I've allowed it." She wanted him to know that she ultimately held the power here.

Governor Harris rubbed his index finger over his chin. "My wife and I have known your family for decades. Harland was one of my best friends. We care deeply about what happened to you, Brooke. We wanted to be sure you were okay."

She actually believed the part about him caring because of his long-time friendship with Harland. "Did you go and see the other girls your son attacked? Did you speak with the woman he raped? How are they feeling after being assaulted that way?"

Mrs. Harris gasped. Tears streamed down her face. She took the handkerchief from her husband and dabbed at her eyes. "He was a good boy. Quiet. Kind. Thoughtful. Something happened to him. He changed. He wasn't himself. He wasn't the one who did those things." The disassociation of her son from the monster struck Brooke like a hammer blow. Mrs. Harris truly didn't believe her son capable of hurting anyone.

She hadn't met the monster Brooke saw the night he attacked her.

Something inside Brooke snapped. "You only see him as your son. You ignored the signs that something was off with him."

Confirmation shone in both their eyes that she was right about that.

"You never wanted to see the monster who attacked me and four other women," she accused. "You only want to cover it up, so no one will ever know the boy you raised is a stalker, rapist, and murderer. You want to avoid the stares I can't escape when people see my scars. You don't want to be shunned because of what he did." She stared down the governor. "You don't want to lose your job and the power you wield."

The governor consoled his weeping wife with a hand on her shoulder. "We don't need to get into the details."

"Why not? The details matter. Your son attended parties with you here. I'd never really taken the time to get to know him. But last Fourth of July, I spent some time talking to him and a few other friends. I thought he was nice. A little sad that he lived in your shadow and that you didn't see him for who he was, more than you saw him as merely another player in your political game."

The governor bristled. "I love my son."

"I'm sure you do, but he didn't feel that love. He felt your judgement and need for him to play his part. He was desperate to be seen and loved for who he is, not as the governor's son, but as Adam. He wanted to feel good enough just as he was."

Governor Harris hung his head, his gaze distant with memories.

Brooke continued. "We spoke for less than an hour. Then he stalked me for six months, intermittently meeting up with me and my girlfriends with his friends, acting like everything was fine and he hadn't been out attacking other women. I couldn't go anywhere without looking over my shoulder, wondering if the gifts and pictures would soon turn into something more sinister. But instead of coming for me, he picked vulnerable women to go after and terrorize. The first two women were lucky. Even though they were drunk, they fought him off. They got away. One of them was in his quantitative reasoning class. The other his government course. The third victim didn't fight because your son brought a knife to subdue her. He put that knife to her neck and scared her so much she lay there fearing for her life while your son tried to rape her. We'll never know if he planned to kill her, because a jogger saw them and he ran away after the sexual assault. I wonder if she knew when she went back to school two weeks later that he was sitting in her international relations class with her. He made the fourth victim pay for all his failed attempts. Not only did he terrorize her with that knife, he did rape her, and beat her unconscious. He left her there, beaten, bloody, and scared out of her mind when she woke up. He did that on my twenty-first birthday." She paused, letting them get the full impact of that. "That student dropped out of the semester. She didn't have to sit in her ethics class, where he'd picked her to be his next victim because she looked like me."

Cody turned to her. "Brooke, how do you know they were in his classes?"

"When the detective investigating my stalker told me the other victims were probably his victims because they looked like me, I started looking into them to see if I could figure out who was doing this. Women are more likely to be raped by a person they know. These women didn't know each other. But Adam knew all of them. So once I knew Adam was the campus stalker, I figured these women had to be in his classes. After you brought me home, and while you were working in your office and assumed I was watching something on my laptop, I emailed a friend willing to break the rules and who works in the counseling office and asked her to get me all of their schedules. It was easy to connect the dots."

The governor looked reluctantly impressed she'd done what the police couldn't. But they didn't know Adam had attacked any of them. They didn't know if they were looking for one person or more.

"Your son did that. He sat there, day after day, watching the women around him, looking for someone who looked like me. He picked those four surrogate women. And then he came for me."

Mrs. Harris violently shook her head side to side. "I can't listen to this. It's just so—"

"True," Brooke snapped. "Tragic. Unforgiveable. Horrendous. Unspeakable." She tilted her head and studied Mrs. Harris. "I think the note he left you after his suicide attempt spelled it all out very clearly. Everything he'd done and why. He confessed to everything. Didn't he?"

She got no response to her guess. But how else would they have known what Adam did and that they needed to hide him away as quickly as they did?

"What happened to the letter, Governor?" She raised a brow.

He stared at her shrewdly, stuffed his hands in his pockets, and remained silent.

A politician knew how to spin things and when to say nothing at all.

Brooke couldn't confirm the existence of the suicide note, but it was a good bet Adam left one behind before he tried to kill himself. Guilt moved him to do something drastic. She bet that same guilt made him leave a confession.

"He is depressed," Mrs. Harris said, trying to defend her only child.

"Depression didn't make him a rapist or murderer," Brooke shot back. She refused to accept any excuses for what Adam Harris had done to her and those other women "He's mentally unstable and should remain locked up for the rest of his life."

"He's getting the help he needs." Governor Harris took a step toward Brooke.

That wasn't a confirmation Adam would remain locked up.

Cody stepped forward, ready to pounce if the governor even thought about coming closer.

Brooke vibrated with anger and the fear and grief that was never far from her mind. "As far as the doctors know, he's being treated for depression. Right? You're not getting him the help he actually needs. So when the doctors say he's stable and can go home, what then?"

The governor didn't respond. Mrs. Harris's gaze dropped to the floor.

Governor Harris gave her his diplomatic answer. "Brooke, it's obvious our son was suffering, and he lashed out at you and those other girls."

That was as close as he'd come to calling his son a murderer and a rapist.

As a parent, you never wanted to think of your child in that way, but you couldn't hide from the truth either.

The governor touched his chin again. "Mr. Wagner has remained in touch with me, the police, and campus security and is keeping track of the investigation. Have you instructed him to reveal my son's name as your attacker?"

She tilted her head and stared right at him. "You mean the murderer of my baby."

"Our son is sick," Mrs. Harris pleaded, not wanting to truly believe her son capable of all he'd done as she made excuses for him. "You can't blame us for what happened. You can't make us pay for his mistakes. This will ruin us."

Brooke looked down at the woman sobbing on the couch, trying to salvage a life that had never really included her son. Brooke could muster enough compassion for the woman's grief at discovering her son was the worst sort of person and not the boy she thought him to be. Almost.

"Your son is sick. That doesn't exonerate him from what he's done."

Governor Harris's frame went rigid. "But if you'll just listen to reason. I'm the governor of the state. People depend on me. I'm up for reelection next year. This will ruin my career. Every good thing I've ever done to serve the people of this state won't matter. I'll only be remembered as the father of the man who attacked five women and killed an unborn baby."

"Yes." She nodded and wrapped her arms around her middle. "A baby who never got to take a breath, or see the light of day."

"He knows what he did was wrong. He's sorry he did it," Mrs. Harris wailed. "He's distraught and anxious to make things right. He's sorry."

"I don't care if he's sorry!" she raged. "I don't care if he was the kindest boy there ever was. I don't care what changed him, or the reasons why he decided I was the woman of his dreams, and he had to have me at all costs. None of that mattered when he held a knife to my face." She traced the scar on her cheek. "It didn't matter when he dragged me into the bushes and trees and attacked me because I had the audacity to love someone else."

Governor Harris held his hands out to her, palms up, pleading, "Brooke, we understand your anger and your sadness over the loss of your daughter. It's understandable, expected, and perfectly reasonable. I see your anger is directed at the person who did this to you. It wasn't our intention to come here and cause an open wound to bleed even more." He pulled a piece of paper from his pocket and held it out to her. "This is for you."

Brooke eyed the check as if he were holding out a rattlesnake. She actually took a step back before she caught herself. "Do you actually believe you can buy my silence?"

"No," Governor Harris said quickly. "No, Brooke. This is our way of doing...*something*," he said for lack of a better word. "Nothing will change what happened, but this money is for you to use to build a future."

Mrs. Harris gazed up at her, with watery eyes, imploring her. "Please take the money. There's no reason to ruin my husband's career and life over *this*." Mrs. Harris had gone too far turning what happened to her and those other women into simply "this."

The fury she'd kept in check to this point hit the boiling point and spewed out with her next words.

"Over *this*," Brooke repeated. "*This* that we're talking about is my murdered daughter. *This* is about me and Cody and a little girl who never got to be here with us."

She wished she could make them understand. They'd lost their son, but they were more worried about a job and a reputation. Granted, the governor had worked his whole life to earn both, but it shouldn't matter at a time like this.

"Why couldn't you have just come here to tell me how sorry you are for what happened? Why couldn't you express your sympathy for my daughter in a way that made me feel like you understand all that I've lost? You're parents. Yet I just don't think you get it."

She snatched the check out of the governor's hand and glanced at the amount. "I've had a lot of time to think about what your son cost me." She faced Cody. "About what we've lost." She turned to Mrs. Harris. "A half a million dollars. In your estimation, this is what compensates for a life lost. A life never lived. This is what my daughter's life was worth. This is what your son's life is worth to you."

They looked helpless to answer.

"You just don't get it." The anguish washed over her. "I never got to see her face. I don't know what color hair she had, or what color her eyes were. I never got to hold her in my arms after she was born and count her fingers and toes. I never heard her voice, or saw her take her first steps. I'll never walk her to her first day of school. I'll never get to play the tooth fairy or Santa Clause for her. Cody will never get to put together a dollhouse, or a new bike for her the night before Christmas. We'll never know if she wanted to be a doctor, an engineer, a cowgirl, a writer, a chef, or a lawyer like her dad. I won't talk to her about boys in high school, or help her pick out her prom dress or wedding gown. I'll never see her father walk her down the aisle and marry someone she loves beyond words. I'll never hold my grandchild in my arms, knowing they're a part of that beautiful girl I lost."

The tears streamed down her cheeks unchecked. The sadness welled to overwhelming proportions. "Do you get it now?" She wanted them to understand. To feel her pain. But how could they? Their son lived.

"You carried your son for nine months and gave birth to him. You had twenty-plus years of making memories with him. You got to watch him grow up and go off to college. It may have turned out badly, but I bet you wouldn't trade those twenty-plus years for anything." She shook the check at them. "Certainly not a half a million dollars." *Maybe for prestige and power*, she thought bitterly.

She sucked in a ragged breath. "You've got a million memories stored up to pull out to console you and remind you of what you had with him. You have years ahead of you to make more memories. I didn't get a single day with my daughter!" She sucked in a ragged breath, letting the tears fall. "Not even an hour with her," she added miserably. "The last thing I remember before your son attacked me is her rolling and kicking inside my belly. That's the only memory I have of my daughter, what it felt like to have her move inside me." She pressed her hands to her stomach. "And now I'm empty. I'm empty all the way to my soul."

Cody moved behind her, put his hands on her shoulders, squeezed, and kissed her on the head, letting her know he was there, backing her up, grieving with her.

She held up the slip of paper. "This check is to buy my silence. I want you to know that I know it. And if you want me to even contemplate giving it to you, then I want something in return. And I want it before I agree to anything."

The room remained completely quiet and still, except for the soft weeping of Mrs. Harris and her own mom.

Tears spilled down her face. Brooke didn't even bother to wipe them away. Each one was like another event she'd miss in her daughter's life.

"You will go to the women your son attacked and tell them he's locked up and will never hurt them again. You will offer to pay for whatever medical or mental health aid they need because of what your son did to them."

Governor Harris looked at Cody, surprised.

Cody bowed his head and touched it to her shoulder.

She went still, wondering what they knew and she didn't.

"I didn't want to upset you, or set back your recovery. It was a calculated risk and one that's coming back to bite me in the ass." Cody turned her to face him. "I didn't say anything *yet* to give you more time to heal."

"What is it?" Her stomach fluttered with dread.

"The student Adam raped committed suicide. Her family said she was devastated after the rape and unable to cope with what happened. I didn't want to tell you and bring back all those horrible memories. You were doing so well... I wanted to talk to your psychiatrist about how and when to tell you."

"You should have told me," she snapped, fisting her hands at her sides. "We don't keep secrets from each other. Remember?"

"Yes." Cody hung his head, then looked at her again. "I wanted to wait for the right time to tell you in a way that softened the blow as much as possible, or at least didn't send you into a downward spiral. I love you. Hurting you isn't easy for me."

Of course Cody tried to protect her from any more bad news and tragedy.

She frowned even as the tears came again.

That poor girl.

She turned back to the governor and his wife. "So your son is responsible for two deaths. If that doesn't motivate you to keep your son under lock and key for the rest of his life, I don't know what will."

The governor sighed. "Brooke, I'm not heartless, and when I said I care about you and how you're doing, I meant it. And I certainly could have handled this conversation with more tact and compassion. This is hard for us, knowing what he did and that, as his parents, we bear part of the responsibility. I've promised you he'll never get out. I get that you have reservations that I'll keep my word. When it comes to this...you...I will.

"In fact, I also discreetly did what Cody's been asking for on your behalf. I had an attorney contact the other victims. In exchange for them signing a non-disclosure agreement, the attorney would tell them who attacked them and let them know he was locked up. Only the first victim wanted to know. The other two declined the offer. The fourth...we didn't get to her in time. I don't know if it would have made a difference to her, if she would have still... I don't know. And I'll have to live with that the rest of my life."

Brooke allowed that maybe they were too concerned about their reputations, but the governor had done the right thing in the end. "You protected your ass but gave them a chance to know they were safe. I hoped you would do something behind the scenes to ease their pain and suffering and you did."

Cody stepped up next to her and faced off with the governor. "I assume you have an NDA for Brooke."

The governor pulled it out of his suit jacket inside pocket. "The money is yours no matter what. This is more than just an NDA; it is an insurance policy that Adam will stay locked up in a psychiatric facility for the rest of his life."

Cody eyed the governor with suspicion. "Did you stipulate it in the NDA?"

Governor Harris handed the document over. "Brooke is only held to the NDA terms so long as Adam is locked up. If he is released, so is she."

Cody turned to Brooke after he read through the document. "It's true. It's very specific. If Adam is released, you are free to tell the police, or anyone you want, what he did to you. With no statute of limitations on murder, you could send him to prison for life."

Brooke sighed with relief. "I've already instructed Mr. Wagner to continue to tell the police I did not see my attacker. The story will remain as it's been reported. Whoever the stalker might have been has moved off campus. End of story. So long as Adam never gets out."

The governor gasped. "You did this already."

"Yes. I'm not always as out of it as people think. I hear and see what's going on. So long as you keep your son locked up in that psychiatric hospital under a qualified doctor's care, I will remain silent. While I don't think you should have to pay for what he did, I will hold you responsible for ensuring he pays for what he did by never letting him go free again. He will never be allowed to hurt another person. Is that clear?"

"Yes. He will never leave that place, or one like it," Governor Harris assured her. "Keep the money, Brooke. I need to know that I did something, however inadequate it is. I wish I could...do something to ease your pain and suffering." He took the few steps to her and stood in front of her, as humble as he'd ever been. "I'm sorry you were hurt. I'm sorry you lost your daughter. I'll think of you, I'll think of her, every day for the rest of my life."

"I hope you do." Brooke turned to Cody, handed him the check, then walked out the back door, past the governor's security guard, and to the lawn, where the lights from the house couldn't reach her. She put her face up to the dark sky, stared at the stars, and let the tears fall. The anger she'd carried around with her eased with each tear streaming down her face. Telling the governor how she felt about her daughter and all she'd lost made it a little easier to carry.

Cody came up behind her minutes later and wrapped his arms around her with her back pressed to his chest. He leaned his head down on her shoulder. "They're gone, honey. I had no idea you'd contacted Doug about not turning Adam in to the police."

"You left the office the other day to get me a bowl of ice cream. Your phone rang. I went to grab it and take it to you in case it was a client or your office, and I saw the governor's name. It felt like my burden had been placed on your shoulders to carry alone because I simply checked out on dealing with the very present issues facing me and what happened."

"The governor could wait until hell froze over as far as I was concerned."

"He can't fix his son. He can't fix what his son did. So I knew he'd try to hold on to what he still has. His job. His reputation. His ability to help others." She didn't let politics or his outstanding record cloud her judgement on that, and tried to hold on to the fact he was a very good public servant and maybe this situation would make him even more sympathetic and empathetic in the future.

"When I thought about what I really wanted to happen to Adam, I realized I already had it. He's locked up and getting the help he needs. So long as he remains at the hospital, I can live with no one knowing he's the one who—" Her throat closed on saying the words again. "But I wanted the other women to have the same sense of safety I feel knowing he's not out there watching or coming for me anymore."

She turned in his arms and looked up at him. "When I do feel that way, I have you to remind me I'm safe. I don't know if they have someone to do that for them, but I could force the governor to make that assurance."

"I knew you were getting stronger, I just didn't realize you'd come so far so fast. It is so good to see you standing up for yourself and them. And I'm sorry you're hurting. You carried her inside you. She was so very real for you. I feel like she's fog. I can see her, but then I reach out to grab her, and she slips through my fingers."

Brooke cried even harder from his words. He got it. He might think she felt more deeply, but he'd described how she felt perfectly. The baby had become something so close to being solid and real, then she'd faded and disappeared before her eyes.

She held him so tightly her arms ached.

"What do you want me to do with the check?"

"I don't want to talk about it tonight. I don't want to talk at all. Just take me to bed and hold me."

He hooked his arm around her shoulders, pulled her close, and walked her back to the house.

Susanne met them in the living room and wrapped them both in a hug. "I am so proud of you, Brooke, and how you handled yourself tonight." She kissed Brooke on the head. "Goodnight, you two."

Brooke turned and buried her face in Cody's neck.

"Come on, sweetheart, you've had a hell of an evening." He scooped her up into his arms and carried her up the stairs to their room, set her down by the bed, and undressed her like she was a child. She simply didn't have the energy to do it herself. He helped her under the covers and joined her a minute later after stripping to the skin. She went into his arms the second he lay beside her. She didn't speak or sleep that first hour. She cried, then rested quietly against his chest. He kept his grip tight around her and whispered soothing words to let her know he was there for her. They fell into an exhausted sleep hours later as the moonlight streamed through the window.

When she woke to a slightly graying sky before dawn, she quietly left Cody's loving embrace and snuck away to her favorite spot to think.

Chapter Thirty-One

Cody had woken up every morning wrapped around Brooke for weeks and he loved it. And her. More each and every day. So when he opened his eyes to the bright sunlight and saw Brooke's side of the bed empty, his happiness at greeting another day with her dimmed to concern. Especially because of the turbulent visit they'd had with the governor last night.

Something was wrong. He felt it to his bones.

He threw off the covers, grabbed his slacks from the chair beside the bed and pulled them on, then ran from the room. He pounded down the stairs and rushed into the dining room, hoping to find Brooke eating breakfast with her mom.

The room stood empty, amplifying his fears.

He found Susanne in the kitchen with Janie. "Where's Brooke?"

Susanne set her coffee mug on the breakfast table with a thump. The hot brew sloshed over the edge onto the counter. Her eyes went wide, sweeping over his bare chest to his pants barely hanging on his hips. "I haven't seen Brooke this morning. I thought she was upstairs with you."

"I woke up alone."

Janie wrung a dish towel in her hands. "Maybe she had a bad dream and needed some air. She probably walked down to the stables to see the horses."

It could be true, but anytime she had a bad dream in the past, she turned to him. Why not this time? "I'll call down to the stables and see if she's there."

Cody rushed to his study to make the call. Out of the corner of his eye, he noticed the truck Brooke liked to use when she was home wasn't in the driveway and stopped short.

In his haste to find her, he hadn't considered what Brooke would do if she was really upset. It hit him all at once. He knew where to find her. He ran up the stairs, taking them two at a time, and went straight to his bedroom to change and gather what he needed.

Ready to leave, he pounded down the stairs again.

Susanne waited at the bottom.

"I know where she went. I'll bring her back. Don't worry, everything will be fine."

Susanne nodded, completely trusting in Cody. "Go get her."

Cody ran out the front door. He had everything he needed, except Brooke. He refused to let her sink back into depression and live in the dark world that sucked her away from him. He'd find a way to pull her back to him again. He'd done it before. He'd keep doing it until she found a way to live in the light and enjoy her life again. A life he wanted her to live with him.

The sleek sports car roared over the road. The comforting rumble of the engine helped settle his mood. The turnoff to the dirt road came into view, along with Brooke's truck, parked just where he knew he'd find it.

Skidding to a stop, he killed the engine and got out. He walked the trail through the tall grass and trees, winding his way down to the creek. He walked into the clearing and sighed out his relief. Brooke had brought a thick blanket and spread it on the bank by the rushing water. Lying on her side, facing the water, she slept soundly in her favorite spot. Soft hiccups punctuated her shallow breathing. She'd cried herself to sleep.

His heart clenched with sadness. She'd turned away from him, rejected him, deciding to be alone instead. Why?

He slid down onto the blanket beside her and pulled her against his chest. Holding her close, he listened to the water and her soft breath. She didn't stir, but snuggled closer into his embrace. He had to admit, he liked her pretty spot. The hypnotic rhythm of the tinkling, gurgling water settled his nerves and steadied him. The quiet solitude became a part of him.

Maybe that's what Brooke needed.

Still, he didn't like waking up alone, not knowing where she'd gone.

The cadence of her breathing changed, alerting him she was finally awake. Brooke rubbed her hand over his on her belly and scooted closer to him.

"I woke up alone and you were just gone." He held her close and buried his face in her hair. "Why?

Brooke reached back and slid her fingers over his head. "You missed me."

"Always." He kissed her neck. "But you scared me."

She turned and looked back at him. "I'm sorry. I didn't mean to do that."

"Don't do it again," he grumbled.

"You haven't had your coffee," she teased.

He was always a bear in the morning until he got his caffeine fix. "No. I haven't. I came after you."

"You must really love me if you gave up your coffee just to come and find me when you already knew where I'd be."

"How did you know I'd know where to find you?"

She leaned back and looked up at him. "Because you know me better than anyone."

He did. And he loved that she'd counted on him to come after her this morning.

"Yeah, well, you know me, and you knew I'd be concerned when I woke up without you, but you did it anyway."

"Truthfully, I wasn't thinking clearly. I couldn't sleep and I didn't want to wake you. I needed to be alone to sort out my thoughts and feelings."

"Alone, huh?"

"Yes, but that doesn't mean I don't need and want you."

Thank God. She wasn't pulling away from *him*.

"Next time, tell me you're going out. After last night, I didn't know what to think. You weren't in the house and I thought..." He'd thought the worst. When he drove out here, he expected to find her in bad shape. She didn't seem to be. In fact, she'd joked with him. Her words, her mood, everything about her seemed steady.

Her gaze dropped. "You should have told me about the woman who committed suicide." Her sad eyes met his. "I'm not so fragile that I'll shatter."

"I know you're not. You proved that last night when you handled the governor with such strength and conviction."

"I needed him and his wife to understand. They never saw their son for who he really was. And I don't mean the bad part of him. His life was stunted by expectations and living up to an image he didn't want any part of and never fit him." She stared out at the water. "He turned my understanding of that into an obsession and a need to possess the one person who saw him as an individual. Everyone needs to be seen for who they are and to be appreciated by those close to them. He took it to a dark place."

"You've really thought about this." He brushed his fingers over her soft cheek. "You sound different, Brooke."

"I'm better. As much as it hurt to talk to the governor and his wife about what their son cost me, I think it helped me to accept it. I will always miss her. I'll forever wish for her. But I need to live my life and not live to grieve her."

He let that sink into his battered heart. "I feel the same way, sweetheart. I can live with the hole in my heart because you fill up all the other places inside me."

"You do the same for me, Cody. Maybe you don't believe that, but it's true."

"I want to be the one you can always count on." He hadn't been that for her in the past, but he meant to be that from now on. "I want you to believe in me. In us."

They were together, but she hadn't made a commitment to him. He wanted that more than anything.

"Cody."

"Yes, sweetheart?"

Her gaze locked with his, her eyes so earnest, a fathomless depth of how she felt. "I love you."

He cupped her cheek and held her loving gaze. "I love you, too. More than I've ever loved anyone. And I know you love me. But when you say it...man, it hits me. Every time. I can't get enough of hearing you say it." He dipped his head and kissed her softly. Reverently.

God this woman owned him, heart and soul.

She brushed her fingers through his hair. "Right now my feelings are raw and all over the place. The only thing I know for sure each day is that you love me. That's part of why I came out here this morning. I've spent the last several weeks surviving in the aftermath of what happened. My psychiatrist kept telling me to find a way to live *with* what happened and not *in* what happened. I didn't truly understand what that meant until I came out here and thought about what I want for myself and my life. I think I needed these last few weeks to grieve for everything I've lost. Not just our girl, but the person I used to be. I don't think I'll ever be her again."

"Honey, if you tell me the Brooke I've known for more than ten years is gone, I won't believe you. You're still you, just stronger, more independent. Someone who goes after what she wants. You're the happy, nurturing, loving woman I've always known and so much more now because of what you've been through."

Her lips tilted into a soft grin. "I'm not the naïve girl I used to be. I played a lot of childish games chasing after you." She put her hand over his on her belly. "It was selfish and callous not to tell you about the baby. You were her father, and I regret not telling you and dealing with the situation head-on."

He appreciated that. "It was a complicated situation that I didn't handle well either. We were both trying not to hurt each other and not to get hurt. In the end, we realized that the only way to be happy was if we were together, because we love each other. That's what really matters."

She pulled him into a hug. "I love you so much, Cody. Loving you and being loved by you has gotten me through these last few weeks. Your steady and constant love has made it possible for me to wind my way through all the crazy twists and turns of my thoughts and emotions. No matter how hard I pushed you away, I knew you'd stand beside me. I knew you'd understand I wasn't in my right mind and I needed you to just hold on to me."

He pressed his forehead to her soft hair, his lips next to her ear. "I will never let go, Brooke." A promise he'd never break.

She turned in his arms and looked him in the eye. "I know. I believe it, because you show me every day."

He traced his fingers across her forehead and tucked her hair behind her ear. "And I will keep showing you how much I love you for the rest of our lives."

"About that and our life together..."

He raised a brow. "What about it?"

"I want to use the money the governor gave me and buy the pizza place I told you about. Instead of a partnership with Mrs. Marino, I want to buy it outright, so she can let the place go after it's served her family all these years, and she can do what she wants now, instead of carrying on a legacy for her late husband that she doesn't want anymore."

"Sounds like a plan."

She rubbed the back of her fingers over the scruff of his stubbly beard. He hadn't shaved this morning before chasing after her.

He smiled and kissed her fingers when she brushed them over his lips. "You're smart and organized and can accomplish anything you set your mind to, like making me fall head over heels in love with you." That made her giggle. "I think it's perfect, Brooke. Whatever I can do to help, I'm in."

"I can already see the renovation and the new menu. I want to add an ice cream counter, where kids can pick out their favorite flavor and toppings. For her. Because she made me crave ice cream every day."

He smiled and brushed his nose against hers. "I love it."

"Now that I've told you and you're excited about it, too, I feel like I can really do it."

"Of course you can."

"I'll have my bookstore, the café, and Italian place with ice cream as the cherry on top. And we'll run the ranch together. It's our home. It's always been ours. Someday soon, we'll get married, and as soon as it's possible, and we're both ready, I want us to have another baby. Or two. Three tops." Her vibrant smile brightened her green eyes. "We'll make a real life together." She was practically doing the proposing for him.

"I want you to be my wife, the mother of my kids, my partner in everything. I want you in my arms every night and to wake up to you every morning." He squeezed her to him and stole a kiss, then slipped his hand into his pocket and pulled out the red velvet box. "Will you make me the happiest man on the planet and in the universe and marry me, Brooke?" He flipped open the box and showed her the sparkling round pink diamond solitaire ring. Pink for their little girl. A reminder she didn't need but she'd carry with her every day.

She gasped. "Yes," she squealed. "I can't wait to marry you."

He kissed her so passionately she was panting and curled around him in seconds as they celebrated and poured their love and excitement into the kiss.

Brooke started giggling against his lips. "I can't believe you asked me." Her eyes were bright with joy. "You know you're the only man I'd ever marry."

"Absolutely. You can't resist me." He slid the ring onto her finger.

The diamond caught the light and sparkled as bright as the smile on her face.

"It's so pretty. Why a pink diamond?"

"To remember what we lost and what we have. Forever, Brooke. Me and you."

The smile she gave him was full of love and joy, touched with the sadness they'd always feel when they thought of the missing piece of them.

He kissed her again and held her close to his chest, and breathed a huge sigh of relief. Things were finally as they should be.

They'd only get better now. They'd turned a corner.

"I can't resist you." She reached up and cupped the back of his neck and brought his mouth to hers for another scorching kiss.

He smiled down at her. "I like your quiet spot by the creek."

"It's so pretty here. *And private*. I can share a quiet moment among the flowers with the man I love."

He gave her a wicked grin. "Let's make the moment count."

She smiled right before he took her mouth in a searing kiss and made love to her right there on the bank of the creek with the birds chirping, butterflies dancing from flower to flower, and the sound of the water carrying their soft sighs and moans away as he showed her how much he loved her.

This was how he planned they'd spend the rest of their lives. Happy. Together.

Chapter Thirty-Two

A dam had been planning for this day since the moment he woke up in this place. His parents wanted to keep him trapped. He wanted out. Of this place. Of his life. He was done.

He needed to see Brooke.

This was the only way.

He didn't want to hurt anyone else, but what could he do?

His mom and dad had gone to see her. She'd agreed to keep quiet. That's all they told him, despite him asking a million questions about how she looked. Did she ask about him? Did she want to see him? What had she said?

No matter what he asked, they didn't answer.

They told him to work on himself and getting well.

They told him to keep quiet about what really happened to put him in this place.

They didn't think he knew what was really going on—that his father had covered up everything. Nurse Nell was a talker. And since she didn't know about what he'd done, she had no problem telling him what was going on in the outside world. And since she knew he'd gone to the university, she was all too happy to supply him with answers to his questions about the campus stalker after he gave her a boo-hoo story about a girlfriend thinking she'd been watched on her way to her dorm one night.

The police were still looking for the campus stalker. There had been no new attacks.

Of course not. I'm in here.

But the poor girl from his ethics class had committed suicide. That was his fault. He never meant for that to happen. He'd never thought about those girls after he used them.

His sole focus had always been Brooke.

Which was why he wanted to be there for Brooke's big bookstore and café opening the day after tomorrow.

He needed to see her. He wanted to be a part of her big day.

Would she think about him?

Yes. She was thinking about him.

She probably couldn't stop thinking about him.

He needed to see her. He needed to be near her.

She deserved what was coming to her.

He wouldn't fail.

Not this time.

Good ol' Nurse Nell walked into his room for one last night check and he made his move.

He was getting out of here. Finally.

"Anything I can do for you before I head home, Adam?" she asked, so politely.

A prison guard wouldn't give a shit if he needed or wanted anything.

He sat on the edge of his cozy bed with his back to her. "I…" He didn't say anything more, drawing her closer.

She must have thought something was wrong and walked around the bed. She'd gotten so comfortable with him, she sat next to him. "What is it, Adam? You can tell me anything." She thought he'd tried to commit suicide because he was depressed. Lonely.

If she only knew the truth. If anyone in this hospital knew the truth, he'd never be allowed alone with a female nurse.

His father had sacrificed the safety of the staff here in favor of keeping things quiet so he could hold tight to his career with ruthless ambition.

He turned to Nell and looked into her pretty face, those sweet, trusting brown eyes, and said, "I'm sorry I have to hurt you."

It took her a second to understand his words, but it was too late. He already had his arm around her neck as he choked her out. Her feet kicked against the floor, her shoes scuffing on the hardwood. No simple white linoleum tiles in this place. His room looked like a suite at a five-star hotel, less the frivolous decorations one could use as a weapon. Still, he had fine linens, soft blankets, a sofa where he could relax and read or watch TV.

He didn't belong here.

This place was too good for him.

Nell stopped fighting and soon went limp.

He gently pushed her back onto the bed and checked her pulse and the rise and fall of her chest. She'd be out for a little while.

Until then...he tucked her into his bed on her side, facing away from the door, and covered her up. Anyone looking in would think it was him. Hopefully. At least for a little while.

Long enough for him to use her security card and the keys in her purse that she always left outside the door because he was her last stop each night before she left through a convenient side door just outside his room.

No one would be the wiser as he drove away.

He pulled up the hood on his sweatshirt, flipped off the light, and checked the corridor as he opened the door. He grabbed the purse, found the keys, then tucked it under his sweatshirt, and made his way to the end of the hall. He pressed the badge to the reader and heard a buzz. He opened the door, didn't hear an alarm go off that security monitoring the cameras noted he wasn't Nurse Nell, and booked it to the employee parking area. He used the key fob to find Nell's older model Toyota Corolla. He got in and drove out of the lot with one thought for Brooke: *We're not over.*

Chapter Thirty-Three

Brooke had spent the whole morning training her new employees in preparation for the big opening tomorrow. She couldn't wait to start working in the shop and café. Nervous butterflies swarmed in her belly.

What if no one came?

What if she failed?

What if she had to close?

Those were the same questions she'd asked Cody this morning over breakfast—which she could barely eat—when he'd tugged her out of her chair and into his lap and told her in no uncertain terms that she was going to be a rousing success. He assured her she had nothing to worry about. Everything was going to be amazing, because she'd planned and executed everything to ensure success.

She loved him so much for being so supportive and one of her biggest cheerleaders. Her mom had also been right there to echo Cody's thoughts.

She was so lucky to have them.

And since she hadn't eaten very much of her breakfast, she'd left her mom in the café overseeing the final prep for tomorrow's grand opening and headed out to grab some lunch.

She loved the downtown area but not the traffic. Even at this hour, just as the time was nearing the end of lunch for most, who'd head back to their nearby offices, the car and pedestrian traffic was rather busy.

She hit the end of the street and stood with a group of others waiting for the light to turn green so she could cross the street and meet Cody at the pizza place on the corner. They would check it out before she made her offer next month.

Cars were whizzing by as she stood shoulder to shoulder with about six other people. Just as the light turned yellow for the cars driving past them, Brooke felt a hand slam into her back, sending her into the street. A minivan came barreling at her as her feet hit the pavement and she fell forward.

Tires screeched. People gasped.

Someone yelled her name, though it seemed to echo.

Her right hand hit the pavement first. The brace still on her arm took most of the hit. She held her left hand up toward the car skidding toward her and her palm connected to the hot grill. Her knees hit the ground just before the force of the car pushing on her hand shoved her back. She landed on her hip and side and slid a couple feet.

Suddenly, everything stopped and she crumpled to the ground, her heart pounding as she heaved for breath.

Then it seemed like chaos with so many bystanders asking if she was all right.

The driver rushed out of the car and squatted next to her. "I'm a nurse. Don't move. Stay still until we assess your injuries." She ran a shaking hand through her long brown hair. "I didn't think I could make the yellow, so I started slowing down. Thank God. But then you jumped out in front of me and I slammed on the breaks."

Brooke locked eyes with the nurse. "Someone pushed me."

"What?" Cody suddenly appeared next to her.

She nearly smiled with relief, but caught a face in the crowd of bystanders on the sidewalk she'd just been pushed from. Her gaze locked on the monster who starred in all her nightmares. "Adam." His name barely came out a whisper.

From one blink to the next, he was gone.

She searched the crowd with her gaze, but it was like he'd never even been there.

Cody cupped her cheek. "Brooke, baby, are you okay?"

She grabbed Cody's shirt and shook him. "Did you see him?"

"Who?" He pulled her hand from him and stared at it. "You're bleeding. What else hurts?"

Nothing hurt. She couldn't feel anything but the cold, paralyzing fear. "Did you see him? Did you see Adam?"

Cody's gaze followed hers to the crowd, then they stared at each other. "Baby, he's locked up. You were in a car accident. You fell in front of a car and nearly got killed. I saw it from the window of the pizzeria."

She shook her head. "I didn't fall. I was pushed from behind."

"What?" Cody's eyes filled with fury. "Who the fuck would do something like that?"

She grabbed his shirt again, smearing more blood on it. "Adam."

Cody shook his head. "It can't be him."

She pleaded with her eyes. "I saw him."

He shook his head and brushed her hair behind her ear. "It was just your imagination. You're scared. I get it."

"I saw him."

Cody scooted closer and put his leg under her head. "Okay. I hear you. Be still, baby. Did you hit your head? What hurts?"

"My hand. Maybe my knees and hip." With the adrenaline still running along with her fear, it was hard to tell.

A police car pulled up and two officers took over the scene, ordering bystanders to be on their way after they got their statements. The driver was distraught but consistent with her story that it appeared Brooke had stepped into the road.

Cody held her hand as a paramedic checked her out. The worst she'd suffered was scrapes on her palm, ripped pants, bruised and scraped knees, and maybe a few bumps and bruises on her hip and thigh from when she landed and skidded.

After Cody gave his statement to the cop, it was her turn, and it was obvious Cody had told the cop what she'd said about Adam and that Adam was locked up because the cop's first question to her was, "At the time of the accident, did you have any thoughts of harming yourself?"

Tears gathered in her eyes as she looked up at Cody. "You don't believe me?"

He squatted down next to her as she sat on the curb. "Sweetheart, I love you. I will always have your back. No matter what. But what you say you saw can't be true. And if you were having some sort of waking nightmare or something, I could understand that."

"Someone pushed me." The cop and Cody both stared at her with pity in their eyes. "Why would I want to harm myself now? I'm about to open my stores. You know I've been excited about it for days." She held up her left hand, showing off her ring. "I'm going to marry you. Do you think there is anything I want more than that? Because there isn't. I'm not suicidal. I'm as happy as I can be. I'm looking forward to my life with *you*. I don't want to end things. I'm anxious for our dreams to start right now."

Cody brushed his hand over her hair and kissed her on the forehead. "You scared me half to death. I thought I lost you there for a second and my heart stopped. My mind is just...stuck on that."

She couldn't blame him for that. "I would never do that to you, Cody. Ever. I swear it."

"Promise me you'll call your therapist immediately and talk to him about this. I need to know that you're okay."

"I will. I'll call him once this is cleared up."

"Promise.

"I promise, Cody, but I need you to listen to me." She hooked her hand at the back of his neck and looked him dead in the eye. "He. Was. Here."

Cody stared at her for one long moment, then turned to the cop. "Can you pull any video from this corner to see what happened? If someone pushed her, that's...a crime." It was like Cody couldn't bring himself to admit that someone tried to kill her. Again.

"It'll take some time, but yes, we'll check out her story." The cop went off to talk to his partner.

Cody squeezed her hand. "We'll figure this out."

The paramedic finished cleaning her scrapes and bandaging her knees. "You're all set, Miss Banks. Are you sure you don't want to get checked out at the hospital?"

"I'm sure. But thank you for taking care of me." She signed the forms he held out to her and gave her a copy.

Cody took them and stuffed them in her purse, which he must have pulled out of the street because she didn't remember dropping it or whatever during the accident. "I'm taking you home."

"I still have some things to do at the café before tomorrow."

Cody clenched his jaw so tight the muscle along his jaw twitched. "Fine. I'll take you back there, where your mother can tell you you need to go home and rest."

She stood and dusted off her pants with her left hand, then walked right into Cody's chest. His arms immediately wrapped around her and held her close, without crushing her, probably because he was afraid of hurting her. "I'm fine. Just some scrapes and bruises."

"Not if someone tried to kill you," he bit out.

"It was Adam."

"He's going to be sorry he ever touched you." Cody pulled back and stared at her. "Can you make it down the street to your shop? I can grab my car and drive you."

"I'll walk. I feel like if I stay still, everything will seize up."

Cody growled under his breath.

She patted his chest. "I'm fine."

"Yeah, well, I'm not. Let's go." He put his arm around her shoulders and walked her down the street. Several people asked if she was okay as they passed. She assured everyone she was fine, but that only made Cody's body tense even more.

They walked into the café and Susanne grinned at both of them before her smile fell with one look at Cody and then the rips in Brooke's pants. "What happened?" she asked as she came around the counter.

"Brooke nearly got run over by a car."

"What?" Her mother dropped into the seat next to where Cody deposited her in a chair at one of the café tables.

Brooke took her mom's hand. "I was standing at the crosswalk waiting for the light to change when someone pushed me into the street and oncoming traffic. Luckily, the driver was able to stop before she hit me."

Cody scoffed, his eyes narrowed. "She did hit you. But it could have been a hell of a lot worse."

"Who would do such a thing?" Her mom stared at her with shocked eyes and the same panic Cody still bore, that she'd almost lost Brooke again.

Cody fell into the chair next to her and took her hand, pulling it up to his mouth so he could kiss her palm. "Brooke saw Adam there."

"What?" Susanne gasped. "No. That's not possible. He's supposed to be locked up."

Cody pulled out his phone and hit one of his frequent contacts. "Doug. You've been in touch with the psychiatric facility. I need you to verify that Adam is still on lockdown. Someone just tried to kill Brooke. She's okay. No major injuries, but she swears she saw Adam at the scene." Cody listened for a moment, then said, "Thanks." He hung up. "We'll know for sure in a minute."

Susanne stood. "I'll make you something. Coffee? Tea? How about a hot chocolate?"

"I'll take the hot chocolate." She didn't really want it, but it would give her mom something to do.

"Coffee, Cody?"

"Sure." He gave her hand a gentle tug. It didn't take much to get her to rise and slide into his lap. He wrapped her up close in his strong arms and rested his chin on her shoulder. "I'm sorry it took me a minute to believe you saw Adam. I don't want it to be true."

"I know. It's the last thing I want, too. I can't live with him out there stalking me. Not again, Cody." She shook her head and squeezed him tighter.

Cody kissed her forehead. "I'll protect you. I can't lose you again."

She leaned into him. "Never going to happen."

His phone rang and Cody answered, putting it on speaker. "Tell me he's there."

"Funny thing. Last time I spoke to the director, they confirmed he was there immediately. Today I was told Governor Harris has rescinded my authorization. They won't give out patient information to me anymore."

"Fuck." Cody raked his fingers through his hair. "He could have done that after Brooke signed the NDA."

"Or he did it to conceal the fact that Adam is out."

"But we don't know that for sure. That would mean that Brooke could go to the cops."

"What good would that do if the governor gets Adam out of the country?"

"Fuck." Cody slammed his hand on the table.

"After I called the facility, I tried the governor. He's not answering. Maybe he's busy. I don't know. But if I were you, I'd keep a close eye on Brooke. Cancel the store opening."

"No!" Brooke shook her head. "I'm not letting him ruin this for me. He took her. He's not taking this, too."

Cody's arm tightened around her. "Brooke."

She stared hard at him. "No. I'm opening my stores. There will be a ton of people here. People we know. He won't get to me. We'll talk about what happens after the opening if he's not caught." Because she had to believe that if Adam was out, the governor would get him back, or at least warn her.

Cody sighed. "I'll agree to the opening, but after, you'll have to let your employees take care of things until we know for sure what's happened with Adam."

"I'll see you two at the grand opening tomorrow," Doug said.

"The more eyes on her, the better. Thanks, Doug. As you can imagine, I'll be working the rest of the day from home with Brooke."

"Not a problem. I've got you covered. I've got some contacts at the PD. I'll make some calls about the accident and see what they have to say."

"Thanks. Appreciate it."

"Partners, remember. Take care." Doug hung up.

Susanne arrived with Brooke's hot chocolate and Cody's coffee. "What does this mean? Is he after her again?"

"If he is, he's not going to live long enough to regret it." Cody looked Brooke dead in the eye. "I'll do whatever I have to do to keep you safe and happy."

She turned fully in his lap, wrapped her arms around him, and hugged him close. "I love you."

"I love you more than anything. I will do anything and everything to protect you."

Susanne brushed her hand over Cody's head and smiled at Brooke. "Seeing you two together makes me so happy. I wish Harland was here to see it, too."

"He knows," Brooke said. "Before he passed, he told me, 'keep loving Cody hard.' And I did. I always will."

Cody's eyes met hers. "He said that?"

She nodded. "I think maybe he knew I'd never let you go." She took a sip of her hot chocolate, getting a milk mustache from it.

Cody hooked his hand at the back of her neck and drew her in for a kiss, where he licked off the sweet treat and melted her panties.

The man knew how to kiss.

Then he stood, effectively scootching her right off his lap. "Susanne, if you'll excuse us, I'm taking my fiancée home and putting her in a hot bath after her ordeal today."

Cody walked out of the bathroom and found Brooke finishing her call with Dr. Wick. She put the phone on speaker. "Can you please tell Cody that I am of sound mind and not having any self-harm thoughts?"

"Hey, Cody, Brooke told me of your concerns after what happened today and I'm glad you encouraged her to reach out to me. We've had a really good talk and I am satisfied that while Brooke still needs to process what happened and how she reacted to seeing Adam, whether he was real or imagined, that she's not a danger to herself or others. In fact, she seems excited about opening her shops tomorrow despite her fears that Adam could be out there trying to get to her. I hope the police will have a solid answer soon. Until then, keep supporting each other through this and talking to each other."

Cody hugged Brooke to his side. "Thank you for re-assuring me. I appreciate you taking the unscheduled call and making time for Brooke."

"Talk to you at our next session, Brooke. You both have a good night."

Brooke hung up and sniffed the air. "Do I smell vanilla?"

"Come with me. Your bubble bath awaits." They were in his room because he had a freestanding bathtub big enough for two. Up until now, they'd shared Brooke's room because she was more comfortable in her surroundings after her attack. But there was nothing he'd like more than for her to be in his bed.

Brooke started shedding her clothes on the way to the tub. "Do you have a bag to go over my brace?"

"Everything is ready."

They stepped into the bathroom together. She discarded the rest of her clothes and stood naked before him and the full-length mirror as she twisted her dark hair up into a floppy bun. He stood in just his boxer briefs behind her, mesmerized by her gorgeous body reflected in the mirror. The scars were mere pink lines. Badges of her strength, ability to fight, and her survival. They didn't detract from her beauty; they made her magnificent.

His warrior.

Even now, she stood proud and defiant against Adam. She wouldn't let him scare her away from accomplishing her goals. She'd fight. And she'd keep on fighting until he paid for what he did.

But tonight...Cody got to hold her in his arms. Love her. Be loved by her.

She raised a brow and gave him a flirty grin. "Like what you see?"

"I love everything I see." He slipped up behind her, nibbled kisses from the outside of her shoulder to her neck and up to behind her ear. "You are so fucking beautiful. And mine." He bit her neck and soothed it with his tongue as he held her hips between his hands. He slid one around her hip to her mound, sliding his fingers down her slit, then back up to her clit. He used his foot to tap hers to get her to open her legs wider. She obliged, her eyes locked on his in the mirror as he stroked her soft folds, his fingers sliding deeper and deeper until he had one finger, then two thrusting into her.

She rocked against his hand and he thrust harder and deeper as she rode his fingers.

"That's it, baby, take what you need."

"More," she begged.

"You want my tongue."

"Yes. Pleeease."

"Keep watching." He stepped around her, shifted her so she could see him and her in the mirror, then kissed a trail down her neck, over her chest to one taut nipple, then the other, sucking it deep and licking it while he rubbed his thumb over her clit and fucked her with his fingers.

He kissed his way down her belly as he fell to his knees on the white marble floor. He nuzzled his nose over her pussy and inhaled her heady scent. "Fuck, Brooke. The things you do to me." He pulled his fingers from her dripping channel and sucked them into his mouth. "You taste so good, baby." He hooked her leg over his shoulder, opening her wide to him, then pressed his face into her heat and licked her slit, diving his tongue deep.

Her fingers slid through his hair as she held him to her. "Oh my god, yes."

He worked her over good, licking her sweet pussy and nibbling her swollen clit until he knew she was close. To send her over the edge, he sucked her clit and thrust two fingers deep inside her, hooking them to hit that sweet spot that sent her right into oblivion.

Her walls clamped down on his fingers as the orgasm quaked through her.

He wrapped his arms around her hips and lifted her up before her legs gave out. He set her in the tub filled with hot water. "Sink in. Relax."

"What about you?" She eyed his hard cock, then reached for it.

He dropped his boxers and stepped into the tub before she could wrap her fingers around him and sank down across from her. "You need to soak and relax."

She shifted forward. "I need you." She pushed his legs down and straddled his lap.

"Baby, are you sure?" No sooner were the words out of his mouth than she was sliding down his hard shaft with a satisfied moan.

He didn't need to worry about a pregnancy. She'd taken care of that at one of her many doctor appointments.

"That's what I need." She rode him slow and deep, rocking her hips against his as they kissed, their tongues sliding over each other's the way their bodies were gliding against each other's.

It was a slow rise to the razor's edge, where they both kept themselves until he couldn't take it. He reached between them and rubbed his finger over her clit in circles, setting off her orgasm as he thrust into her hard and deep, once, twice, then over that edge and into bliss he went with her.

They stayed like that for a few minutes, holding each other before he lifted her off him, helped her turn around, and she sat between his legs, her back to his chest, and they soaked away the day and languished in tranquility a little while longer.

Tomorrow they could think about the opening of the bookstore, the car accident, and Adam. Right now, they had each other.

Tomorrow Cody would go after Adam if he truly was the one who'd tried to kill Brooke.

Until then, he'd love her through the night and keep her nightmares at bay.

Chapter Thirty-Four

B rooke had advertised in the local paper, online, with mailed postcards, and on social media. She and her mom had hung a banner out front announcing the grand opening. Still, she worried no one would show up.

Those fears did not come to fruition. There had been a line at the door when she arrived thirty minutes before opening. The place had a constant flow of traffic. Her mom was ringing up book purchases at a steady pace and the café was filled with patrons sitting and enjoying their beverages and baked goods, and flipping through the books they'd already bought while the line remained at least ten deep.

It was a huge success.

Brooke couldn't be more proud. And relieved.

She'd done it. She'd opened not one, but two businesses despite the hardships in her life right now.

The thing with the push and the car and seeing Adam yesterday...that was still fresh in her mind. But she didn't let it deter her from greeting her invited guests at six o'clock for the party she'd planned to celebrate the opening. Customers were welcome to join in.

Mindy Sue rushed her with Julie right behind her. "Look at this place! It's amazing!" Mindy Sue wrapped her in a hug. "You did it, Brooke. You own your own businesses. And that children's section...I want to play in that cute little fort and sit and read in the boat. And the teen section...all those fantasy novels and romances! Now that I'm out of college, I'm going to start reading for pleasure again. I can't wait to pick out some books."

Brooke pulled out two tote bags with the bookstore logo printed on them and held them up. "I thought I'd get you and Julie started. Romantasy for you, Mindy Sue. Super sexy romance and paranormal for you, Julie."

They squealed, hugged her again, then took their loot.

"I'm still buying more books," Julie announced, heading toward the cookbook aisle because she also loved to cook and bake.

Mindy Sue bumped shoulders with her. "Super sexy stepbrother hasn't taken his eyes off you."

"Don't call him that."

"Oh, come on, he's like every taboo romance we ever read. You've been lusting after him forever. And now...that man is yours."

Brooke held up the ring.

Mindy Sue's eyes went wide. "How did I miss that pink sunset sparkler? When did this happen? Why don't I know?"

Brooke told her how Cody had proposed and got another huge congratulatory hug. "You two were meant for each other. But something seems off with you. Aren't you happy?"

"Ecstatic. But something happened yesterday. Someone pushed me off the curb and I nearly got run over by a car."

Mindy Sue's eyes went wide with shock. "What? No way. Did they catch whoever did it?"

"No. But…" She bit her bottom lip, not wanting to share the rest and have her friend look at her like she was crazy.

"What?" Mindy Sue stepped closer.

"Please don't think I'm nuts."

"Never."

"I saw Adam in the crowd right after it happened."

Mindy Sue gasped. "What? No." She dropped her voice to a whisper. "That's not possible. He's locked up. Right?" Mindy Sue glanced around at the crowd.

Brooke held Mindy Sue's forearm. "I hope so."

The shock came back. "What does that mean?"

"Cody and your father have been trying to get confirmation on that, but the hospital is citing patient confidentiality and the governor won't answer their calls. They think the governor may be trying to get him out of the country."

"But he promised you." Indignation filled her eyes and words. "If he does that, it voids the NDA." Mindy Sue knew all her secrets.

Brooke shrugged. "Maybe he thinks I won't come forward in order to preserve my privacy, but there is no way I'll let *him* go free and hurt someone else."

"What are you going to do?"

"If we can't get confirmation tomorrow, I'll have no choice but to give the governor an ultimatum. Either he confirms Adam is locked up with proof, or I go to the police."

"Shit. That will blow up your whole life in a whole fucking shitstorm kind of way."

She shrugged it off like it didn't mean what it really meant. "I know. But what else can I do?"

"Be careful, Brooke. Threatening the governor could have dire consequences."

Brooke shivered with the thought.

Mindy Sue glanced around the room. "What if it wasn't Adam? What if it's someone else?"

She let that roll off her. "Who else could it be?"

Cody finished his conversation with a couple of his buddies he'd invited and walked toward them.

"What about the scorned ex?" Mindy Sue whispered.

"She's stopped texting him," Brooke said under her breath as Cody snuggled up to her side, wrapping his arms around her from behind as he kissed her on the head.

"I'm so happy you and Julie made it tonight." Cody smiled at Mindy Sue, oblivious to their more serious talk.

"Julie and I wouldn't miss it. And congratulations on the engagement. I'm so happy for both of you."

Cody released Brooke to hug Mindy Sue. "I'm so lucky she said yes."

"No luck necessary," Julie said as she joined us. "Brooke was only ever in love with you. No one else stood a chance. And there's always been something special about your relationship. 'Inevitable' comes to mind."

Cody kissed Brooke. Soft and quick. "She had my heart the second we met. Just in a different way until it grew into what we have now."

"You two really are the perfect couple," Julie announced. "I wish you had a brother." She and Jeremiah had amicably decided to go their separate ways after graduation.

Tony joined their group with an autobiography about one of his favorite rock gods. "I paid for this," he mentioned to Brooke before turning to Mindy Sue. "Can I add this to your bag?"

"Absolutely." Mindy Sue dropped it into the bag.

"What did you get?" Tony asked her.

"My very awesome friend gave me a couple of romantasy books."

Tony grinned and hooked his arm around Mindy Sue. "So, inspiration for later. Lucky me."

Everyone laughed at Tony's comment as he pulled Mindy Sue into his arms for a steamy kiss.

She swatted his shoulder. "Save that for later, when we're alone."

"Can't wait," he shot back.

Cody leaned into her ear. "Me either."

Susanne and two of the café staff walked in carrying trays of champagne-filled glasses.

All of her guests and customers took glasses as Cody led her toward the front of the assembled group. Then he took one step away to give her space to give her speech.

Brooke took in a breath and addressed the assembled group of friends, family, and neighbors. "Thank you for coming today. The bookstore and café have been a dream in the making for many months. It started with the idea of carrying on my stepfather's kindness in sharing. He believed in helping his neighbors and building up his community. I wasn't sure where to start, until I heard about the bookstore possibly closing. I always loved coming here as a kid. Books were a way to travel to other places, learn new things, and a way to set my troubles aside for a little while and immerse myself in someone else's life."

She glanced at Cody, then Mindy Sue, Julie, and her mother watching her, all of them so proud of her. "Some of you know the last seven months have been difficult. Tragic. I lost someone I loved very much." She brushed away a tear. "And then the love of my life helped me heal, helped me open this place, proposed, and loved me with everything he has. This place wouldn't have been possible without you, Cody." She held up her glass to him. "You believed in me. I will never forget that. I love you."

"I love you, too, sweetheart."

There were several sighs and aws from the crowd. A few tears, too. From her friends and mom especially.

"I want to thank all of you for coming tonight, for supporting me. Especially you, Mom. Doing this together...it's been everything I needed and more." She turned her attention back to the crowd. "Please, enjoy the bookshop, and café. I hope I see you here often. I hope these places mean something to you and it's where you come to escape and find each other when you need a good book or a friend to hang out with. I appreciate each and every one of you. I'm so grateful to have you all in my life."

"To Brooke," Cody toasted, holding up his glass.

"To Brooke," everyone echoed.

Brooke sipped her champagne with everyone else before she noticed something in the back. *Smoke! Oh God! A fire!*

She dropped her glass and ran for her back office.

Cody called out to her. "Brooke?"

The blast and whoosh of a fire extinguisher went off, confusing her. Who was back here?

Maybe someone else had seen or smelled the smoke and rushed to help.

She skidded to a halt in the hallway when she spotted Adam, in the same hoodie and jeans from yesterday, coming out of the office and stopping in the open back door.

"Brooke," Cody called again, this time closer.

Adam's eyes went wide when he spotted Cody, and he ran.

Cody spun her around. "Stay back, sweetheart, it could still be burning."

She turned back to the open back door, and then spotted the fire extinguisher on the floor just inside her office.

Cody rushed past her into the office.

Tony came up behind her with Mindy Sue, her mother, and Julie behind him. "Fire department is on their way. I told everyone else to evacuate out the front."

"The fire is out," Brooke said, trying to see around Cody.

He turned and tried to make her back out of the office. "The damage is minor."

"Let me see."

"There's nothing to see." Cody blocked her view by staying really close to her. His height and the width of his shoulders made it so all she could see was him.

"Cody. Stop. It's my office. Let me see."

He cupped her face. "I don't want you to see it."

"What did Adam do?"

Cody's eyes went wide. "What?" He must have been too focused on getting to her to see Adam dashing out the door.

"Adam. I saw him just before you came up behind me. What did he do?"

Cody seemed frozen for a moment before he slowly shifted sideways and let her see the smashed picture frame on her charred desk and the ashes of what remained of the picture of her and Cody kissing with her hand on his cheek, her diamond engagement ring sparkling.

Her mother had taken the picture the morning they'd come home from her creek-side retreat where he'd proposed.

There were a bunch of other wadded-up papers all over the desk and floor.

"This doesn't make sense." She looked at everything and still couldn't come up with what Adam intended to do.

"He torched the picture of us and could have burned down the whole fucking place." Cody seethed.

"And then he put the fire out before it really got started?" She gripped Cody's arm. "That makes no sense. Even more strange...he was wearing the same clothes as when he pushed me into the street. Why do that, then put out this fire? What's he trying to do?"

Cody pulled her into a hug. "I don't know. But we'll figure it out." He took her hand and walked her out of the office and down the hall to gather with their friends as the fire department pulled up outside. "I'm taking you home. I can't protect you here. Too many people. Too much going on."

"We have to deal with all of this."

"We'll give our statements, then Susanne can lock up. I need to get you somewhere safe. Please, Brooke."

She stepped in close and put her hand on his cheek, her thumb resting on his bottom lip. "I'm safe, right here with you. With all the firemen and cops right outside. Nothing is going to happen to me."

"You don't know that. He was here. In your store. That's too fucking close." He pressed his forehead to hers. "I want to take you home. Now."

She appreciated his protective streak. "Let's deal with this first. I will stay right by your side the whole time. I promise."

The firemen poured into her store.

She pointed them to the back.

Cody walked her out front and to the first police officer they found.

"Hi. I'm Brooke Banks. This is my store. I saw the person who I believe set the fire."

It took forty-five minutes for her to tell the officer what happened, repeat it to the fireman for his report, and to hand over the surveillance video from the hidden camera in her office and by the cash register, along with the two very obvious cameras that overlooked the store. The police would see whatever Adam had been doing in her store.

She didn't want to see his face again.

Chapter Thirty-Five

B rooke held Cody's hand as they trudged up the stairs toward the bedroom. Susanne would be home soon. She'd stayed behind at the bookstore with a policeman protecting her to lock up once the police and fire department finished their investigation.

Exhausted yet amped on adrenaline, Brooke wasn't looking forward to the crash. Or the nightmares of seeing Adam again, bringing up everything from the past.

"I'm going to draw us a bath, sweetheart."

She stopped outside her bedroom door, not remembering closing it. She'd been anxious and in a rush to make it to the store on time. "Let me grab some fresh clothes."

"You won't need them." His sexy smirk made her belly flutter. Cody's plan to distract her from what happened tonight made her body hum with anticipation.

Maybe she'd slip into something sexy for him to peel off with his teeth. "I'll need something to wear in the morning. I'll join you in a few minutes."

He gave her a soft kiss on the forehead, then headed down the hall to his bedroom and the amazing soaker tub she couldn't wait to slip into with him, so she could climb on top of him and forget everything for a little while.

She didn't know why, but she approached her closed door cautiously, reaching for the handle and turning it slowly. She sucked in a deep breath, mustered her courage, and slowly opened the door to the dark shadows in the room.

Adam Harris stepped into the open doorway and grabbed her with one hand at the back of her neck, the other over her mouth. "Don't scream. I just want to talk to you."

She didn't believe that for a moment, but nodded.

Her insides went cold. Her bones turned to ice.

Flashes of memories of his attack on her assailed her mind and made it hard to think.

He pulled her into the room, kicking the door shut with barely a sound, then turning them so his back was to the door. He walked her backward, toward the bed.

Cold terror paralyzed her mind. She needed to fight, but couldn't make her body respond to that order as a cold chill ran through her.

Her knees hit the bed, and he pushed her down so she sat on the edge, then pulled a gun from behind his back and pointed it in her face. "I'm going to take my hand away. Don't scream."

She scrambled back on the bed, ended up on her knees, and held up both hands, palms up to block a bullet that would rip right through her. "Don't shoot, Adam. Please. Leave me alone," she begged, tears welling in her eyes.

He shook the gun at her. "Do you see me?"

She stared at him, from his black hoodie down his black jeans to his black boots. "Yes, Adam. I see you."

He pointed the gun at the window. "They don't. No one does." He pointed the gun at her. "Only you *see* me."

"I do. I see that you need help. You should be in the hospital." *How did he get out?*

He brushed his fingers through his hair, pulling it when he reached the ends. "Fuck that place. All they want to do is keep me sedated and stupid."

He went to the door, locked it, then turned back, pointed the gun at her again, and closed the distance between them. "I'm not spending my life in a place like that, wasting away."

"Adam, the doctors can help you control your urges."

He shook his head. "After tonight, I won't need that."

Her whole body shook. "What do you mean?"

"My parents want to leave me in that place. Lock me up and throw away the key. Their visits have slowed. It won't be long until they don't come at all. No one will remember who I am, or what I did, and *they* won't have to accept that... *They*. Made. Me. This. Way!" He slammed his fisted hand into his head with each of those words.

She hoped Cody heard Adam's shouted rant. "I understand you're upset they sent you there. They want to help you."

"I don't need help! I deserve to be punished for what I've done." His gaze went soft on her. "I love you. I *never* meant to hurt you." He pressed his hand and the gun to his forehead. "You were supposed to see how much I love you. How good we could be together. But nothing went right. You didn't want to be with me. You want to be with *him*!" Adam pointed the gun at her bedroom door. "I know you love *him*. I heard you say it at the bookstore. And now you're getting married." He stared at the ring on her finger on the hand she had fisted, clutched over her heart with her other hand. The one he'd broken.

She tried to explain her side of things. "Adam, I loved Cody long before I met you. But that doesn't mean I didn't like you, that we weren't friends. You tried so hard to get my attention. You sent all those wonderful gifts, but you never told me how *you* felt. Not once when we spoke in person. You could have said something at the picnic, the Christmas party, one of the outings with all our friends," she said, reminding him of the good times they'd shared, letting him know she hadn't forgotten.

His eyes went soft as his body relaxed. "I wanted to, but the words wouldn't come. My nerves got the better of me. I wanted so badly to whisper them in your ear, then shout them to the world. But we were never alone. I wanted it to be you and me. I wanted to spend time with you. I wanted so many things." He shook his head with regret. "Now look what's happened." He hit the side of the gun against his head once, twice, over and over again. "I fucked it all up!"

"Adam, please, stop. I don't want you to hurt yourself."

"It hurts so bad, knowing that I hurt you."

"Then why did you do it? Why did you push me off that curb and try to burn down my store?" She knew he'd attacked her in a rage about the baby, but not why he'd tried to hurt her again if he felt this remorseful.

"You won't believe me."

"Maybe I will if you tell me the truth."

His shoulders went lax. "It wasn't me. Yes, I was following you, but only because I wanted to get you alone." He gripped his hair and tugged. "Not like that. Like this, so I could talk to you."

With a gun?

She kept her mouth shut about that. "Then tell me. If it wasn't you, then who?"

"I don't know. Some blonde. She saw you and slipped in behind you with the others. I thought maybe she was a friend of yours, though she's a bit older than you. When she pushed you, I froze. I couldn't believe it. Then I rushed forward, thinking that was it, you were dead. I'd never get to talk to you, to tell you...everything. And it would all be for nothing. No one would care."

"About what?"

"This. Me. You. What happened. I need you to understand. To be with me."

She didn't understand what he meant. "Adam..."

"After you were okay on the street, I followed her back to her car." He pulled out a wadded-up piece of paper and tossed it on the bed. "Blue BMW. That's the license number. I didn't think I'd see her again. Until I did, tonight."

Oh my God!

She leaned toward him. "You didn't try to burn down the bookstore, did you?"

His shoulders went lax. "I just wanted to see you on your big night. I snuck in the back." His mouth tilted into a lopsided frown. "You should really lock that door during business hours."

She thought she had, but maybe her mom or Cody had forgotten when they came through that way. Didn't matter now.

Adam stepped closer. "I stayed at the back, so no one would notice me. But then *she* slipped out from one of the aisles while you were speaking and snuck into your office. I tried to grab her, but then I saw the smoke and saw the flames and rushed to put them out. That's when you saw me. She'd already gone out the back door. I thought I could catch her, but she sped away in her car again."

"I think it was Cody's ex."

His gaze narrowed. "She's really got it out for you."

"That bitch won't get away with it. I have you as an eyewitness."

"Who would believe me?"

"I do."

He shrugged. "It's finally over for me. Now you know, you can stop her."

"What do you mean it's over for you? What do you want? Why are you here?"

His gaze swept over her scarred arms. "I hurt you. I killed your baby." Tears streamed down his face. His eyes pleaded with her. "It could have been our baby if I'd only done things the right way."

Okay, now that was crazy. But who knew...maybe if Cody and Kristi hadn't lost the baby and married, she could have moved on with Adam, and she and Cody would have simply been co-parents to their child.

No. For her it had always been Cody.

She shook off any thoughts of Adam being her baby's stepfather.

"Brooke?" Cody rattled the nob. "Why's the door locked?"

"Do you *see* me?" Adam raised the gun and pointed it at her again.

"Brooke!" Cody pounded on the door after hearing Adam's voice, shaking it in the frame.

Adam held the gun steady. "All I wanted was you. I love you. You're my everything."

He's going to kill me, then himself.

"Please, Adam, don't do this. Please."

"I love you. I never wanted to hurt *you*." He put the gun to his head.

She had only a second of relief before his teary eyes locked on hers.

"Do you think you ever could have loved me?"

"Adam. Please."

"Do you see me?" His soft, anguished voice broke her heart.

She held her hand out to him, hoping he didn't do what she thought he was going to do. "Yes, Adam. I see you. I see you. Please, don't do this. I'll help you. I see *you*." She reached for him.

The gun went off. The side of Adam's head exploded in a burst of blood.

She flinched and her whole body froze in that moment, her eyes glued to Adam's soulfully sad gaze.

Cody kicked in the door. It swung wide and slammed against the wall. Cody ran toward her.

Adam fell to his knees, hit the floor, his head bouncing on the carpet, his cold, dead eyes staring at her.

Cody wrapped his arms around her, pulled her off the bed, and ran out of the room with her like she weighed nothing. She stared back over his shoulder. One last glimpse at Adam's dead body lying sideways on her floor, blood staining her cream carpet deep, dark red.

No. She didn't want this. She'd never wanted this.

Chapter Thirty-Six

Cody stood on the porch steps and watched the coroner's van and police cars drive away. Governor Harris stood beside him, silent. His pale face remained pensive, his mind turned inward, leaving his eyes blank.

"Go home," Cody ordered.

The governor shook himself out of his stupor. "Huh. Right. Nothing left to do, I guess."

"Except cover this up too, right?"

"How do I explain away my son breaking out of a mental institution, stealing a gun from *my* home, and coming here to terrorize Brooke, the last victim of the campus stalker, and committing suicide in her bedroom?"

"I don't know. Seems to me, the truth always comes out, no matter how much we deny it or try to hide it."

Cody had done that with Kristi, uncovering her treachery to get him to marry her. He'd done it with Brooke, denying his love for her until he just couldn't do it anymore. She saw right through him anyway. So did Kristi. So did everyone else.

This went far beyond denial and went straight to unhinged.

You just couldn't make these things up.

Governor Harris might have gotten away with covering up the attacks on campus by hiding Adam away in the mental hospital, but Adam coming here tonight and doing what he did made him look guilty as hell. No reporter worth their salt would buy that he came here for any other reason than that he needed to see Brooke—the object of his obsession. That his guilt put that gun to his head.

"I don't know what to do. My wife is so far gone with grief and guilt that we couldn't help Adam, I'm not sure she'll recover from this."

"Give her time. Love her. Spend time with her. Remind her of all the good times. But never forget that this could have been prevented if he'd been in a cell. Still, I'm sorry for your loss."

Governor Harris stared at him, his eyes wide with surprise.

"What? Adam was mentally unstable. I may have wanted to kill him for hurting Brooke and killing my daughter, but deep down, I never wanted this."

"I'm sorry for everything he's put you through. Everything he's done to Brooke."

Cody stuffed his hands deep in his pockets. "Me, too."

Governor Harris held up the phone in his hand. "The police chief left me a message. After Brooke told us about Adam's confession, they tracked Kristi to the airport, where they apprehended her ten minutes ago with her passport in hand and a ticket to Montenegro."

"Let me guess...no extradition treaty."

Governor Harris nodded. "Seems you like smart women." He looked up at the house. "What are you going to do about Kristi?"

"I went to college with the DA's son. I'm going to take a page from your book and use that connection to make sure Kristi is held accountable to the fullest extent of the law for what she tried to do to the woman I love."

"I understand that desire to protect someone you love. I hope you understand that's all I was trying to do with Adam. I thought he would come home after he snuck out. Or even turn himself in to the police. I don't know which one I hoped for more as I looked for him."

Cody knew now that the governor had been discreetly using his resources to find Adam the last two days. He wished the governor and his people had found Adam.

But then again, without Adam's help, he wouldn't have known Kristi started the fire. He'd found out tonight that surveillance footage from street cams and neighboring businesses by the corner where Kristi pushed Brooke into the street had captured the moment it happened. Plus they had the license number from Adam and his confession to Brooke that he'd seen it all go down.

Cody planned to visit Kristi soon.

Governor Harris backed down one of the steps. "I hope you and Brooke will be very happy together. I wish you nothing but utter joy from here on out. And if either of you ever need anything...don't hesitate to call. I owe you."

Cody shook his head. "One day, I might collect, even though Brooke and I know you were only trying to protect your child."

They shared a long look of understanding.

Cody rolled his tired shoulders. "Would you like me to call someone to take you home?"

"No. The drive will do me good. Give me time to think of a way to explain all this to my wife."

"It's simple. Adam couldn't live with what he'd done. For all he did to those girls, to Brooke. He felt remorse. He didn't want to hurt them. He just couldn't help himself. You're the governor of the state. At least for now. You implement policy. You have the power and the platform to help the mentally ill. Turn this tragedy into something good. Maybe what your wife needs to get over this is a cause to champion."

"Yes. Do something positive. Make a difference for those in need."

"I hope you do. I'd like to see it. But it also wouldn't surprise me if you spun what happened tonight into another tragic story about how you were getting Adam the help you thought he needed, never knowing what he'd done on campus, until he came to apologize to the one person he couldn't leave without telling her how sorry he was for what he'd done." It wasn't like the governor hadn't already thought of this scenario. Of course he had. Cody just wanted him to know that he knew the governor's mind and what was coming.

The governor eyed him. "I would keep Brooke's name out of it if I could."

"Victims should always be protected." He put the warning in his voice.

Uncertainty clouded his shrewd eyes for a split second. "I don't know if even I can keep her name out of this."

Cody gritted his teeth. "You can turn the focus from her and keep it on Adam and helping those in crisis." He hated everything about this conversation, but if it helped keep Brooke out of the spotlight faster, then he'd suffer through it and whatever came next. Anything for her.

"It will be difficult, but nothing's impossible." Governor Harris stared off in the distance. "Goodnight and good luck. Congratulations on your upcoming wedding."

"Thanks." Cody didn't need luck or the congratulations. He only needed the woman he loved.

He worried he'd lost her again tonight. If she faded back into the darkness, lost herself in the nightmares Adam left her with, he didn't know what he'd do.

Actually, yes, he did.

He'd love her back to him.

God, he hoped Brooke had it in her to fight her way back one more time.

The governor drove away and Cody walked into the house and made his way to his office well past three in the morning. He found Brooke curled into the corner of the sofa. She stared at the black windows, only able to see the dim room reflected back at her. Susanne sat beside her, holding her hand. He closed the distance and kneeled beside the sofa in front of her.

He placed his hand on her leg.

She flinched away, sucking in a quick breath, staring wide-eyed at him. The second she realized it was him, she sighed and put her hand over his.

"The police and governor just left."

"It's all done?"

"Yes, honey, they took Adam away."

"Okay." She leaned forward and traced her fingers over his brow and into his hair, holding on to his head. "You look so tired. We should go to bed."

He laid his head in her lap and wrapped her in his arms for a moment. He needed her close, to feel her breath wash over his skin, her body pressed to his.

She brushed her fingers through his hair over and over again, then sighed. "It's going to be okay."

He believed her, because she believed it.

Chapter Thirty-Seven

C ody walked into the police department holding cells the next morning bright and early with two very important people in tow.

He walked all the way down to the last cell, where Kristi was trying desperately to squat over the toilet and pee without touching the not-so-clean seat. There was vomit on the floor from another woman, who was passed out on the bench, probably picked up for being intoxicated in public, or something similar.

Kristi spotted him and pulled up her panties and black leggings to cover up. Her neck, face, and ears flushed crimson with her embarrassment and probably a heaping dose of fury. But she held it back when she saw the two men with him. "Cody?" The question was in her voice. *What was he doing here with them?*

"You remember my good friend Brad Whitlock."

As in District Attorney Devin Whitlock's son. He didn't have to say that last part though. She knew.

She took a tentative step toward the bars. "What is this?"

"I told you to leave Brooke alone. She was grieving the loss of our child. But you couldn't do that. You went after her because I canceled the wedding."

"No I didn't." She wrapped her arms around her middle. "I don't know what you're talking about. You'll see. I didn't do anything. They're lying."

He opened the folder the DA had handed him before they walked in here. He pulled out a photo and turned it toward her. "This is you standing right behind Brooke at the crosswalk. That's your hand on her back."

She gasped and her eyes went wide.

"Let me guess what happened. You were downtown for some lunch meeting or whatever. You saw me. Then you saw her. You followed her to the corner. Then you pushed her and just backed away."

Her eyes remained wide as saucers. "How?"

"Nearly every move you made was caught on surveillance cameras from local businesses and the street cams. But there was also a witness. One you didn't see. But he saw you. He followed you back to your car and wrote down your license plate number. He knew Brooke. In fact, he was *stalking* her."

"What?" She crossed her arms over her chest.

"That's right. The man who attacked her on campus came back. But this time he didn't want to hurt her, he wanted to talk to her and tell her about *you*. He was at the bookstore and saw you come in through the back and start the fire."

"The guy in the hoodie," she whispered to herself, but not quietly enough that they didn't hear her.

Cody nodded, then pulled out another photo. "This is you in your car, leaving the parking lot." He pulled out another. "This is you at the nearby traffic cam." He pulled out another. "This is you standing in Brooke's office, setting the picture on fire that her mother took of us the morning I proposed, of us kissing and showing off Brooke's engagement ring."

"That fucking ring was bigger and nicer than mine."

"Its worth is in the fact that it's a symbol of my love for her and our daughter, and my promise that I will be hers, and only hers, forever." He glared at her. "You used yours as a trophy you'd won. Or at least manipulated your way into getting it on your hand. It never really meant what it's supposed to mean."

"I loved you and you threw it all away for *her*."

"Because I *always* loved *her*." He tried to rein in his rage. "And now you're going down for attempted murder, arson, and a few other charges you won't be able to get out of, right, DA Whitlock?"

"That's right," he agreed. "There will be no deal in this case. I will prosecute you to the fullest extent of the law."

"My father is getting me an attorney. I'll tell him that when I pushed her, I wasn't in my right mind. I lost it when I saw her ring."

DA Whitlock smirked. "And how will you explain starting a fire in her office with over fifty people inside the building, all of whose safety and well-being you disregarded when you tried to destroy Brooke's business."

"No one would have gotten hurt. They'd have left through the front, but her pretty little shop would be ashes."

DA Whitlock shrugged. "We'll see what the jury thinks after they hear what a jealous woman you are and how you coerced Cody into a proposal, then callously didn't tell him you'd lost his child for two weeks. No one is too busy to hear something that important."

Kristi's face turned ghostly white. "Cody, please, you can't do this. I've never done anything wrong."

"I have no mercy for someone who goes after the woman I love. I will do anything to make sure you never have a chance to hurt her again."

"Cody, don't do this."

"*You* did this to yourself." He walked away from Kristi's pleas and angry words and threats.

He had somewhere else he'd rather be. Home with Brooke. Better yet, back in bed with her and his arms wrapped around her.

Two days later, he walked into the courthouse and court-room 3 for Kristi's bail hearing and stood at the back of the room. Kristi was sitting next to her attorney with her hair up in a twist, her back ramrod straight as she faced the judge. Her parents sat behind her.

Her attorney pleaded her case. "Miss Randall is an up-standing member of the community. She has a job and has no prior record or arrest. Miss Randall will hand over her passport and post a reasonable bail if it is granted."

The DA stood up. "After a witness saw Miss Randall set the fire at the bookstore and she knew she was going to be caught, she tried to flee by plane to a country with no extradition treaty. She is a flight risk and a threat, not only to Brooke Banks but to the community at large. She set the bookstore on fire when it was packed with people. If not for a bystander putting out the fire quickly, who knows how many people may have been hurt or killed. There was a tenant upstairs and people in the adjoining café. She had zero regard for any of them."

The judge rendered his ruling quickly. "Bail denied. The suspect will be remanded to prison until her trial date."

Brad was standing next to him, showing his support, and smacked him on the shoulder. "Yes. She's going down."

Cody turned to his friend. "Thank you for getting me in to see your dad the way you did."

"Cody, you're a respected attorney. He would have taken your call and a meeting if you asked for it."

"I know he paid special attention because of our friendship. I appreciate it."

"Yeah, well, don't be surprised if he calls *you* for a favor next time."

Cody expected it and he was willing to pay up when the time came. Within reason.

Kristi stood and turned to her parents, but went still when she spotted him. Her face flushed red with anger. "You did this."

The court security guard moved closer to her.

Kirk stood and turned to him. "It didn't have to be this way."

"No, it didn't. She should have left Brooke alone. You shouldn't have tried to have me fired. I guess her need for revenge comes from you. Just remember you both lost coming after me. If I were you, I wouldn't try it again." What he really wanted to say was *if you do, I'll make you suffer*. But with so many witnesses, probably not a good idea.

Kirk turned to Kristi. "We'll figure something out. It's going to be okay."

Don't make promises you can't keep.

Kristi was not getting out of jail anytime soon. He'd made sure of that.

Brad hooked his hand on Cody's shoulders. "Come on, man. I can't wait to see your fiancée."

Cody had invited the DA and Brad to lunch at the house. Mostly so Devin could assure Brooke that Kristi was not going to be a problem anymore.

DA Whitlock followed him and Brad out. "She sounds...resilient."

"Yes, she is." More than she had ever thought she'd need to be.

He couldn't wait to put all of this behind them and marry her.

Chapter Thirty-Eight

They stood in the hallway with her back to her bedroom door, Cody pressed along the front of her, kissing her neck. Well, the room wasn't hers anymore. After Adam's suicide, she'd moved into Cody's room—their room—permanently and they'd had her old room redecorated as a guest bedroom for now. That was five months ago. Nearly Christmas now.

So much had changed since then. She'd gone through another difficult depression that included meds and lots of therapy. Mostly the Cody kind of therapy, where he spent as much time with her as possible, usually naked, loving her. But the talking kind, too, with Cody and her therapist and their grief counselor. They'd stopped seeing the latter in September, both of them feeling like they'd worked through the rush of feelings they'd had when they lost her and had settled into life without their little girl, though they still talked about her with each other from time to time.

She'd gone to Adam's grave at one point to have a chat with him. He'd gotten his say. She hadn't gotten hers. It felt strange but cathartic to have a clear head and heart about what he had done, what he took from her, and how he'd left her behind to deal with the fallout.

Luckily, Cody shielded her from most of it, though reporters had tried to get her to make a comment and tell her story.

But soon there was another big headline they were chasing: the governor had stuck to his word and tried to keep the focus on Adam's mental health issues and what he was trying to do for others.

Last she'd seen, his approval rating was up.

They'd all weathered the publicity storm the best they could and Brooke was happy to be back to just another private citizen trying to make a living.

She'd delayed the opening of her Italian restaurant until after the new year so she could focus on the wedding.

She and Cody had decided in August to put the past behind them and pick a date. They decided on the very special day they had made their daughter. The date of last year's Christmas party and the day they'd finally gotten to share their love with each other. Maybe it had fallen apart the next day, but that special night had been magical and they didn't want to lose sight of that.

So tomorrow she was finally going to marry Cody.

He ran his tongue up her neck to the back of her ear, then growled, "Whose stupid idea was it that I sleep in the primary suite without you tonight?"

Brooke giggled, fisted her hands in Cody's hair, and drew him up to look her in the eye. "You did. Remember?"

"I'm a stupid idiot."

"You're sweet. Tomorrow, we'll be married and never spend another night alone."

"Promise me," he demanded.

"I swear." She crossed her heart with her index finger.

"Seal it with a kiss." His lips met hers, coaxing at first, then demanding. This hadn't changed in the last many months they'd been back together. They were still desperate for each other whenever they were in the same room.

She tasted the passion mixed with the bourbon and strawberry cheesecake they'd shared on the back patio by the fire pit. They'd spent a quiet evening together, just the two of them, after she spent the day out shopping with her mom. They had picked up the wedding gown she bought months ago and left at the shop last week for alterations. She couldn't wait to put it on tomorrow, walk down the aisle to the man she loved, and marry him. She couldn't wait to start the rest of her life with him.

Cody released her hips and planted both hands on the door on each side of her head and pressed back, breaking the kiss. His gaze roamed down her body and back up in one hot sweep of need. "I want you so damn bad."

"Not tonight. That's what you wanted, remember?"

"I can't remember anything when I'm this close to you."

"Go to your room. I'll see you in the morning."

"It's *our* room." He never let her forget it.

"Yes, I know. It turned out beautifully."

Cody had surprised her. A designer had arrived last month just before Thanksgiving and taken measurements and her and Cody's ideas for transforming the room. Two days ago, she'd shown up with her crew and turned Cody's bachelor basics into their honeymoon suite. The room they'd share for the rest of their marriage. Soft cream walls. Dark wood furniture. A massive king-size bed covered in a light blue and navy spread. Light blue sheers and heavy navy drapes on the windows. Black and white photos of them over the last ten years in antique silver frames on the dresser and walls.

A new room for their new life together.

Soon she'd transform her old room into a nursery. One thing at a time.

"It's sweet you don't want to see me until the wedding. Traditions are good," she coaxed.

Cody rolled his eyes. "Not for me. I'm dying here."

She giggled and smacked him on the arm.

He traced her lips with his fingertips. "I love it when you smile."

"You make me smile." All the time. Every day now. He'd helped her heal her heart.

He stole a kiss, pressed away from the door, and walked down the hall, calling back over his shoulder, "You're all mine tomorrow."

"Hey, Cody."

He stopped just outside his door and turned back to look at her.

"I am yours. Always have been. Always will be."

His eyes softened on her. "I love you."

Her heart melted. "I know you do. I love you, too."

"Tomorrow you'll be Mrs. Jansen. My wife."

"I can't wait, Mr. Jansen, because you'll be my adoring husband."

"Always." The look in his eyes told her he meant it.

"Fuck it." She ran down the hall and threw herself into his open arms, wrapping her legs around his waist. He chuckled, then blew her mind with the kiss he laid on her as he took her into the room, kicked the door shut, and followed her down onto the bed, where he made love to her until they were both exhausted and panting for breath, tangled in the sheets and around each other.

Chapter Thirty-Nine

B rooke stood in her mother's room, staring at her reflection in the mirror. She smoothed her hands over the lace and beads sewn into the white gown. Long lace sleeves covered the scars on her arms, but not the one on her face. She reached up and traced it with her fingertip, thinking how far she'd come in six months. The past year, really.

She dropped her hand, stared at herself again, and saw the woman she'd become.

The woman she became when she made love to Cody the first time.

An adult. A mother. Soon to be a wife.

The woman *after* Adam.

Shattered, then more resilient than she ever thought possible as she worked to heal and find herself again.

A business owner. A fighter. A lover.

A daughter to a mother who stood by her through everything with compassion and kindness and support.

A friend to the man she loved more than anything.

And she was the woman he wanted to marry and build a life with. Her.

"God, you're beautiful."

And I am so grateful and lucky to have him.

The smile she couldn't contain at seeing him bloomed on her rosy lips as her gaze shifted to him in the mirror, standing over her shoulder, still by the door.

"You're not supposed to see the bride before the wedding."

"You and I like being together more than we like tradition." *True.* "I'm here to walk you down the aisle."

She turned to him. "Really?"

"We do things together."

That widened her grin. "It's been that way for a long time."

"Yes, it has, so why stop now." He walked to her, took her hands, and held them out to the side, staring down at her gown. "That's a pretty dress for a gorgeous woman. I love your hair like that."

She'd twisted the long length up on her head and secured it in place with the silver and crystal flower clips her mom bought her as something new. She'd borrowed her mother's diamond earrings.

"I know you like it down."

"I love it like this, but it will be my pleasure to take it down later." The suggestive grin made her smile. He leaned in and stole a quick kiss without smudging her lipstick.

The black tux suited her lawyer man. She much preferred him in jeans and a T-shirt, working on the ranch, but this was good, too. The jacket defined his massive shoulders and broad chest and tapered in at the waist.

She slid her hands down the lapels and held her hands over his heart, feeling it thump against her palms. Not quite calm, her cowboy lawyer. "Nervous?"

"Excited. I've waited a long time for this day to come."

She eyed him and tilted her head in surprise and confusion. "I think that's my line. I've been chasing after you since I was a girl. I've dreamed of this day nearly my whole life."

"I've thought about getting married to the woman I love. Maybe I hadn't exactly put you in the wedding dress beside me, but I always wanted the woman to be someone who loved me. Someone who saw the real me. Accepted me for all that I am. Saw the potential in all I could be. A friend as well as a lover. A partner in every way. You are that woman, Brooke, even if I didn't recognize it right away like you did. Thankfully, you balanced my stubbornness with sheer determination."

That made her chuckle. "We make a good team."

He gave her a lopsided grin. "I need you to tell me all those things I don't want to hear in the way you do that makes me listen."

"I need your steady strength to hold me up when my world crashes down. I need you to love me."

"I do. I always will, because you do the same for me." He kissed her again. This time his lips pressed to hers in a long, soft kiss that settled the butterflies in her belly.

Cody ended the kiss, pressing his forehead to hers. "Will you marry me?"

She smiled softly and stared into his sparkling blue eyes. "Yes."

He stepped back, but halted before walking out of the room with her. "I almost forgot. You need something blue." He dipped his hand into his pocket and pulled out a beautiful diamond and sapphire tennis bracelet. He took her left hand, pulled the ends around her wrist, and clasped it in place. He took her hand and brought it up to his lips, kissing the back of it, the bracelet sparkling at her wrist.

"It's beautiful, Cody. Thank you."

"A wedding gift for my bride."

"I have something for you. I thought my mother forgot to take it to you, but I guess she knew you were coming up to get me."

The plastic box sat on the bedside table. She undid the lid and pulled out the single pink rose surrounded by baby's breath. She turned to him. His gaze locked on the flower and something in his eyes told her he understood.

"A symbol of our daughter for you to carry with you down the aisle." She pinned the boutonniere to his lapel.

Cody touched his finger under her chin and tilted her head back, so she met his earnest gaze. "Ready?"

She took his hand and walked ahead of him to the door to prove how ready she was to be his wife. His long strides made it easy for him to catch up and walk beside her down the hall to the stairs. She trailed her fingers over the laurel leaf and roses garland wrapped around the banister. Tiny, twinkly white lights lit their way down to the living room. Vases overflowed with white spider mums and roses. Their sweet and heady fragrance filled the room and calmed her nerves.

"I love it, Cody. The house looks beautiful."

"Wait until you see the garden."

They stepped out the back door and followed the path of red rose petals to the garden patio. Outdoor heaters kept them warm in the brisk evening air.

The wedding march played as she and Cody walked the aisle between their guests. Everyone looked wonderful in their dashing suits and pretty dresses. They'd move into the house once they finished the short ceremony. She wanted to be married in the flourishing garden. The florist had made it even lusher with the huge urns overflowing with greenery and flowers. Twinkling white lights sparkled in the bushes. The fountain's tinkling water added to the peaceful scenery.

Cody walked her right up to the marble pedestal at the front of their gathered friends and family. Their daughter sat on the center of the pedestal with two pink, strawberry-scented candles, one on each side of her. A taller, unlit candle sat behind her.

Brooke stared at the silver vessel, released Cody, and touched her fingers to the small case. Cody's hand covered hers. She looked up at him and he stared down at her, both of them taking a moment to remember all they'd lost and all they were about to promise to share in their future.

She smiled softly, stood tall, and turned to face him. He took her hands in his and the preacher began the ceremony with a prayer she'd never heard. It spoke of love and sacrifice and perseverance. It spoke of love's endurance.

She lost herself in the words and drifted off into the past and all she'd overcome. Cody touched her face to bring her back. She smiled up at him, trying not to make a big deal about the conflicting images in her mind to the beauty all around her. She focused on him and squeezed his hand to let him know she was here.

She was okay.

She'd endured.

She'd persevered.

To settle her mind and her heart, she stepped closer and gave him a quick kiss to take the worry out of his eyes.

"Not yet," the preacher said.

Cody laughed. "She's been stealing kisses from me for as long as I can remember."

And that's all it took to erase all the bad from her mind and fill it with images of them always together over the last ten-plus years.

It made this moment feel inevitable.

"You've stolen a few over the years."

"That's because you stole my heart." Cody gave her that panty-melting grin.

She placed her hand on his chest. "You stole mine first."

Cody smiled back at her, then nodded for the preacher to continue the ceremony. They exchanged vows, speaking the words with a poignancy that brought tears to her eyes.

Cody slid the diamond eternity band onto her finger. "I will love you beyond forever."

She took the ring she'd bought him from her mom and slid it onto his finger. She stared down at it and touched both diamonds surrounded by an infinity symbol. "My love for you is infinite."

This time Cody was the one who didn't wait for the preacher to tell them to kiss. He reached for her, slipping his hand around her neck and drawing her close. She wrapped her arms around his massive shoulders and held him tight, losing herself in the kiss.

"Well, I now pronounce you husband and wife. Kiss her all you want," the preacher said, making the crowd laugh.

Cody smiled against her lips, held her close, turned his gaze to the preacher, and teased, "Thanks, I will," and kissed her again.

The celebration that followed amplified her happiness. Everyone kept the mood light, focused on her and Cody. At dinner, everyone went around the tables telling one story after another about the two of them. A trip down memory lane that led straight to their wedding today.

They cut the cake, drank champagne, and laughed with all their friends. Mindy Sue and Julie hugged her a dozen times, if not more. Cody, Brad, even Doug, and a few of his other buddies all did shots. Then they were all dancing and laughing and having fun.

It was so much more than special. It was magical. It was joyous.

As night closed in and the stars took over the sky, Cody led her to the foyer. She stood on the top step and tossed her bouquet. Julie caught the roses when Mindy Sue shoved her in front, saying, "No way am I next." Julie held the flowers to her nose and inhaled, smiling. "I'll take it so long as I get the kind of love Brooke found." She held the bouquet up and said, "To Cody and Brooke." Everyone raised their glasses of champagne and drank.

Cody took Brooke's hand and led her to the door.

"Wait, where are we going?"

"Honeymoon." He opened the door and held out his hand, indicating the limo waiting in the driveway.

"Where are we going?"

He'd refused to tell her.

"To be alone." Cody smirked, brushed his nose against hers, kissed her socks off one more time to distract her, then hauled her up into his arms to carry her out the door.

But not before her mother hugged both of them together. "Be happy. I love you."

The night they spent in the luxury hotel suite started off their marriage right, but spending a week in Hawaii at a private bungalow with a secluded beach and their own chef made it extra special.

She loved being Cody's wife.

He loved being her husband.

They spent every minute together. By the time they came home to the ranch, she'd forgotten ever feeling like this was all a dream. The reality of loving Cody and being loved in return was so much better.

Epilogue

February blew in cold and windy. Cody pulled his coat tighter around him and buttoned the top to keep the wind at bay. He brushed down one of his favorite mares, enjoying a rare day working the ranch. He liked the methodical process. He did his best thinking when he was alone in the stables, brushing down a horse. Not that he didn't enjoy being a lawyer. Being a partner had its perks and also a heavy caseload. Brooke watched over the ranch with their ranch manager more than he did these days. And it was doing well under her watch.

He couldn't wait for her to get home. Quiet this morning, she left for the bookstore with little more than a quick kiss. It wasn't like her to leave without them getting tangled together for several minutes.

He smiled when he thought about all the changes she'd made over the last thirteen months. After their holiday honeymoon, she bought the pizzeria and turned it into the Italian eatery she'd imagined it could be and the community now loved.

She loved working at the bookstore and café, checking in with the business owners who had moved into the second-floor office space. An accounting firm, tech startup, and graphic design business. She'd embraced being a businesswoman and his wife, supporting him at client dinners and social gatherings they were constantly invited to.

She'd been happier than he'd ever seen her these last many months.

She'd found her direction, and she was thriving.

At least, that's what he thought, until he'd seen her grow quieter and quieter over the last few days. Something was wrong. He wished he knew what it was. He hated the sullen look in her eyes and the way she withdrew into herself.

He wanted to stop her from walking out the door this morning, but couldn't come up with a reason why without possibly making Brooke defensive. When she was ready to talk, she'd come to him. She always did.

Fast footsteps crunched over the gravel road outside. He glanced up, then froze, concerned, as Brooke sprinted toward him. His men were all out checking on the cows and horses. The stables were quiet and vacant but for the horses occupying the stalls.

Afraid something had happened, he stepped out of the stall to meet her, but she didn't stop running and leaped into his arms and wrapped her legs around his waist. Her mouth crushed his in a hard and demanding kiss that he responded to immediately. He cupped her bottom and held her tightly to him, the wave of heat and lust sweeping through his system like wildfire.

Brooke grinded her hips against him until he was hard and throbbing.

"Make love to me. Right now."

Brooke was a wonderfully giving lover, and they had sex as often as they could get their hands on each other. It seemed he could never get enough of her. Right now, she couldn't seem to get close enough to him, judging by the grip she had on his waist and the lip-lock she'd planted on him.

Having trouble holding on to her, he backed her up against a stall gate and kissed her back. He didn't care what had gotten into her. She wanted him, and he was hot on her heels, wanting her just as much.

He managed to get a breath when she buried her face in his neck and kissed her way up the column of his throat to that spot behind his ear that made him groan.

"Sweetheart, not that I'm complaining, but what is this all about?"

"I want you," she said simply.

"It's freezing out here."

"I don't care. Make love to me, Cody. Hurry." She tugged his hair and pulled his mouth back to hers.

Her wish was his command. Pleasing her, making her happy, he lived for that because she did the same for him.

With her wrapped around him, he walked into an empty stall filled with fresh bedding. He slammed the gate closed to give them what little privacy they'd have if anyone came in. He pressed her up against the wall, then it was all heat and flying hands as jackets, shirts, pants, and underwear went flying.

Her hands grabbed at him, and he was in a frenzy when he took her breast into his mouth. Just that one intimate touch sent her skyrocketing. She arched into him, her hands gripped in his hair, holding him to her breast. He slid one hand down her belly and over her mound. He slipped two fingers into her slick core—so wet, she was practically dripping as she bucked against his fingers and ground against his palm. He slid his hand free, grabbed her waist, and picked her up. She wrapped her legs around his waist again, and he buried himself inside her in one hard thrust. Hot and slick, she took him deep, and they kept the passion flowing as their bodies moved in concert.

He didn't know what brought on this bout of torrid lovemaking. He didn't care.

He let her lead him into the fire, but he made sure she burned with him.

Cupping her breast in his hand, he squeezed her nipple between his index and middle finger and thrust hard and deep. He tugged and rubbed at her breast as he kissed her with long strokes of his tongue, matching the beat of his cock pushing into her.

"Oh God, Cody, yes." She burned for him with every pump of his hips to hers. She covered his hand on her breast and squeezed.

Her body tightened around his.

He thrust, nailing her to the wall as she contracted around him. He spilled himself inside her with a satisfying groan. His body sated, he relaxed into her.

Pressed against her, he felt his breath saw in and out in heaving gasps. Her breathing was just as labored. He leaned back just enough to see the smug satisfaction on her face. It made a smile tug at his lips. "Downright pleased with yourself."

A soft, seductive smile curved her lips.

"Promise me something," he gasped out, trying to catch his breath.

"What?"

"You'll do that again. Soon." He leaned in and kissed her hard before pulling back and looking at her swollen mouth. "You're so beautiful."

He put his hand to her waist. She locked her legs tighter around him before he could help her down. "Not yet."

Her bright smile warmed his heart. How could he leave her when she looked at him like that? "You look so happy."

"I'm more than happy. This is the second happiest day of my life. Well, maybe third, if you count our wedding day too."

He brushed his thumb against her cheek. "What are you talking about, sweetheart? This morning you left looking sad. What happened to change your mood? Not that I'm complaining, because, darlin', I love this mood." Her smile infected him deeply, making it hard not to smile back at her.

She cupped his face and grinned even wider. "I'm pregnant."

Cody went completely still. The smile faded from his lips. He couldn't believe it.

"I'm more than a week late. I went to see Dr. Nash this afternoon. He confirmed it. I'm pregnant. We're going to have a baby."

Her excitement, the bright smile, it sank into his heart and made it soar.

They'd been trying for the last two months. The disappointment and sadness he'd seen in her eyes when it didn't happen scared him. He'd worried getting pregnant might make her sad, remembering the baby they lost. He'd worried that not getting pregnant would make her fear they'd never have another baby.

He'd worried it was too soon to try, that something might go wrong, that it wouldn't happen at all.

Most of all, he'd worried she'd spiral into depression again.

All his worries disappeared.

The pregnancy had made her happier than he'd ever seen her.

He had to admit, he was extraordinarily happy, too.

This time, he'd be with her through the pregnancy. This time, everything would be perfect.

He let out a whoop and a holler and kissed her soundly on the mouth, then he spun her around, making them both a little dizzy. "We're pregnant. Sweetheart, I'm so damn happy." He kissed her again.

"Where are my pants? I have a picture."

Cody reluctantly set her down so she could grab them.

She took the ultrasound photo out of her pocket and held it up to Cody with all the pride and joy she had inside herself spilling out in her smile. She pointed to the little round ball in the photo. "It's just a little peanut right now," she showed him. "But in about nine months, it's going to be our beautiful baby in our arms."

His chest went tight. His heart expanded and ached with the pride and joy he couldn't contain. "I love you." He stole a kiss. "We're having a baby." He fell to his knees and kissed her belly, where his baby lay safe and protected under his mama's heart. He kissed her again and again until they were both laughing with joy.

Eight months later, they welcomed their happy and healthy son into the world.

Cody walked into Brooke's hospital room, a huge bouquet of roses under his arm, and found his wife breastfeeding their boy. Beautiful a day after giving birth, she smiled and it lit his heart with love.

He stole a kiss from Brooke, then kissed his son's forehead as he worked his little mouth against his mama's breast.

This was what she'd dreamed of for months. Her whole life, really. She finally had everything. Cody, their son, the happiness both of them brought into her life.

It hadn't been easy getting here, but it had all been worth it. Especially when Cody wrapped his arms around her and their son and said with his whole heart, "I love you, Brooke."

Acknowledgements

I hope you enjoyed the conclusion of Brooke and Cody's tumultuous love story. For more information about upcoming releases and sales, please sign up for my newsletter.

I wrote this book many years ago. I loved it, but never thought a publisher would go for the dark plot. So I left it sitting on my computer while I wrote a whole bunch of other books. When I decided to start self publishing my books, this was the first one I thought to do after I finished the Dark Horse Dive Bar for my fans.

The best thing I ever did was hire an amazing developmental editor. Thank you, Susan Barnes (www.susan barnesediting.com), for seeing the potential in the book. Your suggestion to make it a duet was brilliant. It allowed me to really dive deeper into the characters and separate the tough road Brooke and Cody had to travel to get their happy ever after. These books are everything I didn't know they could be until you showed me the way.

Melissa Frain (www.melissafrain.com), thank you for another great copyedit filled with all the words I don't know need to be hypenated. It is the bane of my existence. I appreciate your hard work. I was so happy to give you and the readers that surprise at the end.

Angela Haddon (www.angelahaddon.com), you are an amazing cover artist. Thank you for the beautiful covers!

To my amazing agent, Suzie Townsend, thank you for always having my back, guiding me through this crazy business, sharing your insights and expertise, and always cheering me on. I couldn't, and wouldn't, want to do this without you.

Steve, I love you. What else is there to say after all these years of support and encouragement, kids, laughter, fun, and everything else that goes into a life together. I can't imagine doing any of this without you by my side.

Chasing Morgan – The Right Bride
Lucky Like Us – Saved by the Rancher
Short Stories
"Close to Perfect" (appears in Snowbound at Chrstmas)
"Can't Wait" (appears in All I Want for Christmas is a Cowboy)
"Waiting for You" (appears in Confessions of a Secret Admirer)

Also by Jennifer Ryan writing thrillers as JENNIFER HUNTER
The Ryan Strickland Series
The Lost Victim – The Rose Reaper

About the Author

New York Times and *USA Today* bestselling author Jennifer Ryan writes suspenseful contemporary romances about everyday people who do extraordinary things. Her deeply emotional love stories are filled with high stakes and higher drama, family, friendship, and the happy-ever-after we all hope to find.

Jennifer lives in the San Francisco Bay Area with her husband and three children. When she isn't writing a book, she's reading one. Her obsession with both is often revealed in the state of her home and how late dinner is to the table. When she finally leaves those fictional worlds, you'll find her in the garden, playing in the dirt and daydreaming about people who live only in her head – until she puts them on paper.

Please visit her website at www.jennifer-ryan.com for information about upcoming releases.

Printed in Great Britain
by Amazon